The Singular Adventure *of* Charles Goodfoote

The Singular Adventure

of

Charles Goodfoote

A Thrilling Tale Of A Perilous Escapade Set In The Old West

*(Not recommended for The Clergy
or Ladies of a Retiring Nature)*

By

Tom Hanratty

edited by

John H. Watson, MD

and

Charles Goodfoote

The Singular Adventure of Charles Goodfoote

© 2012 by Thomas F. Hanratty

© 2019 Revised edition by Thomas F. Hanratty

No part of this book may be reproduced in any electronic or mechanical means without written permission from the author, except by reviewers who may quote brief passages in a review.

Except for famous historical persons, all characters are fictitious and any resemblance to actual persons living or dead is unintentional. And a little silly.

ACKNOWLEDGEMENTS

A book is the product of many people, but those below contributed greatly to the completion of this work and deserve special mention.

To **Jerilyn Kien** and **Toby Bell**, who not only cleaned up the grammatical errors, but gave valuable advice to improve the work significantly.

To **Pam Altendorf** for her encouragement, advice, and support from the very beginning.

To **Dr. Ann Stewart McBee** who taught me the art of the story.

To **Romaine Wood** for his skill in keeping my computer running when the demons came to call.

And to my wife **Ellen** who corrected, edited, encouraged, and held my hand during the times when the muse stumbled. Thank you for your love, support, and honesty.

Thanks to **A. Conon Doyle** for recording the lives and adventures of Sherlock Holmes and John Watson.

"…*his face had resumed that red-Indian composure which had made so many regard him as a machine rather than a man.*"

    Watson on Holmes, *The Adventure of the Crooked Man*

"*I registered his seemingly unusual coldness. It may be a form of madness, I thought, in anyone but an Indian or an Englishman.*"

    Goodfoote on Holmes, *The Singular Adventure of Charles Goodfoote*

PROLOGUE

By John H. Watson, M.D.

"MY DEAR WATSON, how good to see you again," Sherlock Holmes greeted me in our old rooms in Baker Street. "You look fit, if a few pounds heavier. The gasogene is still on the sideboard and we have time for a companionable pipe together before we dine. No, no, I won't join you in drink, but I will offer my tobacco pouch, if you desire a change from your Arcadia mixture of old."

"The fluff on my sleeve, I presume, told you I was still smoking my old tobacco," I said as I poured a small whiskey. "Your eye for detail still amazes me, Holmes."

"You know my methods. They are founded upon the observation of trifles." Holmes picked up his black briar pipe and threw himself into a chair by the fireplace. He looked me over in his singular introspective fashion as I took my old place opposite him. "Your practice goes well, I perceive. New boots, a well-cut suit from Dunn Brothers of Oxford Street, and a small run-about bringing you to the door bespeak of an active practice with lucrative patients."

"My practice is growing daily," I replied, as I settled into the coziness of our solid friendship. "The newspapers are full of your exploits as well."

"Well, yes. Crime seems to be currently on the upswing, and Scotland Yard has its hands full. A few small crumbs fall my way from time to time."

"Have you anything on at the moment?" I asked.

In response, Holmes rose and picked up a pile of glossy photographs from the table. "These arrived just today. Inspector Hopkins has asked me to draw some inferences from them. See what you make of them, Watson."

Holmes handed me the photographs along with one of his strong lenses. "Why, they're pictures of footprints in mud or clay," said I. "I can see no mark on the shoes to give them any individuality. They are worthless as evidence," I concluded, as I handed the photographs back to him.

"Surely not worthless, my dear Watson. You may recall my demonstrating the value of footprints in determining the height of a man. I believe you chronicled it rather incorrectly in one or two of your little tales. If memory serves, you mentioned the length of the stride as the measurement to indicate height, even after I had specifically told you differently."

"It was my editor who got it wrong, Holmes," said I rather heatedly. "I wrote 'foot-length' and he misread it as 'step-length.' My protestations are a matter of literary record."

"Yes, well. It's fortunate your accounts are not published in the *Police Gazette*," he replied. Holmes' vanity regarding his work had lost none of its vinegar. "These photographs are of footprints that were discovered outside the window of Lord Balfour's home in Ludgate Hill, the night of the theft of Lady Balfour's emeralds. Careful measurements show them to be from a man nearly five feet ten inches in height." He placed the photographs on the table next to me.

"You know, Holmes," I said, as I relaxed once again into my chair. I had idly picked up the stack of glossy photographs again and was looking through them. "Your ability to trace footsteps and pull knowledge from mere marks on the ground is a wonderful accomplishment for a man who has spent most of his life on the pavements of London. One would think you were raised by Bedouins or Red Indians."

Holmes dug a red-hot ember from the fire with a set of tongs and lit his pipe. He puffed quietly for several moments, standing with his back to the fire. "Your statement is a remarkable coincidence, Watson," he said. "I received a telegram just today from the very man who, more than any other, guided my early efforts in gleaning clues from the soil. He is making his way to London at this very moment and should be here within a week."

"He is a professor, then? From your old college?"

"Hardly that, Watson. Although, for a man of his origins, he is remarkably well educated." Holmes sat down, a far-off look upon his sharp features. "Our acquaintance pre-dates even my college days."

"A childhood friend, then?"

"He was already a man when I was a boy. I met him in America."

"My dear Holmes," I said, sitting at attention in my chair. "You never mentioned you spent time in America."

"Well, I'm afraid I haven't mentioned much about my early life to my old friend Watson," he said with a smile. "Your meretricious stories have already revealed more of my private life than the British public is entitled to know."

"Really, Holmes," I said. "I have been most discrete when you so requested."

His smile broadened. "Yes, Watson. You have been the model of fair play on many occasions. But the story of my American visit is tied to a secret so profound that only now, with the recent passing of a certain Great Lady, can that period of my early life be disclosed."

"You'll share the story now?"

"I have a feeling it's already been revealed, Watson. No, no more questions. All will be made clear in good time. Now, unless I am badly mistaken, I hear Mrs. Hudson's tread upon the stairs and my nose tells me we dine on Cornish hens tonight."

And there the matter remained until the following week. We were seated at breakfast, my wife and I, when the maid brought in a telegram. It was from Sherlock Holmes and it ran this way:

"Have you a couple of hours to spare? My American friend desires to meet my Boswell. We dine at Simpson's at seven."

"You will go, of course," said Mary, looking across at me.

"I really don't know what to say. I'm fairly busy at present, and I may not arrive home until early morning."

"Oh, Anstruther would do your work for you if you're kept up late. You have been looking a bit pale lately. I think an evening out will do you good, and you are always so interested in Mr. Holmes' cases."

"Well, this is only an invitation to meet a friend of Holmes. No cases this time, I'm afraid. But it will be a welcome break." I rose from the table. "I'll send a note around to Jackson to meet with me this afternoon. I've taken his patients often enough and this will give him a chance to pay me back."

At close to the appointed hour, I arrived at Simpson's in the Strand and found my friend in close conversation with an elderly gentleman.

"Watson, so good of you to come," Holmes expostulated, rising to wring my hand. "I want you to meet Mr. Charles Goodfoote from America. He's the man most responsible for my present occupation." He bowed slightly and introduced me. "Dr. John Watson is my dear friend and biographer."

Mr. Goodfoote rose from his chair to shake my hand. He stood a good half-foot taller than Holmes, rail thin with a sunburned face, prominent nose, and high cheekbones. Although his dark hair shot with grey was cut in the latest fashion, and his suit was of the finest cloth and tailoring, there was something of the wild country about him. It may have been his eyes that gave me a sense of unease, for the right was a clear blue and the left nut-brown, almost black. A full grey mustache added to the picture of a man of the vast American West.

"This is indeed a great honor," said I.

"No, no, Johnny. The honor is all mine," Goodfoote said. "I've followed the exploits of our friend here closely since you began publishing them. And I find them fascinating, and well-written." His unusual eyes twinkled with good humor.

I was somewhat taken aback at the informal way Mr. Goodfoote had addressed me as I hadn't carried the diminutive 'Johnny' since my days in public school. But at the same time, I was pleased with his assessment of my work. Holmes had been criticizing my writing for decades.

"There you are, Watson," Holmes said with a smile. "You have at least one reader of discriminate taste. But I suspect he may have an alternative motive for his high praise."

"You do me an injustice, Sherlock," Goodfoote responded. "I speak from experience, as only another author could. Your criticism is misplaced. These cases of yours are important lessons as written, with a flair that readers find palatable. You, I'm afraid, would bore the readers to death with your lectures on logic and scientific methods. A bit of romance in a story keeps it interesting."

"You are an author, also, Mr. Goodfoote? I don't believe I have read anything you may have written. Is it something only circulated in America?"

Holmes burst into laughter. "He has you now, Watson. The old Scout has laid a trap and you have willingly stepped into it." He turned to Goodfoote. "I notice the satchel sitting on the floor next to you appears remarkably swollen, Charles. Could you possibly have a manuscript inside?"

"Why, I believe I do, Mr. Holmes. If you gentlemen will permit me…" said Goodfoote as he drew the leather pouch onto his lap.

The waiter interrupted us and Goodfoote held the pouch on his lap until we had ordered. "I suppose I could wait until after we've eaten," he said, as he looked directly into my eyes. He replaced the manuscript and dropped the pouch back onto the floor.

"What have you written, then?" I asked.

"Why, nothing more than an account of the very first case of Mr. Sherlock Holmes," Goodfoote responded.

I looked at Holmes, who answered my raised eyebrows with a smile. "Yes, Watson. I am afraid our American friend here has beaten you to it this time. His rendering of that brief span of history is, however, even more sensational than your collection of tales."

"And how has he displeased your sense of literary criticism, Holmes?" I asked, smiling.

"He has erred, perhaps, as you so often do, in attempting to put drama into each of his statements. In this case, a series of lessons for the nascent detective could have been developed. But, after you've read the manuscript, I'm sure you'll agree with me." With that, the three of us turned to other matters and neither man would answer any further inquiries regarding Holmes' adventure in America. We dined well, as we always do at Simpson's, and sat far into the night over cigars and brandy. At last we parted, my baggage enlarged by the leather pouch containing Charles Goodfoote's manuscript.

When I arrived home that evening, I pulled the thick sheaf of papers out of the satchel and placed them on my desk. I intended to read them at my first chance. As fate would have it, a plague of enteric fever broke out in London and all medical men were pressed into service. Days and nights became as one and it was three weeks before I had an opportunity to sleep more than an hour or two a night. Gradually, things returned to normal, but my regular practice, which, of necessity, had been neglected, was busier than ever. With the strain of being called out at all hours and meals hastily grabbed between calls, my usually robust constitution began to fail me and I developed a nagging cough. Finally, a full two months after my meeting with Holmes and Goodfoote, my wife and I decided a vacation was the only solution for my flagging health. We set off for the sunny coast of Spain, Goodfoote's manuscript packed along in the portmanteau as an afterthought.

It was there, in the hot sun of Costa del Sol, that I at last was able to read the remarkable story of Sherlock Holmes' first case. I have added nothing, but felt it incumbent upon myself to edit certain passages for clarity.

 Mr. Goodfoote has approved these changes and he agrees they only enhance the tale. Here then is what I read.

CHAPTER 1

◫ ◫ ◫

...Charles Goodfoote, tracker of low-life villains, cut-throats, and forgers, the crown jewel of the Pinkerton National Detective Agency.

I started this rattle back in the 1880s when Johnny Watson first started putting out stories of our mutual friend, Sherlock Holmes. I thought it might be time for a true telling of Sherlock's first real case.

But this narrative is about me, mainly.

If you're not a reader of the popular literature or you've been living in a cave, you'll not know the name of Charles Goodfoote, tracker of low-life villains, cut-throats and forgers, the crown jewel of the Pinkerton National Detective Agency.

Born of a Blackfoot woman of merit and an Irish free-trapper of little note, I was raised a savage in 'the most primitive of conditions.' That's the literary take on my early years, but I never viewed it that way. An uncle on my mother's side, Keeps-the-Lodge of the Blackfoot Nation, once told me that a Blackfoot didn't exist except in the bosom of his tribe. He worded it differently, of course, but that's the gist of what he meant.

To be separated from your band and family was the worst event that could happen to a Blackfoot, even a half-blood like me. But the wind that blows through the mountains and the thunder that rolls across the plains had a fate for me that even Keeps-the-Lodge couldn't imagine.

When I was still of a young age, the U.S. Cavalry burned my mother's village, killed most of my boyhood friends, but spared me because of my one blue eye and fair complexion. They thought I might be white, but they weren't sure. Being men of a practical nature, the soldiers sold me for a keg of whiskey to a traveling sideshow and I started a career as 'The Wild Boy of the West.' I was put into a cage at night, and shared the stage during the day with a Chinaman with extraordinarily long fingernails, a Black African man dressed in an outlandish Moorish costume, and a toothless lion that roared on command. We toured the large cities along the Eastern coast where the *Kind Hand of Providence*, as a preacher would say, in the form of a gentleman from a genteel family in Boston, rescued me from that life of degradation. Oliver Wendell Holmes, a prominent physician and poet, took me on as a project to cure my savageness, and also serve as a playmate and companion to his own son, Wendell. Dr. Holmes' kindness got me a good education in some of the finer schools in the East, but failed to completely suppress my rambunctious spirit.

My appearance in a glass would show hair like a raven's wing, square jaw and a distinguished nose inherited from my mother's people. An erect carriage and above average height were part of the Blackfoot package. From my father's side came a keen Irish wit and reflective view of life. In short, I'm a true son of the American West with the soul of a wild Indian and the heart of an Irish poet. Gunpowder and flame have no greater explosive potential.

However, it was my own wits and skill on the trail that brought me to my present prominence. I'm equally at home in the halls of President Grant's Washington and the badlands of the far West, each infused with its own brand of malfeasance and treachery. Although more than handy with a Remington revolver, and a rare brawler when fists are called for,

I prefer using the art and science of detection, as my present employer Mr. Allan Pinkerton calls it, to solve the conundrums that Providence and the Agency send my way from time to time.

CHAPTER 2

◘ ◘ ◘

"You'd be advised to keep your hogleg under your pillow, and sleep with one eye open."

This little adventure began on a fair morning in late May shortly after the end of the hostilities of the War of Southern Secession. I had newly arrived in Chicago in response to an urgent request from William A. Pinkerton, eldest son of the founder of the agency. Allan Pinkerton himself had been felled by an apoplexy and his son, a noted man-hunter in his own right, had taken up the reins. While not an official government organization, the Pinkerton National Detective Agency has some broad ranging powers to investigate any law violation or threat to the prevailing peace in the land. Since its inception before the late War Between the States, the Agency has had some impressive successes. Although I had been with the Pinkerton's for two years, a transfer from the U.S. Marshal's Service, William A. Pinkerton, who liked to be called Chief, and I had never had the opportunity to meet. I had been hired by his father and had spent my time in the field, away from the main office in Chicago.

When I entered William A. Pinkerton's chamber in the red brick building on Washington Street, I saw a tall man, somewhat corpulent, dressed in a well-cut suit standing by large windows, looking over the Chicago scene. I was somewhat reminded of a Laird surveying his feudal holdings. Abruptly, he turned, pulled a large gold watch from his vest pocket and looked from the watch to me. His eyes were deep-set in a face that sported a fine bushy mustache, much like my own. He stuffed the watch away.

"Goodfoote, is it? Damnation, Sir, you're late. I expect promptness from my operatives. You've wasted over ten minutes of my time, and valuable time it is."

"Yes, Sir," I responded, as I offered my hand. "I had the opportunity to reflect on the value of time while cooling my heels in your outer office for the better part of an hour."

He paused only a moment before seizing my hand. "They said you were a game rooster, but we have no time for pissing on each other's shoes. Sit down," he said, with a wave at a high-backed chair. "I can give you five minutes. Cigar? No? Just as well, what with the price of tobacco these days. Now, let's get down to business." Cigar in hand, he settled easily into his baronial chair behind his matching desk, bit off the tip of the cigar and spat it in the general direction of a brass spittoon. "I've heard some interesting things about you, Goodfoote. And not all of 'em bad, either. The Denver office says you're a contentious, undisciplined"…here he paused while he put a flame to his cigar and puffed out huge clouds of smoke…"savage, known for your skill with pistol and rifle. Is that fairly accurate, Mr. Goodfoote?"

"A ringing testimonial, indeed, Sir," I responded. "I'll have to thank them for the compliment."

"They also say you can track a tick over bare rock in a howling gale, and you're as quick with your wits as you are with your gun."

"In the Land of the Blind, Sir, the one-eyed man is king," I answered.

"Yes, and the Two-Eyed man is God. Did you pick that up at Harvard? Oh yes, I know about you and Harvard. You left in a bit of a hurry, according to my sources. Something to do with educating the Headmaster's daughter outside the normal curriculum. Well, I'll not hold your youthful hi-jinks against you." Pinkerton waved his cigar, rubbing out the past in a cloud of smoke. "What's important here is you have some genteel education and can converse with a higher class of rogue. I'm assured that's the case." He blew a cloud of cigar smoke toward the ceiling.

"I lasted two years at Harvard," I said, "and have been told on occasion I sound like a Duke."

The Chief put his cigar into a glass ashtray and sat forward in his chair. He rested his elbows on the desktop, and drilled his eyes into mine.

"We have a problem and it involves the British. This problem may be much or may be little, but it's vexatious as hell." Pinkerton stood abruptly and began pacing behind his desk.

"A few months ago," he began, "Scotland Yard foiled a plot to assassinate Queen Victoria and overthrow the British government. The crackpot who hatched this little drama is a shadowy figure known only as 'Mr. Maldrome,' and, so far as the English know, has been seen only once in person. He devised the plot, brought together a band of merry men to carry it out, and was only discovered when a youngster happened to be at the right place at the wrong time. When the lad told Scotland Yard what he had seen, the whole sorry scheme came undone."

I leaned forward in my chair. "And now this Maldrome is in America?"

Pinkerton stopped pacing. "That's right. And so are the British police. Scotland Yard contacted our government and Pinkerton's was approached for our assistance. There is no country-wide detective branch that has our record of success. The Brits damn near had the man in New York, but he slipped away. Our own operatives missed him here in Chicago, and I have an agent, name of Hoople, right now looking for him in San Francisco."

"How do they know what he looks like, if he's never been seen?"

"Oh, he has been seen, Goodfoote. Remember the youngster?

Those English are dragging this young man around the US of A, and following up every lead. The boy gave a good description, but it seems a bit fanciful. Maldrome has a black mole on his right cheek, and a red birthmark on his forehead. He should be easy to spot, but this villain is a master of disguise, probably covering his mole and birthmark with powder. He can be an Austrian Duke one day and a Flamenco dancer the next. In addition, he has nearly unlimited resources and is reputed to speak several languages fluently. The boy is the only hope we have of catching the man."

"Sounds a bit dangerous for the youth. How old is the lad?" I inquired.

"About thirteen or fourteen. He's been kept out of sight for the most part. We feel sure Maldrome isn't aware of his presence in America, although the boy is the one who spotted the villain in New York."

"And what's my role in all this?" I was growing curious. In my two years with Pinkerton's, my job had been mostly going after violent men who had fled into the wilderness. This was building up to be a more cerebral assignment.

"Maybe nothing. Maybe everything," Pinkerton responded, lowering himself back into his chair behind his desk. He pulled his watch and checked the time. "There's another part of this problem that concerns this Agency and you directly."

I reached into my coat pocket and pulled out an old briar pipe and a leather tobacco pouch. After offering the tobacco pouch to the chief, I began to stuff my pipe.

Pinkerton continued. "There are a few trouble-makers the government has been keeping an eye on since the end of the Civil War. This bunch of hardriders is made up of riff-raff of every sort, including ex-Confederate Officers, Grant haters, separatists, segregationists, you name it. What they lack is a leader. For the past several months, members of this group have been seen gathering in a little town in the Arizona Territories called Disenchantment. And we think this Maldrome is on his way to meet with them. Our snake, Mr. Goodfoote, could be getting a British head."

I finished loading my pipe and struck a match. It gave me time to consider what the Chief had said. A master criminal with unlimited resources was afoot in America and was apparently soon to be holed up in a dumping ground of a town in Arizona Territory. The governments of two countries, in their august wisdom, were sending a group of foreigners with a boy not out of his teens, into what would be a dangerous trek in the best of times. With the gang Pinkerton described congealing there, the chances of these Englishmen getting out alive were slim. I was familiar with the town of Disenchantment and rated this little adventure a fool's journey.

The aroma of my tobacco blend filled the air around my chair and drifted upward with the smoke. I sat back and crossed my legs.

"It sounds like a job for the Federal Marshals. You say someone from the government asked Pinkerton's Agency to get involved? Who would that be, Chief?"

Pinkerton wheeled around in his chair so he was sitting sideways to me. He picked up his dead cigar and began to relight it. For a moment, it looked like he wasn't going to respond. With a quick motion, he spun to face me again.

The Chief glanced at the closed door, then continued in a lower voice. "We have a client who prefers to remain anonymous, but he's highly placed in this government. Let's just say he's very highly placed. However, let's also say there may be a weasel who has snuck into the henhouse. In short, our client can't trust his own people on this one."

I puffed quietly on my pipe waiting for him to proceed. What new disasters would he reveal?

"Unfortunately, this agency is stretched a little thin right now. We're spread all over the map," he said, almost to himself. I wondered about that, too. The Agency has a boatload of resources, and I wasn't aware of any great criminal push in the country, with the exception of government scalawags, of course, stealing everything not nailed down in the Reconstructed South.

"So my assignment is…?" Here was the critical question, I thought.

"First, and foremost, keep these English alive. You may carry a Pinkerton Detective badge, but you have the reputation of a shooter. There are two United States government officers traveling with the British. But don't depend on them or anyone else. There's some deep politics involved with this whole pudding, deep and dirty."

Deep and dirty politics. That came as no surprise.

The Chief continued. "These government men are ex-military and are along to provide some guns on the road, should the need arise. You can send them packing after you get to Disenchantment."

"I'll need particulars," I said. And a quick and ready plan, I thought. "For example, who is this boy and who are the men from Scotland Yard?"

"Men? Did I say men? One of them is a woman. The three, two British officers and the boy, are traveling as a family under the name of…" here he consulted a paper on his desk. "Robert Sigerson and his 'sister' Elspeth. The boy is traveling as Will Sigerson."

"Other then Kate Warne of this Agency, I never heard of a woman police officer," I said.

"Remember the women spies in the War? My father helped capture some of them. Certain women can be as crafty and effective as men. But this 'Elspeth' is little more than a clerk, I'm told. Recruited from the War Department to round out the family portrait Scotland Yard is attempting to project." Chief Pinkerton puffed on his cigar. "The Brits are posing as investors, looking for someplace over here to put their gold. So they'll be staying at the best hotel in town and traveling around the countryside looking at ranches and businesses. It seemed like a good cover."

"I won't have any cover in Disenchantment," I said. "I was a Marshal in that area a couple of years back. I made more enemies than friends."

"You are a personal security agent working for the Pinkerton National Detective Agency. Sigerson hired you because he was afraid of the Apache. That's close enough to the truth."

"What about the agent in San Francisco? California is a lot closer to Arizona Territory than Chicago." I'd had some difficult assignments in my spell with this Agency, I thought, but this operation looked impossible.

"Unfortunately, Hoople has disappeared. I have two more detectives on the way to California right now to see if they can locate him." Pinkerton sat back and seemed to droop in his chair. "We haven't heard a word in days."

"Disenchantment," I said. "It's halfway between Hell and Purgatory, in fact and in attitude."

"You'll have your hands full, then" he said, rising to his feet. I stood, as this briefing was obviously over, although I suspected there was much not being said. The Chief came around his desk. "You'll need to go by train to California, then get a horse or stagecoach to Disenchantment. The Sigerson party left San Francisco two days ago, so you're already playing catch-up. Anyway, see my clerk, Mr. Todd, for your travel expenses and details."

We shook hands, more cordially this time. "Get out to this town, Goodfoote. Disenchantment. Keep these English alive and see what's going on with this gang of troublemakers." William Pinkerton took me by the elbow as I turned toward the door.

"So that's your job. And if this Maldrome character shows up, arrest him or shoot him. If you bring him back in one piece, we'll turn him over to the Brits to hang."

"Oh and Goodfoote," Chief Pinkerton said as we paused in the doorway, "one more thing. A band of hostiles has been kicking up a fuss in that area. It would look bad for this agency if these Brits got themselves scalped while under your protection. You'd be advised to keep your hogleg under your pillow, and sleep with one eye open."

So with that fanciful admonition, I boarded the next train bound for the West.

CHAPTER 3

◙ ◙ ◙

*He saw a blood covered Apache woman-warrior,
black hair streaming, bounding at him with
a huge knife in her hand.*

THE WIND GENTLY shook the scrub pine of the high country, and picked up speed as it skipped across the parched desert sand and rocks, whirling dust-devils into the air. The oppressive heat of the cloudless sky was undisturbed by the breeze, and the vast distance slowed its movement. By the time it reached the dry wash where the Apache girl lay on her belly, the waft was barely a movement of air. But she noticed it, her nostrils flaring to take in any stray smells.

For the past three hours, Kaya-Te-Nse, as she was now called, lay concealed next to the trail, shifting only her dark eyes, and once, when a hunting hawk had cried out, her head lifted slightly to follow the bird's long sweep across the sky. The hawk was her messenger bird, it told her about the movements of her enemies. Kaya wore warrior's clothing, the long shirt of the Chiricahua, washed to a dun color, a fawn-skin loincloth, and high desert boots with a cut fringe on the top. With her long black *hair held in place by a grey headband, the only real color on her was her face paint, a strong yellow stripe that ran across her face and eyes from temple to temple*

The sun was blistering, but Kaya had oiled her skin, and then carefully poured baked clay dirt over herself so she was nearly invisible where she lay in the shade of the rocks, away from the talus slope where she knew their gaze would rest. Halfway up that very slope, a spark of reflected sunlight could be seen where Kaya had carefully placed a single spent rifle cartridge. The Papago scout would see it and all eyes would be seeking the Apache on the high ground, not on this side of the dirt trail where little cover was to be had.

Barely twenty-five summers lay across her strong shoulders; powerful shoulders because she had worked for many of those summers to build her body. She had strengthened her legs by running, and her sinewy arms by drawing the bow until she could put more arrows into the center of the circle than any of the men warriors. And finally, seven winters ago, her brother, the great Apache war chief Lupan, had let her ride along on a war trail against the hated Mexicans. Since that time, she had ridden with her brother's band as a warrior, and her reputation among her people had grown. Even the Bluecoats feared the name Kaya.

Once more, the hawk called, and a breeze brought the smell of the enemy. Kaya sunk even lower to the ground, her dust-covered body blending with the rocks, her mind clear of anger or hatred, concealing her feelings as Lupan had taught her.

She heard the horses' hooves against the ground and the jingle of harnesses. The Bluecoats were coming.

For many days past, Kaya had watched the fort with its American soldiers. These were the new enemy, dressed in blue uniforms, hot under the desert sun. They were hairy, smelly men, and their sweat stung her Apache nose. And they had come with the disease that killed whole villages. Mangas tried to talk to them and treat the Bluecoats with respect, and look what happened to him, she thought. They shot the old man while he lay, and cut off his head. When Nana went to them with a white flag to ask them to leave, they tried to kill him and they shot his nephew and brother. These Americans were crazy, and Kaya fought to rid her land of them. But these thoughts must be put away or her enemy would feel her hate and be cautious.

Kaya watched them come up the trail. They would send three Bluecoats and a Papago scout out ahead of the main column. The scout would die by the first shot, then, when the horses were jumping, Kaya would get her second shot off. Two of the enemy would die today. Kaya had only two bullets and each must count, but she knew the remaining soldiers would bolt and ride hard back to the column. They were afraid of the Apache and would not stand and fight. By the time the column caught up, Kaya would be long gone.

Just as Kaya had thought, the Papago came first, watching the sky and the trail. The other men, three in number, rode behind, seeing nothing. Suddenly, the group halted and the Indian scout pointed at the glint in the rocks up the slope.

The first shot from Kaya's rifle knocked the Papago scout from his horse, causing his pony to back into the other three men's mounts. Kaya rose from her hiding place while she levered a second round into the chamber of her rifle. With only a quick sight down the barrel, she fired again, aiming at the nearest Bluecoat. The bullet went high and struck the man in the neck and jaw. Blood splashed over the shirt of his nearest companion. As the horses bucked, neither of the remaining men turned to run; instead, they jumped from their horses and ran towards Kaya.

At first, Kaya thought they were charging her, and she grasped her empty rifle by the barrel, ready to swing it like a club. She braced herself to receive the attack. But the men suddenly dropped into the dry wash and fired their rifles at the talus slope where the Papago had been pointing. They hadn't even seen the Apache girl, and now they had their backs to her.

Both men yelled and pointed up the slope. The nearest to Kaya, a few feet away, tried desperately to cram a cartridge into the breach of his rifle. His hands shook so badly that he nearly dropped the round. The horses had bolted a little distance away, ears back, their heads turned *toward the sound of the rifles.*

Kaya slipped carefully behind the first trooper, her large scout knife in her right hand. She laid her rifle aside, as the bluecoat shouted and fired at the rocks above. With one swift practiced movement, Kaya grabbed the soldier by the hair, pulling his head back to expose his throat. Her slash nearly decapitated the man, and he died instantly.

The second trooper turned when Kaya roared a war-cry. He saw a blood covered Apache woman-warrior, black hair streaming, bounding at him with a huge knife in her hand. He screamed and dropped his rifle. Kaya leaped like a great cat, knocking the trooper to the ground. She drove her knife into the Bluecoat's chest as she straddled him. Her free hand held the man by the throat as she jerked the knife free and plunged it again into the flailing body. Slowly, Kaya disengaged herself from the fallen Bluecoat and dropped to her knees, suddenly weak. The moment passed and quickly the Apache woman checked each of the slain men. She collected only their rifles and cartridge belts, tying them swiftly into a bundle that she slung onto her back.

Kaya jogged to her pony hidden behind a ridge. As she swung up onto her pony's back, she recalled a duty awaiting her. The young girl, Chula, was about to have a baby and Kaya was needed as her midwife.

CHAPTER 4

◨ ◨ ◨

*The town is a dry scab in the Sonoran Desert between
the aptly named towns of Hell and Purgatory in the middle
of the Arizona Territory.*

Two weeks after my meeting in Chicago, I found myself aboard a Butterfield stagecoach, bouncing around like an apple in a cooking pot until we came to a halt in Disenchantment.

The town is a dry scab in the Sonoran Desert between the aptly named towns of Hell and Purgatory in the middle of the Arizona Territory. It can be reached from the West across two hundred miles of parched alkali desert and a series of dry stage depots, or from the East through the mountains where hostiles reside when not burning ranches, attacking stagecoaches, or engaging in other rude behavior. Fort Crawford, an Army outpost, lies a two-day hard ride, due west, and the territorial capital of Tucson sits four days to the southeast. It's rough country and only dreamers and the greedy flock to its supposed riches.

The spur line of the California Pacific Railroad deposited me in

Pueblo de Las Cruces, California, the closest station in the West. I had expected to pick up a mount in that town, but none were to be had for another month since the Army had taken all available horses and mules. It was there that I received a telegram from William Pinkerton informing me that Hoople, the agent in San Francisco, had been found floating in the Bay. He had an extra smile, ear to ear.

Five days heading back south and east from California on the Butterfield stagecoach brought me and the other four passengers, tired and irritable, into this part of the Arizona Territory. The ninety dollar fare was exorbitant, and I much preferred the saddle, but despite the usual hazards of the road, such as flooded rivers and an assortment of road agents, I arrived without injury. However, I again questioned the wisdom of sending a woman and a boy from the peaceful pastures and dales of England into this lawless wilderness, even with their escort.

Disenchantment. The town hadn't improved much in the two years since my last visit. Before the silver began to play out, it was a booming metropolis of some ten thousand people. When built, the founders had had the good sense to make the main street wide enough for four wagons to roll side-by-side without scraping each other. The buildings were of good frame structures, painted blue mostly, with a few whites and reds to add variety. Most of the private dwellings, of which there were a couple hundred, were spread across a section of desert behind the business district, east of town, and as far away from the mayhem of the 'deadline' or 'red-light' section as possible. Goods from as far away as San Francisco and Chicago had been brought in by teamsters who braved the heat, dust, and hard work of driving forty mule-team rigs from the riverboat docks at Fort Yuma. Occasionally, some hostiles would get the notion to raid one of the convoys, but it was rare they were successful. Disenchantment even had had a semblance of law in the person of a middling honest sheriff named Jake Platt, and a somewhat useless town Marshal. But all that changed when the supply of high-grade ore in the surrounding mines began to play out.

Now, Disenchantment was a cesspool that attracted every low-life gunfighter, gambler, drunk, and road agent looking to plunder the hard-earned money from the local miners, of which there were still a fair number. It had been reported, in the *Boston Herald*, that innocent and unoffending men were shot down or bowie-knifed merely for the pleasure of witnessing their death agonies. According to the reporter, who had left town with an Army escort, there were one hundred thirty graves dug in the town's Boot Hill, and only two were filled with men who had died of natural causes. The exaggeration was prodigious, even for a newspaper, but not without some merit.

Behind the boards of the town runs the Tomorrow River, dry for ten months of the year and a raging torrent from the mountain melt-off in the spring. It's also the dumping ground for any dead cat, dog, or unidentified traveler who has succumbed to the violence of the local citizenry without the money in his pocket to pay for his burial. When the breeze comes out of the West, which is often, a miasma overlays the town like a buffalo fart. I sniffed the air. Welcome back, I thought.

After a brief discussion with the driver regarding his skill in hitting every pothole in the road, and his family resemblance to the hinder parts of one of his mules, I entered the front door of the Silver Lode Hotel and walked stiffly into its cool, dim lobby.

A cut above many frontier hotels, the Silver Lode boasts thirty-two rooms, hot water baths on Saturday and clean linen upon demand. It was still the best bed in town so the hotel was nearly filled with the middling wealthy and somewhat powerful, and the saints and sinners who float around gold and silver like stink on a skunk. Most badgers can't afford its high rent, so gamblers and business owners fill much of the establishment's available space. The rest of the rooms are rented out by the hour to the 'fallen flowers,' for sin is a brisk trade in Disenchantment. In short, not a bad place to spend the night with a chair propped under the doorknob and a six-gun within easy reach.

"Welcome back to Disenchantment, Marshall Goodfoote," the desk clerk muttered, without reading my signature in the registry. "We have your room ready."

I was not surprised the clerk remembered me, for I had stayed at this very hotel back when I was Marshalling for Federal Judge Jeffords. The clerk, who I recalled was named Pottle, had a cadaverous look about him, pale of face, dark thinning hair and dressed like a mortician's helper. His voice was scarce above a whisper.

"This way, please."

If Pottle is Disenchantment's idea of a town greeter, I thought as we climbed the stairs, God help me when I run into the local undertaker. Little did I realize how soon that meeting was to be, for suddenly a scream like a puma in heat ripped from the hallway above. "Murder," a woman shrieked. "Blood! Murder!"

CHAPTER 5

🔳 🔳 🔳

"The key's still on the inside. We'll have to blow the damn door down."

Keeps-the-Lodge of the Blackfoot Nation often said there was a time to quietly watch the enemy camp, and a time to mount up and count coup. This seemed like a time for the latter, so I pulled my wheel-gun and took the remaining stairs two at a time. The staircase ended in a hall that ran off to the right and left. Standing outside the last door at the far end of the right-hand corridor was a young woman dressed in a green silk dress and matching hat. A gangly lad in a grey suit and vest stood nearby, a flat boat hat in one hand. A gaggle of 'low-flying doves' had emerged from their various 'frolic rooms' and huddled together in the hallway, like orphans in a blizzard. The scream had come from one of the strumpets who I recognized as Mavis, attired in the abbreviated finery of her trade. All were staring at the floor in front of the door where a thin stream of blood was soaking into the faded runner carpet. The other rooms on the floor were emptying into the hallway, as some half-dressed men ran toward the back stairs, probably the married ones, while others were drawn to the smell of blood and disaster. Calamity is a great attention grabber.

As Pottle and I hurried down the hall toward the crowd, the lady dressed in green raised her fist and pounded on the door, screaming "Robert! Robert!" The young man stayed back, staring at the blood pool. He then knelt and touched the blood with his forefinger.

"What's this, Madam?" I shouted as I approached. Pottle followed behind. Mavis was preparing to let loose another wail, but choked it off when she heard my voice.

The lady who had been knocking gave me a quick glance with blue-gold eyes and returned to her pounding. The boy stood to watch us.

"My brother is in there," the lady exclaimed. Her voice was high and strained.

"Use your passkey!" I ordered the desk clerk who had gone a shade paler. I stepped aside as he pulled a ring of keys from his belt. He jangled the keys in the lock, but couldn't open the door. I bent quickly and looked into the keyhole. The door had been locked from within and a key still remained in place on the inside of the lock.

I straightened up and turned to the desk clerk. "Get an ax," I ordered. "We'll take this door down."

"Hold it right there, Pottle, damn your eyes," a harsh voice carrying authority stopped us cold. "This looks like my business." A thin man with a face like an ill-used hatchet pushed roughly past me. Tobacco and whiskey smells wafted from his black suit and a thatch of dark hair stuck out from his black flat-crown trail hat. A heavy-gauge double-barreled shotgun was cradled in his left arm. A dull star that proclaimed him sheriff was pinned to his left coat lapel. With him were three men, armed with revolvers, who smelled like stables and cheap rotgut whiskey. All three wore deputy badges.

"Open up in there, Mister," the sheriff yelled as he pounded on the door with his free hand. He turned to the desk clerk.

"Give me that key, Pottle, and get away." He grabbed the key and we all spread out to give him room. After he handed his shotgun to one of his deputies, the lawman stepped up to the door, turned the knob and gave a shove. The door didn't budge. "It's locked," he announced, somewhat unnecessarily, to the group of gawkers. Next he tried to insert the key with a great deal of rattling, but it wouldn't go. Dropping to a squat, the sheriff peered through the keyhole. "The key's still on the inside. We'll have to blow the damn door down."

With that, the peace officer grabbed his shotgun from the deputy holding it, stepped back, and discharged both barrels into the lock. A quick kick sent the door crashing inwards, nearly splintered off its hinges. The sheriff and his deputies crowded around the doorway.

When the black powder smoke from the gun finally cleared, I was able to glimpse into the room through the phalanx of lawmen. My attention was drawn immediately to a body that lay sprawled on the floor at the foot of the bed, nearly at the windows. It was that of a stocky man, face down, well dressed in a dark jacket, gray pants and polished black boots. Even a glance showed that his clothing was awash in blood and an Indian tomahawk was embedded in the back of his head. A red river flowed from the body to the door, and nearly every place else, for the gentleman had bled copiously and even the walls were covered with gore. A rumpled sheet, also stained with blood, lay on the unmade bed. I noted a bowler hat was on its side against the far wall, partially crushed. The light from the windows filled the room and seemed soaked up by the crimson splashes.

"Ain't seen this much blood since Fredericksburg," the sheriff offered, half turning to the crowd that had gathered at the door. "Dub, and the rest of you deputies, get in here and keep the rabble out." I wanted to get a better look but was rudely pushed back with the rest of the crowd.

With a start I remembered the woman who had been pounding on the door. I couldn't spot her, at first, but then saw her green dress and bonnet. She had taken the lad back down the hall. I pushed through the crowd until I reached her.

"Miss Sigerson?" I asked, although it could be no other. She nodded nearly imperceptibly while searching my face. I noted she clung to the arm of the tall young man, leaning into him. For his part, the youth seemed nonplussed, but his thin face was pale and his jaw set. He had turned to watch the crowd as it gathered near the door to the murdered man's room.

"I'm Goodfoote," I said. "You'll have been expecting me. We better get clear of this mob. They may get playful when they get the full smell of blood in their nostrils."

She looked at me hard for a moment, then seemed to make up her mind.

"I have a room just up the hall. The boy is in the adjoining room."

"One moment," the youngster said. "There is only one way this could have been done. I prefer to wait and confirm my theory."

I looked at the lad like he had lost his wits. His age was perhaps closer to sixteen than fourteen, but his lack of emotion after seeing the murder of his friend and traveling companion struck me as odd, even for an Englishman. I took the lady's arm and moved her toward her room. The boy followed, though reluctantly. Within minutes, the three of us were in her comfortable suite, the door closed and locked behind us.

CHAPTER 6

◘ ◘ ◘

*"My name is Sherlock Holmes," the youth said,
in a voice with a clipped English accent.*

Miss, my name is Goodfoote. Charles Goodfoote. I think we can drop the pretense now." I helped the lady to a rose colored settee and removed my hat. I was struck by the symmetry and beauty of her face, wide blue eyes with a glint of gold, and a clear complexion that a princess would give her castle to possess. "It's always awkward dealing with aliases."

The sitting room was large and furnished with several chairs, a table, and the settee. The boy walked to the window, his flat hat in hand, and stood with his back to us, staring down into the street.

"I'm with the Pinkerton National Detective Agency and deputized to act as an agent of the American Government," I started. "I regret my arrival was ill-timed, but if you'll be kind enough to share your real name and the lad's here, we'll get down to business."

The woman glared up at me, her eyes filled with flame. "Ill-timed? Yes, I should say so. I was told you'd *meet* us here." Her teeth clenched and her eyes hardened. "Ill-timed, indeed. Another incompetent American detective. A respected detective from Scotland Yard lies dead within feet of where you now stand. And you most certainly are 'ill-timed,' Mr. Whatever-Your-Name-Is." She stood up and strode to the opposite wall before turning.

"You're all barbarians in this savage country. Stupid, low-life, odious miscreants." Her eyes flashed blue fire. "This town is full of cut-throats, thieves and murderers." She was no longer talking, but yelling, and I noted tears glistened on her lashes. "Just pirates without ships." I reached for her, but she pulled away and turned to face the wall, sobbing, an embroidered cloth clutched in her hand.

"My name is Sherlock Holmes," the youth said, in a voice with a clipped English accent. He turned from the window, placed his hat on the table top, and clasped his hands behind his back. "And this is Inspector Elspeth Kane of the British War Office."

Miss Kane gave him a sharp glance which he ignored.

"Thank you, Sherlock Holmes," I responded with a slight bow. "And I deeply regret the events in this hotel." I looked the boy over. Even with the natural reticence of the British taken into account, his composure was noteworthy for any man, and remarkable for one so young.

"How did this happen?" Miss Kane asked no one in particular. "Sergeant Davis was to meet us for a late breakfast. We've had no warning…"

"It's a tragedy about the policeman," I responded, fearing the young lady might start up again at any minute. "This bunch is damned quick, and not above a little murder. How long have you been in town?"

"Five days," Holmes answered, glancing at Miss Kane. "We have found no signs of the man we were sent to find, even though this town is a haven for criminals. It makes Seven Dials a Vicar's garden."

I nodded. "It's the low end of a buffalo wallow," I agreed. "No argument there."

Inspector Kane moved back to the settee and sat down. I took a position directly in front of her. "The man who calls himself the sheriff," I said. "Have you had any dealings with him since you arrived in town?"

"Yes," Inspector Kane was regaining color in her cheeks. She thrust out her jaw like the prow of a schooner and hissed between clenched teeth. "The sheriff. He's as worthless as the rest of the inhabitants of this rathole."

"It's apparent the sheriff is in the employ of some of the criminal element," Holmes said. "One look at this town, with its surfeit of villains, tells us that much. It's not a stretch to note that a constable who would tolerate the lawlessness apparent in Disenchantment would of necessity be party to the malevolent force that controls its activities."

"Would he have known your real identity?" I turned to Miss Kane and kept my voice soft.

"No," Inspector Kane said. "We informed him we were the Sigersons, seeking to invest in the silver mining in this region. He was most rude and abruptly terminated our conversation."

There was a commotion in the hallway. I unlocked and opened the door. The body of the murdered man was just being manhandled out of his room by four men. Young Sherlock pushed past me to observe the sheriff watching the procession move toward the staircase. I motioned Sherlock to come back inside with me and quietly closed the door.

"The sheriff will be along any minute to find out more about you and your plans. Keep to your story about looking for businesses in this area, but make it clear that you intend to leave town with 'your brother's' body."

Miss Kane stood and put away her handkerchief. She set her shoulders, glanced in the mirror over the washbasin and straightened her hat. A stray auburn curl had escaped and she pushed it back. "I apologize for the way I behaved just now. You will not see a repeat of it. I'm glad you're here, Mr....?"

"Goodfoote, Miss Kane," Sherlock Holmes said. He had begun to pace, seemingly unable to stay in one place for long. His tall figure passed to and fro in front of the windows. "He identified himself as Charles Goodfoote. The Pinkerton Detective sent to meet us, I believe."

He crossed the room toward me, grey eyes jumping from my face to my boots. "You just arrived on the stagecoach, I see, Mr. Goodfoote. Why didn't you come by saddle horse? It's obvious you have Red Indian blood, probably from the Northern plains, so you'd be used to travel by horseback."

"Sherlock," Miss Kane snapped. "Your cheekiness is impertinent at such a time."

I said nothing, but noted that this lad had an uncommon gift for reading much into details. Even in the confusion of the violent murder, young Holmes had noticed that I wore no riding boots, was not covered in dust, and dressed for a stagecoach and not the trail. He had also correctly identified my mixed-blood heritage. I wondered what else his sharp eyes had noticed.

Elspeth Kane seemed to gather her thoughts. "Well, Mr. Goodfoote. I will need to send a telegram. While I am doing that, I will not let Master Sherlock out of my sight. He will accompany me. And you will come with us. I was informed that a man proficient with a sidearm would meet us here. That is apparently you, so you may be of some use after all." She opened her purse and removed a telegram, and studied it carefully.

"Your description from the Chicago office is rather detailed. Let me quote: 'Charles Goodfoote. Tall, lean, black hair, contentious personality. Carries a revolver in a cross-draw holster. Dresses like a Philadelphia lawyer. Often sports a large mustache. Right eye blue, left eye dark brown.'" She looked me full in the face. "It says you are a shootist. Is this summary accurate, Mr. Goodfoote?"

"Except the part about a contentious personality. I'm a bedrock of diplomacy and congeniality."

"I'm more interested in your skill with a firearm," she replied, looking up at me. "This town is a sewer, and the sheriff is the largest sewer-rat of all." She took a deep breath. "I will find the miscreants who killed Sergeant Davis. And I will not be leaving Disenchantment until I see them hanging from a gibbet."

I nodded. That may be easier said than done, I thought, but said, "The telegraph office is up the street." I moved to the window and peered out. Below, the town bustled. "We need to be mindful of any telegrams we send or receive. This town, including the telegraph, is owned by the sheriff or one of his cronies, and anything you send will be read by them."

"All of my telegrams are in code, Mr. Goodfoote. Including the one I received in California with your description." She sat down again, but was ramrod straight on the edge of the couch. "You have been appraised of our mission in this part of the world, Mr. Goodfoote. The wire I quoted reveals as much. So you know it is a villain named Maldrome whom we are here to identify and bring to justice. Our duty is clear, though made more difficult with the death of Sergeant Davis."

A loud knock cut short our conversation. I looked from young Sherlock to Miss Kane as I moved to the door. The sheriff stood in the hallway with his hat off. Behind the sheriff was a man a half head taller than the law officer, a deputy badge pinned to his shirt pocket.

"Now, who might you be, Mister?" the sheriff asked. He stepped into the room, his face inches from mine.

I moved back and closely watched the man with the sheriff. His pock-marked, glowering countenance was not even a country girl's vision of handsome. A scar ran the length of his face, his right eyelid pulled down over the socket. When his good eye, a dark brown, fastened on me, his mouth dropped open exposing blackened stumps of teeth. But he said nothing.

I pulled my attention back to the sheriff.

"Goodfoote's the name. I'm a Pinkerton Detective hired to guard these folks from the hostiles."

"Seems you're a little late," the sheriff smirked. He eyed me closely. "We don't get too many Pinks out here. And, mister, one is too many."

"He ain't a Pink, Sheriff," the man with the scar said. His face had turned red, and I noticed a sheen of sweat coated his forehead. "He's a half-breed Federal Marshal."

"Your deputy is only half right. I was a Federal Marshal until two years ago. Now, I'm with the Pinkerton National Detective Agency." I showed my badge, which the sheriff examined. The deputy kept his one eye on me.

I turned to Miss Kane who had remained seated. "I believe you've met Miss Sigerson and her younger brother."

The sheriff nodded. "Lady," he said, "I grieve for your loss. You may remember my name is Bodkin. Sheriff Bodkin. This man is my deputy." He turned to stare at me. "You look like an Apache yourself. And that hatchet stuck in the lady's brother is Chiricahua. Maybe you know something about that," he said, again stepping close to me. His whiskey breath was as hard as kerosene.

I shook my head. "I just got off the stage, Sheriff. I don't know a thing about this unfortunate event. And I'm not Apache."

The sheriff bobbed his head slowly, never taking his eyes from mine.

"Some folks think it was a heathen ghost." He turned and walked to the door. "Better keep your door locked up tight. That ghost don't seem to like strangers." Bodkin glanced at Miss Kane. "We took the body to Swann's Mortuary. It's 'round back of the Furniture Shop."

Elspeth raised her head. "I'll be taking my brother home as soon as I can arrange transportation," she said with her head held high.

"You might want to bury him here, Miss," the sheriff said, opening the door. "He'll be pretty ripe in this heat in a day or two. We ain't got no ice house."

Elspeth Kane simply stared at him.

The sheriff put on his hat and stepped into the hallway. He didn't glance back again, but his deputy backed out slowly, still glaring at me. Just before he closed the door, the deputy gave me a half grin, raised his index finger and pointed it at me.

When they were gone, Elspeth slumped onto the couch. "He'll be worthless in helping us find either the murderer of Sergeant Davis or that villain Maldrome. And that man with him makes my skin crawl. I'd like to hire the man who gave him that scar."

For the first time since the arrival of the sheriff, young Holmes spoke up. "I believe we already have," he said.

CHAPTER 7

◉ ◉ ◉

*"Each link in my chain of deductions must be
tested against observations in the crime scene itself.
There is nothing like first-hand evidence."*

I simply nodded. I was becoming impressed by this lad's sharp eye. "The deputy goes by the name of Blade," I said. "You may have noted that he doesn't carry a gun. He's as quick with that Bowie knife he has strapped to his shoulder as most men are with a sidearm. And he enjoys cutting up folks."

Young Holmes settled into a chair, his fingers forming a steeple. "You apparently have a long, and possibly violent, history with Deputy Blade," he stated.

"I do," I responded. "Was it that apparent?"

The young man smiled. "Mr. Blade was obviously unhappily surprised when you opened the door. His hand immediately flew to the scar that runs down the right side of his face. As you and the sheriff conversed, Mr. Blade's complexion went from pale to pink to positively red, until he burst out with his loud denunciation of you as a Federal

Marshal. It takes little ability to deduce that here was a man who had suffered a grievous injury by your hand. Hence my statement of your previous history with him."

I nodded. "I was a Marshal for the judge who administered justice in this part of the territory. There's a small town north of here called 'Hell.' Its proper name has been lost, or maybe changed by someone who visited there. If you think Disenchantment has some hardcases, a visit to Hell would make this place look like a Baptist retreat center." I walked over to the door, opened it quietly and peered into the hallway. Nothing stirred. I closed the door again and locked it.

"I'll make this short. I went into Hell to find a cut-throat by the name of Mange, who had killed a family along the Brazos and fled to Arizona. I was jumped and dumped into a fighting pit. Blade climbed in after me, armed with that big knife he carries. Someone tossed another Bowie knife into the pit for me to use, and the men started betting on who would crawl out alive. It's one of the sporting events in that town." I paused for a moment. "Kind of like bare-knuckle fighting, but the scoring is a bit rougher. I probably should have killed him then and there, but I had no warrant on him and nothing against him."

"Other than the fact he was trying to kill you," Miss Kane said.

I waved away her comment. "Like I said, for him it was a sporting event. Anyway, I came out of the hole and he sat there holding his face."

"Did you ever find the man you were after, Mr. Goodfoote?" Sherlock asked.

"I did," I responded. I took a seat in a chair opposite Holmes. "What did you make of the sheriff?" I asked.

"He goes about unshaven with hair that is unkempt, yet he has a coat made of an expensive material, a vest of silk, and Foster boots, hand-made in a small village in the Kent region of England," the boy said.

I again nodded. "The coat is tailored by Scoffer and Dunkirk of Boston. I have the same tailor. The Foster boots would require him to travel to England for fittings, or buy them second-hand."

"His sidearm is a Colt with mother-of-pearl grips."

"Hand-crafted, if I'm not mistaken. Made especially for the wearer. And his holster and gunbelt are hand-tooled split cow hide," I finished.

We sat in silence for several moments pondering what we had observed.

Miss Kane, who had remained silent during our analysis, stood. "I must send that telegram."

Holmes and I both jumped to our feet. "You and the boy better stay in the room." I said. "I'll send the wire and pick up some food for you two."

Miss Kane hesitated, then turned and sat at the writing desk. The silence was broken only by the sounds coming up from the street and the scratching of her pen. When she finished, she handed me her slip of paper covered in neat, clear handwriting.

"These are the people who must be notified, and the messages for each," she said. "We're trusting you, Mr. Goodfoote. Please don't let us down."

I retrieved my hat and turned at the door. "Are either of you armed?"

In response, Sherlock Holmes pulled a strange looking revolver from his suit coat pocket.

"It's self-ejecting," he said. "A .450 caliber."

I merely nodded. I'm not fond of British handguns in general and self-extractors are too cumbersome for my work.

Miss Kane took a pocket model Colt Navy revolver from her purse. She handled it with confidence, but didn't pass it over for my examination. The three inch barrel and small .31 caliber usually requires a dead-on shot to do much mischief. It would do, I thought, as I didn't expect either to do any serious shooting.

"One more thing. You came here with two U.S. government agents. Where are they?" I asked.

"We don't know," Elspeth Kane said. "They left us at the hotel and we haven't heard from them since the day we arrived."

The sun was directly overhead and the heat in the dry desert air was becoming intense as I walked the two blocks to the telegraph office. Old Silas was still running the place. He was a bit timid, but as honest as any man in Disenchantment. It was a low bar. Within minutes of a warm, if somewhat nervous, greeting from the man, we had sent the telegrams for Miss Kane.

"I'm obliged to tell you, Mr. Goodfoote, that things are not as you left them," Silas said. "The Sheriff or one of his deputies come in regular to read all the messages sent and received. I can't stop 'em."

I put my hand on his boney shoulder. "Nothing to be done, Silas. Let them read whatever I send." When I had sent Elspeth's wires to the Chicago office of the Agency, to be forwarded on by The Chief, I had used the Pinkerton's code. The messages would be useless to the sheriff.

Silas stepped up to me at the door. He lowered his voice. "You may want to know that Marshal Sam Thompson is coming here, Mr. Goodfoote. He should be arriving in a day or two." With that, Silas scurried back behind his counter.

After leaving the telegraph office, I stopped at The Blue Cup, an eatery I had frequented in my Marshalling days. Mrs. Nelson still ran the place, and she sold me several sandwiches along with a pot of coffee to take back to Miss Kane and young Sherlock.

I returned to the hotel, climbed the stairs, and knocked quietly on the door to Miss Kane's room. It opened a crack, and I was quickly admitted by the lady.

"Where's the lad?" I asked.

"He's next door in his room, reading."

I walked through the bedroom to the connecting door and knocked. In a moment, Sherlock opened the door, a book in his hand.

"What are you reading, boy?" I asked. The book was bound in paper, much like a dime novel. He held it up so I could read its cover: *Journal of Speculative Philosophy*.

"There's an article in here by a man named Peirce," he said, "which has to do with the laws of logic."

Miss Kane had come up behind me. "The laws of logic, Master

Sherlock, were laid down for all by Aristotle. There are no others worthy of the term."

"Aristotle covers only deductive reasoning, Miss Kane. What of Bacon's inductive logic?"

"I brought some sandwiches and coffee," I said, stepping further between the two. "It's a poor lunch, but it will serve." I had no interest in their discussion, but I found it curious that they both could so readily lay aside their grief.

"Hardly logic, young man," Elspeth said, pouring some coffee into a cup. "Mathematically, only Aristotle measures up. Bacon's work leaves too much to chance, as does Charles Sanders Peirce's. His theories of semiotics or 'signs' are mere speculation."

"You've read Peirce, Miss Kane?" Sherlock asked. "He just recently published."

Elspeth took a sip of coffee and made a face. She put the cup down. "When one is concerned with true mathematical thinking, one keeps up with recent ideas."

The sandwiches were tasty, but I was the only one with an appetite, the other two more interested in their philosophical views on mathematics.

"I'm going to take a quick look into Sergeant Davis's room," Sherlock Holmes informed Miss Kane, after about an hour. "There may be something there with which I can test my theory of the murder."

"The body is gone and nothing can be gained from looking at that horrible room." Miss Kane stood to face the boy directly. "This is not one of your Cambridge science experiments. This is Detective Sergeant Robert Davis of Scotland Yard. Brutally murdered."

"Nonetheless," Sherlock said, turning away. "I intend to see for myself."

"I'll go with him," I said as I opened the door. "It can do no harm." I turned to the boy. "But I must warn you. It's not a pretty sight. And by this time, that blood will smell like an outhouse on an August day."

"I insist, Sir," he said. "Each link in my chain of deductions must be tested against observations in the crime scene itself. There is nothing like first-hand evidence."

My expression revealed nothing, but I wondered what a pup from the cloistered public school system of England could possibly know about evidence, first-hand or otherwise.

CHAPTER 8

◩ ◩ ◩

"My old uncle, Keeps-the-Lodge of the Blackfoot Nation, used to tell me to listen to the tracks."

Entry to the room was no problem for the door barely hung from its hinges. The lock had been blown off by the shotgun blast, and when I found it on the floor, the key was still in it. Bright sunlight flooded the room.

I watched Sherlock pull a hand lens from his pocket. He then took the lock mechanism from me and held it close to the window while he peered at it intently, turning it over several times. Then he took the key out, put it back in and worked the device three or four times. Finally, apparently satisfied with his examination, he put both the lock and key into his coat pocket.

We inspected the door, then the two windows set in the west wall. Both sashes were fastened from the inside, sporting a layer of dust that indicated they hadn't been raised in some time. I wondered what Sergeant Davis had done for air when the afternoon sun had baked his room.

The blood smell filled the room with a coppery odor. I pulled a heavy-bladed knife I keep handy in my boot and pried open both windows. They creaked upward only a few inches before becoming stuck.

"Well, we've eliminated one means of egress for the killer," I said, as I slipped the knife back into its sheath. "With that door locked from the inside, in front of witnesses, we have an impossible crime."

"Unlikely, Mr. Goodfoote, but not impossible, because it did happen," Master Sherlock said sharply. "If we eliminate the windows and doors, we are left with one possibility. All the rest are impossible." He moved quickly to knock on the walls and climbed on a chair to examine the ceiling. "The walls and ceiling are solid, although I didn't suspect we would find a secret passageway in a frame hotel of this sort."

I nodded sagely. "What is the one possibility, young Sherlock?"

"I would like to look around further, Sir," he said. "I will discuss it later, when I'm certain of my theory."

I continued nodding my head sagely. "Very well, young man. I'll be interested in your idea. Now, let's look for tracks, for that's my specialty."

Holmes' grey eyes lit up. "Signs. Tracks are signs, and we can use inductive reasoning to interpret them, regardless of Miss Kane's repeated objections. I can apply Peirce's semiotics to them and prove my solution to this mystery."

Being more comfortable with physical tracks than speculative philosophy, I immediately began my examination. There were plenty of bloody boot tracks. I was particularly interested in a set of tracks that were not bloody, but were prints in a clear area. They were a bit more difficult to find on the bare wooden floor on the far side of the bed, away from the body, but by getting down on all fours, and putting my head to one side, I was able to study them.

"My old uncle, Keeps-the-Lodge of the Blackfoot Nation, used to tell me to listen to the tracks," I said. "He meant, of course, to view them with my head to the side. Here, Sherlock, try it."

The lad got down carefully, avoiding the blood, and scanned the floor with his head tilted. "Yes, I can see the value of the method," he said. "But it is logic that will give us valid conclusions."

I pulled a measuring tape and got busy, examining several prints.

"Exactly twelve and one half inch," I said, as Holmes wrote down the number.

"Will that give us his height?" he asked.

"Yep. Just about six feet three inches," I responded. "Measure the track in inches and divide by two to get the trackmaker's height. You can see from the shape of the heel that these were tracks made by town boots, not boots worn for riding. And you can see a cut on the inside of the left sole. That makes it unique to a specific boot."

"The mystery here, Mr. Goodfoote, is your locating faint tracks on a hardwood floor, and finding a cut in the footprint. How did you find them so quickly?"

"Trick of the trade, young man. Make sure the track is between you and the light. And I looked where I expected them to be."

Holmes put his hands on his hips. "Why would you expect tracks on that area of the floor? It's not close to where the body was found."

"I'll let you chew on that point, Mr. Holmes."

My non-answer didn't seem to bother him as he smiled thinly. "I can see the value of reading footprints," he said. "They can reveal many clues as to how a crime was committed. Once one has the skill to observe the marks."

I nodded. "Tracking is important in detective work," I said. "It's also the most neglected."

"Is there anything else in this room to which you wish to call my attention?" His eyes swept the room.

"The sheet on the bed," I said. I took the rumpled bloodstained sheet and held it up for him to see. "You'll note the blood pattern on the sheet. It's not consistent with the wounds to the victim."

Sherlock nodded. "The bloodstains look more like wipes."

His eyes narrowed as he bent over the sheet. "This is another area of study for a detective," Holmes said as he examined the stains. "How blood behaves when it leaves the body under force."

"Does your logic reveal any other indications of the killer?"

"I'm working on why you were looking for tracks away from the body. The killer would have stood there to…what? Why would the killer have stood there, Mr. Goodfoote?"

"To get dressed, of course."

"Dressed?" He looked at me narrowly with eyebrows raised, then continued as he worked it out. "You suspect the murderer removed his clothing and boots to prevent himself from getting bloody. That line of regress ratiocination does make perfect sense." He thought for a moment, then added with a slight smile. "Unless it was a woman who was undressed for a different purpose."

"If so," I expounded, "It was a woman wearing a large-size men's boots." I looked quickly around. "We'll talk more later," I said. "Let's finish our job here. This stink is making my eyes water."

The lad moved around the room. He picked up the crushed Bowler hat and turned it over in his hands. Then, after an examination with his pocket lens, he put it on the dresser. He wrinkled his long nose.

"There seems to be a great deal of blood," he said. "And much of it on the walls is darker than the blood near the body."

"Excellent observation, boy. Blood darkens as it ages. The blood on the walls is much darker than that on the floor near the door. And the patterns on the wall look like someone threw it up there, possibly from a pail."

The youngster dropped into a squat. He peered closely at the bloodstains. "There are some hairs here," he commented. "We should study them closely. Is it possible a microscope exists somewhere in this town?"

"I know of two, one close at hand. For now, your pocket lens will do. Use it to find more hairs, and we'll take them with us." He took the white envelope I handed him. "I keep a few of these envelopes in my pocket, just in case," I explained.

I watched the young man at work. "Cambridge? You seem a bit youthful for so selective a university," I ventured.

"I won the Newton Award for science when I was twelve and the

Diogenese Prize in Mathematics a year later. By special arrangement, Cambridge allows me full access to their lectures and laboratories, although I'm still enrolled at Westerly." He moved to the damaged door before turning around. "They have had no reason to regret their decision."

"I have one more stop," I said, as we left the murder room. "I'll do it by myself. You return to Miss Kane and explain what we have found."

"We need to examine the body of Sergeant Davis," Holmes said, straightening his shoulders. "I'm prepared for that task."

"It's not necessary for you to attend," I said. "I didn't know the man, so it'll be easier for me."

"No, Mr. Goodfoote. Sergeant Davis was my companion and friend. He was foully murdered and I insist on doing everything I can to bring justice home to his killer. I will examine the body."

I looked him in the face for a long minute, noting his clear eyes and the resolute set of his jaw. I gave a shrug.

CHAPTER 9

◘ ◘ ◘

*The shaman turned to the woman warrior. "It is time
for you to go on a journey," he said.*

AS SHE EXITED her grass wikiup in the morning light, Kaya saw the old Shaman, Dasod, sitting alone under his grass arbor staring straight at her. His eyes pulled her toward him. The two had been close ever since Dasod had helped Kaya develop her special Power, explaining what it meant and how she was to use it. Only Dasod and the aged woman, Tu, knew the secret of her great gift, and how it had kept her people safe from their enemies.

"Fetch me water from the spring," Dasod said when Kaya approached. She picked up the water-bag that hung on the pole of the arbor, noting it was at least half full. Kaya knew then that the old man wanted to tell her something important. The fetching of the water was like the opening signal that a significant event was about to take place.

Kaya ran to the spring and filled the water-skin with fresh water. A feeling of foreboding had accompanied her as she ran. Dasod often had visions of disaster. The last time he had sent her to the spring, the old shaman accurately predicted the death of Lupan at the hands of the Comanche. She remembered staying behind in camp attending to a young woman who needed healing while her brother Lupan and his band set out upon the trail to Mexico to steal horses. Since that time, months ago, Kaya had spent most of her days performing her duties as a midwife and healer. Only twice had she taken the war trail alone, and then only when her Power had sent her a dream that Dasod had interpreted as a war dream.

She returned with the water, hung the water-skin on the pole, and sat down near the old man. For a time, the two sat in silence. Dasod would speak when he felt it appropriate, and Kaya was a patient woman.

The shaman turned to the woman warrior. "It is time for you to go on a journey," he said. He took a necklace from around his neck and motioned to Kaya. She leaned forward and Dasod placed the necklace over her head. She took a deep breath for she recognized the gift. It was a leather thong that held a single bear claw and several trade beads of red, black, and yellow. Kaya knew that it was the old man's most sacred Power, the bear medicine protection he had worn since he was a boy. Her mind went blank.

A hawk's hunting call sounded above the camp. Kaya looked up and shaded her eyes with her hand. With a second, clear cry, a red-tailed Sun Hawk sailed out of the bright sun, its wings spread for his landing. The bird, his white chest puffed and its wings and tail outstretched, landed on the top of the arbor, just above the head of Dasod. With a third cry that sounded throughout the village, the raptor folded his wings and fixed his yellow eye onto Kaya.

"This bird will guide you," Dasod said. "It is Usen's wish that you take this journey. You must leave tomorrow when Holos shows his face. That is all I know."

He reached behind him and pulled out a bundle wrapped tightly in rawhide. He handed it to Kaya with both hands. "You will know what to do, when the time comes," he said.

And the next morning, Kaya rode out of her village with the rising sun at her back. Dasod stood outside his lodge and watched her go. He knew it was the last time he would see the woman warrior on this Earth.

Dasod returned to his lodge. Soon, he would put his own plan into effect. The Sacred Grandfathers may dictate their wishes to the old shaman, but he wasn't bound to do only what he was told. He could help matters, as long as he didn't get in the way of the Spirit World's plans. Dasod's idea called for the cooperation of one man, the man once called 'Mischief Maker,' and now called Neva.

CHAPTER 10

◘ ◘ ◘

The flickering flames of the candles playing on the dead bodies gave the room a Gothic feel.

Swann's Undertaking Parlour was, as the sheriff had said, located behind Swann's Furniture Shop, just off Compton street. Mr. Swann must have been at lunch, as the place was unlocked and no attendant was present. Holmes and I had the funeral home to ourselves. Other than the current group of corpses.

"It seems peculiar to have no impediment to our entering," Holmes said.

"Might be Mr. Swann felt it was one place no one would willingly enter," I responded as I stepped through the door. "And those inside would find a lock the least of their difficulties in leaving."

We moved to the back room, behind the office. For a town the size of Disenchantment, the undertaker's parlor was a crowded establishment. Two bodies were laid out on wooden tables, still fully dressed in the clothes they had been wearing when admitted. Another three were embalmed and in coffins.

The place was dark, with heavy drapes on the windows. If we pulled back the curtains, I reasoned, passers-by would see us at work and that was something we wished to avoid. So we lit candles at first, but soon found oil lamps in sconces that helped with the lighting. The flickering flames of the candles playing on the dead bodies gave the room a Gothic feel, and I wondered how my young companion would handle seeing his friend in this setting.

I needn't have worried, for Master Holmes could have been standing in Trafalgar Square for all the notice he took of his surroundings. He quickly pointed out the body of Sergeant Davis, and I moved a candle resting in an elaborate holder close to the dead man. The mortician hadn't had time to administer his talents, as Davis was still clothed as he had been in the hotel.

I continued to keep an eye on the youngster, as he appeared distant and unemotional. Still, I knew the policeman and Holmes had traveled long distances together and they must have struck up a relationship of some sort. The young man exhibited only intellectual curiosity which made me wonder if he was protecting his emotions. Not for the first time, I registered this remarkable boy's seemingly unusual coldness. It could be a form of madness, I thought, in anyone but an Indian or an Englishman.

Notwithstanding my musings, we started at the head of the body, I describing, and Sherlock taking notes. The wounds were extensive, three in number, to the top and back of the head. The hatchet had been removed, but lay on a nearby table.

"Whoever struck him must have been tall. The wounds are all near the crown of his head," I said.

"That would agree with the height you calculated from the footprints in the room." Sherlock looked up at me. "The placement of the wounds on his head would indicate he had his back turned to his killer and was therefore probably killed when he entered his room, by someone already waiting there."

Sherlock looked down at his notebook. "And there's the matter of the bed sheet. Most probably used to wipe off the blood on the murderer."

I nodded. "That's my thinking. But why all the blood in the room? Far more than these wounds, extensive as they are, would produce."

"I drew a rough sketch of the room," he said, ignoring my question. He showed me his notebook. "It helps me understand the sequence of events."

I continued to examine the body and noted that stiffness was confined to the face and arms, with the larger muscles of the legs still loose. "He must have died shortly before you and Miss Kane found the blood coming from under the door."

"Yes," Holmes said. "The blood was still liquid and flowing, so I estimated the time of death at under an hour." I looked at him, eyebrows raised. He explained, "A little experiment I performed at school on the drying time of bloodstains."

"You attend an unusual school, Boy," I said. "And are you familiar with the rate of stiffness in a body?"

"Only from my reading. Corpse examination is not part of the curriculum at Westerly."

"Neither is bloodstain drying time, I'll wager," I answered. "But, just a quick note, rigor can be noted in the jaws and fingers in an hour. It takes ten to twelve hours to become completely stiff, and he's nowhere near that." I continued to watch the boy for signs of grief or some show of feelings. I observed none, so I asked, quietly, "What time did you last speak to the Sergeant?"

"Sergeant Davis went out early, at about seven o' clock, to meet someone who had information on Maldrome. We were to call on him when we were ready for a late breakfast, sometime around ten o'clock."

After registering this information, I closely examined the dead man's hands, then his clothing, but found nothing of significance. We collected some fibers from his suit and found dust along the cuff of his trousers. It resembled the dust we had already obtained from our examination of the sergeant's hotel room, but it's part of the Science of Detection to be attentive to all details. I paid especially close attention to his shoes, noting that the soles were clean. I found some dirt on the upper part of his shoes and this went into one of my envelopes. I then removed hairs from the man's head and put them into another envelope.

"This hatchet is of some interest," I said to Holmes, as I held it up to the lamp light. "It has Chiricahua markings on it, but I doubt it's Apache. The Apache don't use hatchets as a rule. They're given more to war clubs and lances. You'll also note that the head is stone, lashed on with rawhide. The Apache have gone nearly entirely to iron weapons, so if some Apache had decided to copy the design from another tribe, it was from a long time past. And the handle is likewise old, with dust trapped in its rawhide bands."

"Like a museum piece," Sherlock offered.

"Probably some local collector, I would say. The hatchet is an important piece of evidence, but we've gotten all the details out of it for now."

Holmes took the hatchet and examined it. "Why a hatchet?"

"It's another conundrum, all right. But let's get back to the hotel. The undertaker will probably be back shortly." We extinguished the lamps and candles and made our way out of the dead house.

Back at the hotel, we climbed to the second floor. There was a crowd of gawkers in the hall outside Sergeant Davis's room, and the gasps and comments told me the large amount of blood was having its effect, even though the body was long gone. The sheriff's story of an Apache ghost had spread like wildfire, probably believed even among the hardcases in town. No one is more superstitious than a gunfighter, except maybe a gambler. And there were plenty of both in Disenchantment.

While Sherlock unlocked his door, I stopped to knock gently at Elspeth Kane's room. She opened the door and searched my face, her hand to her chest. When she saw young Holmes entering his room, she gave a deep sigh. "You both left the hotel without telling me," she said. "I was concerned. Please keep me informed of Master Holmes' movements at all times."

"Of course, Miss Kane," I replied. "There are one or two things that we found, and we'll be looking at them in the next room."

"I'll come along then," she said. She stepped into the hallway, closed her door softly, and locked it with her key. We entered Sherlock's room and found he had cleared the top of his dressing table.

"My bags are in my room down the hall," I said. "I'll be back in an instant." Nothing had been disturbed in my chamber, and I retrieved a hard-sided case I always carry. I returned to the room with Miss Kane and Sherlock, put my case on the bed and popped it open. Inside was a complete science kit I had assembled with the help of a professor at Harvard. Smiling at young Sherlock, I set up a microscope that was fitted with lenses that had been ground in Switzerland. Slides, bottles, and jars came out next and I placed them on the dressing table. Miss Kane moved in to get a closer look at the array of laboratory glassware.

"This is interesting," she said. "But I don't see how it will help us find the murderer of Sergeant Davis."

"My uncle, Keeps-the-Lodge of the Blackfoot Nation, had me track mice to get my eyes adjusted to small sign," I said, as I adjusted the scope. "By the time I worked my way up to humans, I could read the tiny cuts and cracks in a man's track that spin his whole history." I put one of the hairs from the room on a slide, covered it with a thin piece of glass, and slipped it under the low power lens. "The lesson the old man was trying to teach me was that there's nothing so important as trifles." I adjusted the mirror on the base of the scope so it reflected the afternoon light.

I turned to Holmes. "Anytime someone enters a room, something is left behind and something of the room is taken away." I observed that Sherlock wrote my words in his notebook. "First, however, we'll compare the coarse hair we found in the dark blood to some samples of animal hair I have."

After studying the shaft of the hair found in the room, I pulled four slides from my case. These were slides of various types of animal hair I had prepared and use to compare to samples I find. I put them under the lens one at a time, then turned to Sherlock.

"Pig hair," I said. "Have a look."

"It's very coarse, isn't it," he said, as he peered into the eyepieces.

"Now, we'll take a look at the hair from Sergeant Davis's head," I said.

Holmes seemed to know a bit about microscopes, so I had him prepare the specimen.

"The hair from Sergeant Davis is completely different in many ways," Holmes said. He sat back in his chair and turned to me. "The blood then is pig blood. But why go to such considerable lengths?"

"Perhaps it's a rather strange ritual killing," Elspeth said. "Mr. Davis' death may not be tied to Maldrome at all." She began to pace up and down as she spoke, her hands clenched in front of her, staring at the carpet. "The Apache hatchet, the excess blood, all add up to a bizarre slaying of some sort." She turned to me. "We told no one who we were. Not even the sheriff."

"The two government men who accompanied you have disappeared," I said. "They may have been taken, and we don't know what they may have said, either voluntarily or under duress."

Holmes spoke up. "We need more information," he said, echoing my thoughts. "Where are pigs kept in and around Disenchantment? Are any missing? Who has access to pig blood?" He stood and began to pace, his head bent and chin lowered. Finally, he approached Miss Kane. "We must find out more about this town and its citizens. We can't just stay in this hotel. We must roam about and meet people, make inquires. One can't make bricks without clay."

"That may be too dangerous for you two. I'm familiar with this town and can move about more freely. And a woman and boy won't be admitted to the saloons where most of the villains and information can be found."

Before they could object, I picked up my hat. "Mister Sherlock Holmes, I leave my microscope and slides in your care." I gave a slight bow. "Use them to study the dust we collected. Use the lamp for reflected light when the windows go dark. I'll be back in one or two hours."

The sun was dropping behind the desert hills to the west, turning the buildings of Disenchantment red, then purple. A chilly breeze came in from the alkaline desert that surrounded the town, and I was glad I had retained my suit coat. For part of the early evening I stood on the hotel porch and watched the citizenry pass by. Compton Street was filled with rough-looking men of all sizes and shapes, from burly teamsters and buffalo hunters, to thinner gamblers and sinewy miners. Most of the men, I noted, were at least partly drunk, liquor being a common way of coping with the boredom of their workaday world. Few women were about, and none of them looked like schoolmarms. I put a match to my pipe after awhile and strolled along the board sidewalk. Exhausted from the day's activities, I postponed my visit to the saloons. The town was coming awake with the setting of the sun and lamp light became the only illumination. I returned to the hotel and bid Miss Kane and Sherlock Holmes a tired goodnight.

CHAPTER 11

🔳 🔳 🔳

*The white-eyes called the village of evil by
the name of Disenchantment.*

THE DESERT WAS *ablaze with spring flowers when Kaya rode her war pony down the steep trail and out onto the flat bottom land that bordered the Silent Sister Mountains. It had been a dry period 'When the Thunder Sleeps,' but a female rain two days ago had turned the otherwise barren flat country into a garden of colors. Red, yellow, and purple blossoms spread across the rock-strewn floor of the valley and Kaya paused to view their beauty and savor their fragrances. The cry of the Sun Hawk brought her head back to watch the circling bird with his red tail.*

She touched her heels to her pony's sides and the animal moved into a gentle lope. The hawk had been in front of her for four days, all the way from the mountain camp of the Aiaha Apache. At night, when the moon was the only light and she and her pony were weary, she made cold camps and ate meals of dried pemmican. Each morning, before the first rays of Holos turned the jagged peaks of the mountains from gray to purple, the hawk's call brought her from her sleep to resume her journey.

The Sun Hawk was leading her closer to the hated town of the white-eyes, the village of witches. She wondered why her Power had brought her to this place, near such evil, but the hawk with the red tail was a messenger directly from Usen, not to be challenged or ignored. From the time of her puberty ceremony when she was given her Power, experience and her elders had taught her to listen and follow, not to question the Sacred Ones. And, in the world of Kaya, all things in nature were sacred.

In the distance, just as Holos was beginning his journey toward the western horizon, Kaya saw the dark smudge ahead on the desert floor. The village of the witches. The place where evil held sway. The white-eyes who brought the guns and whiskey to the Apache called the village of evil by the name of Disenchantment.

CHAPTER 12

◙ ◙ ◙

*"I had an uncanonical enjoyment of the
sacramental wine, I'm afraid."*

We were up and moving by mid-morning the next day. Elspeth looked prim in a white shirtwaist with a brown and gold skirt, while Sherlock had changed into a safari outfit, complete with knee-length shorts, a tan shirt festooned with pockets, and sensible shoes. With his pith helmet clamped on his head he looked like an English Lord on holiday. After a less-than passable breakfast in the small café across from the hotel, we strolled up Compton street to the freight office and made arrangements for the transportation of the body of the Scotland Yard detective. Following Sherlock's notion of getting out and moving around the town to gather information, an amble up Compton seemed in order. We made no attempt to enter any of the saloons. That would wait until the evening when I would be going out alone. One of our destinations was the local newspaper office, but we found the door closed and locked.

Young Holmes studied the faces of all we passed without seemingly recognizing the villain Maldrome. We spotted Sheriff Bodkin at one point across the street talking with a large man in a plantation hat who was dressed like a banker, but we made a point of steering clear of them. Later, we had lunch in the hotel dining room, which was a better repast than breakfast, and Miss Kane spent the hot afternoon at the writing desk in the relative coolness of the hotel lobby. Holmes and I used my microscope to examine the dust and fibers we had gathered and worked until the room became uncomfortably warm. We then joined Miss Kane in the lobby. None of us had any appetite for supper, and we settled for tea brewed by the hotel cook. As the light faded, I left my two charges in their rooms and prepared myself for the serious information gathering I knew would be necessary to understand how Disenchantment related to my assignment. The murder of Sergeant Davis added urgency to my mission. Maldrome, who I suspected was behind it all, was moving fast, and I needed to get my feet under me.

I stepped from the porch of the Silver Lode. Grey and blue shadows had emerged as the sun had once more slid under the low western hills, and the desert air had taken on a definite chill. The main boulevard, Compton Street, was not about to bring the Champs Elysees to mind, but the waxing moon coming up in the east gave it an underserved sense of tranquility. Light spilled out of saloon doors and dusty windows. Along the street, kerosene lamps had been hung at irregular intervals over the planked walk.

My first destination was the newspaper office. If the press of Disenchantment was similar to most towns, gossip and occasional news would be found there. Although the town had the same bustle and smell, much had changed in the two years since I was last through here, and I needed to catch up on the local villainy. I was in luck, for a small man sporting a derby was just locking the front door of *The Disenchantment Dispatch*.

"Excuse me, Mister," I began, as I approached. The man turned and squinted up at me in the dim light. He adjusted his glasses and his eyes grew wide.

"Well, Marshal Goodfoote. I'll be damned," he said. I looked him over, for his face didn't seem familiar. He wore a grey suit, somewhat wrinkled, dusty spats and shoes, and a frayed collar that had once been white. Small, round framed glasses settled on his bulb-like nose that was covered with fine veins. His grey mustaches connected to long sideburns and he sported a three day growth of white whiskers.

"Leviticus Langlade Winthrop," he said, answering my blank expression. He pumped my hand with both of his. "No reason you should remember me. I watched you frog-march Everett McGill down Compton Street when you were Marshaling for Hanging Judge Jeffords. It was my introduction to this Rome on the Tomorrow. I had just gotten off the stagecoach when McGill cannoned out of the Board of Trade Saloon head-first with you right behind him."

"You have a good memory. That was over two years back."

"It was memorable. A week later, you were gone and I had bought me this newspaper…such as it is."

"Any chance of you opening back up and letting me take a look at some newspapers from a few weeks ago?" I asked.

"Interested in what has changed in Disenchantment, I'll wager. *Facilis descensus Averno; sed ad auras evader est labor*. 'Going to Hell is easy; coming back is hard.' Virgil," he added. "You still a lawman?"

"Well, yes and no. Right now I'm with the Pinkerton Detective Agency, riding security on a couple of British investors." Half a truth is better than a lie when dealing with the press.

The newspaperman smiled. "I was just on my way to the Silver Slipper for an aperitif. Join me and I'll bring you up to date on all the glorious events in this thriving metropolis."

The Silver Slipper Saloon had once been the watering hole for mine owners, local businessmen and the upper crust of the town. Now it was a little like going into a pit mine. The darkness seemed to follow us into the place as only a few lamps were lit. I stopped at the door and let my eyes sweep the gloomy cavern. The walls, covered with flocked wallpaper, were a dingy, oily yellow from countless cigars. In a far corner, a fat lady wearing a brown derby pounded out a riverboat show tune on a battered piano, her tits bouncing along to the ragged melody. A long oak bar flanked one wall and was crowded with serious drinkers. A couple of early drunks, three cowboys in long dusters, and a bunch of loud miners made up the drinking group. Gamblers of all shapes and dress were dominant, many wrapped around the whirling wheels of chance. A fair number were seated at the Faro table, while others bent over small piles of poker chips. Some had the pale, hunted look of men desperate for a fair turn of the cards. Others, professionals, knew the odds were long… but gamblers always believe they can outsmart the house. The clicks of the Chuck-a-Luck and Roulette wheels added to loud laughter from the working girls in bright get-ups as they massaged the suckers. The smell of spilled beer mingled with the stench of unwashed bodies and cheap perfume. Even at this early hour of the evening, gambling and whoring were in full swing. One group of five toughs sitting at a table in the rear particularly caught my eye as we elbowed our way up to the bar.

The bartender had a tired, bored expression, and barely nodded when I ordered a beer and Winthrop requested a straight whiskey. A huge gilded mirror was at the back of the bar so I was able to keep an eye on the activity behind me without turning around. One of the gunsels rose from the group of rogues I had spotted in the back of the barroom. He was short and scrawny, sporting clothes that looked well slept in. A greasy thatch of mouse-colored hair stuck out from under his battered flop-hat. The handle of a revolver protruded from his right pants pocket.

"I thought I recognized you. You're Johnny Law. A Goddamned half-breed lawman," he said, as he shambled up to the bar. He was speaking loudly enough so everyone nearby couldn't help but hear, and I noted a drop in volume of the surrounding noise. Then, the piano went silent. Winthrop, a large whiskey in hand, scurried to an open table against the wall.

"Hello, Mange," I replied, as I turned to face the villain. "How's the family?"

Mange squinted his eyes. "You go to Hell, Breed. I told ya, I never kilt them kids. You wasn't able to hang me then, and you can't hang me now."

"Ease up, Mange. I'm not after you. If I was, we wouldn't be standing here palavering." I looked around at the smoky room of sweating men, pale whores, and overflowing spittoons. One of the drunks at the end of the bar took this opportunity to throw up on the floor. "I'm here for the delicate scenery and enlightening ideas, a Disenchantment conversazione. Let me drink my beer in peace."

"They got no business serving no liquor to Goddamn Indians. I've a mind to tell the sheriff. He's a friend of mine, Breed. A real good friend."

"This beer is more creek water than liquor." I glanced at the barkeep before turning back to Mange. "But you run along and tell whoever you want, Mange. I'm taking my beer to that table over there, so I won't be hard to find."

And I was as good as my word. History had taught me that Mange was a back-shooter, so I made sure I had a solid wall behind me. Mange stayed at the bar and tried to stare a hole into me until his friends ran out of patience. They cast looks of pure malevolence in my direction, then filed out of the saloon. Mange was the last to go. The cacophony of the barroom swelled back up, but I watched the swinging doors in case Mange got up the courage to come in shooting.

"I see you still have some admirers here in Disenchantment." Winthrop pulled a notebook from one pocket of his coat, a capped ink bottle from another, and a stylus pen from a third.

"Mange and I go back a few years," I said.

"What made you leave the Marshalling business, Mr. Goodfoote?" Winthrop asked. He had opened his pad of paper and poised his pen. These newsmen are a nosy lot by nature, and giving them something is better than letting them make up their own stories.

"Mange there had something to do with it." I shifted so I could watch the front of the saloon as well as the tables of gamblers. "He rode up to a ranch house one day down in West Texas and found a widow woman whose husband had been killed in the War. Mange moved in and lived there off and on for a year. One day, he got tired of his home life so he took an ax to the woman and her three kids, then fled into Arizona. I found him up in Hell, living with a whore."

I took another sip of the beer. "When I dragged him back for trial, the jury said there were no living witnesses, so they let Mange loose. That's when I quit the Marshaling business and took up with the Pinks."

Winthrop scratched away, then took a short pull of whiskey. "An instructional tale, to be sure," he said. "But Mange there is Sheriff Bodkin's little terrier. The fact that he has already singled you out doesn't bode well for your old age retirement, Marshal. People who Mange or Bodkin notice unfavorably either disappear, or end up dead."

"You needn't call me Marshal, Mr. Winthrop. As I said, I'm now with the Pinkertons." I took a sip of beer. "What happened to Sheriff Platt? He was the law here, such as it was, when I left."

"Disappeared," Winthrop exclaimed. He leaned back and spread his hands. "*Postquam docti prodierunt, boni desunt.* 'When the evil men appeared, the good men went missing.'" He took another drink. "Seneca the Younger." The journalist wrote quickly for a few moments, put down his pen, and sipped his whiskey. "The sheriff vanished during a rainstorm about a year ago. Bodkin and his gang rode into town a week later and just took over. Not much here to stop him with Jake Platt out of the way. A few men tried to stand up to Bodkin, but they were goaded into gunfights and killed by his deputies. They're all gunhands of the first order. The mayor, Timothy Smithers, objected, but wouldn't fight. He never carried a gun. One day he was gone. Vanished. Never came back. He was headed for the Capitol to get some help, according to old Silas in the telegraph office." Winthrop took another pull on his glass of whiskey. "Guess he never made it. His horse and buggy were found a couple of miles out, but no sign of the mayor. His wife stayed around awhile, but finally left for back East."

One of the *grande horizontale*, bursting out of her red satin dress, stopped by the table to kiss Winthrop wetly on the cheek. She set down a full shot glass of amber fluid, which the journalist downed in one swig. The 'girl' tossed her head back and laughed loudly showing blackened, broken teeth.

"You gonna introduce me to tall-in-the-saddle here, Lev?" she said. She bent forward over the table to afford me a glimpse of ample promises to come. The cloying smell of her fragrance filled the air between us. I took a sip of my beer and let my eyes drift around the room. I'm not a man who is opposed to a bedchamber frolic under suitable circumstances, but this dainty prairie flower had calamity written all over her face in the form of syphilitic cankers on her lips, a jaundiced cast to her eyes, and a breath that would drop a dray horse in his tracks. Only a newspaperman well into his cups would find her appealing.

"This man is on a mission, Bess my dear," Winthrop said. "He has no time for dalliance. Right now, at any rate." The smile on Bess's face disappeared, which did her beauty no harm. "Allow me to introduce you to this siren of the desert, Mr. Goodfoote. This is the famous nightingale and *paramour*, Beautiful Bess. Bess, my dear, Mr. Goodfoote. He was once the Marshal of this Godforsaken territory." I watched him slip her a bank note that quickly vanished into her bosom. The siren of the desert thrust out a bountiful hip nearly knocking 'Lev' off his chair. After a few lewd remarks that I won't sully these pages with, she tossed her head, shot me a look of contempt over her shoulder, and moved on to the next table.

"Let me refresh your beer, Marshal," Winthrop said as he rose. He staggered a little, but straightened up quickly. "I feel the need for liquid libation."

"No thank you, Mr. Winthrop," I said. "You go ahead."

I watched the passing scene. The woman who had been banging away on the piano gave it up and was replaced by a young man who had been engaged in sweeping the floor moments before. The noise in the barroom died down as the man began to play a classical piece from one of the Russian composers. He played brilliantly and held the attention of the bar patrons for a full five minutes before the chatter started up again.

"Abel Slade," Winthrop nodded toward the young man when he returned. "He's a complete idiot in everything but music. Can't even tie his own shoes, so Bess and the other girls take care of him. Sad case."

"I've seen it before," I ventured. "Men with great gifts in one or two areas, and minds like children for everything else."

Winthrop raised his glass in mock salute.

"*In vino, veritas*, Marshal. *In vino, veritas*," He smiled. "The more *vino*, the more *veritas*, you might say."

I noticed that the more Winthrop drank, the more Latin he spouted. "You seem to have a vast knowledge of the classics," I observed. "Is that a common trait among you scribblers?"

"Not rare, Marshal. We members of the fourth estate are a varied lot. *Nulla placer diu nec*…etc., etc…'Water drinkers don't write good verse.' Horace is pithy, especially in his *Epistulae*." He paused to gulp down the last of the rotgut in his glass. "I had the advantage of a classical education in Boston." Winthrop raised his empty tumbler. "You see before you a man who once had the Priesthood as his calling. Or damn near, anyway. My mother's idea to send me to Catholic grammar and secondary schools."

"But you became a newspaperman?"

"Saved by the press. I had an uncanonical enjoyment of the sacramental wine, I'm afraid." He was looking around for another drink as he spoke.

"Other than Bodkin and his gang, anyone of note in town?" I asked. Winthrop was going to be useless in short order. He was drinking hard liquor out of a tumbler and his Latinizing cant was getting on my nerves.

"Oh, you could say that. Right after Bodkin set up camp here, Count Von Herder, an Austrian duke, arrived and bought up half the expired silver claims. He has more money than brains." Winthrop wiped the inside of his glass with his finger to get the last drop. "*Malleum sapientiorem*. 'Dumb as a hammer without a handle.' He owns three saloons, an eatery and the Silver Lode Hotel. Most of the whores in town are run out of his stable." The journalist shook his head. "When the silver plays out, this town will just dry up and blow away. The Count will be sitting on a ghost town and worthless silver mines, mark my words."

Winthrop went up to the bar and got another drink. One of the men came out from behind the bar and moved around the room lighting more wall lamps in a failed attempt to keep the thick gloom at bay. The new smell of kerosene now competed with the seasoned odors of spilled beer and cheap whiskey.

Abel Slade went back to his sweeping, his head oscillating slightly with the movement of his broom. When Winthrop returned to the table, he motioned Slade over to the table. "Here's something I'll wager you've never seen, Mr. Goodfoote. Come on over here, Abel. Here's a penny. Tell the Marshal here what the product is of three hundred and twelve times one thousand and twenty."

"Three one eight two four zero," Slade said without pause. He didn't smile and his oscillations continued.

"For a penny," the newspaperman said, "Abel will tell you any mathematical computation instantly. That and the music are all he can do. The rest of the world is a fog to his mind."

A neat parlor trick, I thought. But I played along for several minutes until I ran out of pennies. There was no question that the man was unusual in his mathematical skill. Finally, Abel went back to his sweeping and I encouraged Winthrop to continue his story.

"You may remember Ezekiel Crump. Grizzled old fart who spent most of his time with his rosy snout in a whiskey glass. He owned old number three mine. There wasn't much silver left, just low-grade stuff. Crump hated that mine. His wife and son were buried in it when a gas pocket blew."

Winthrop drank half the amber liquid in his glass. His words were beginning to slur. "Von Herder decided he wanted that mine. Not worth a nickel everyone said. He offered Crump enough money to keep the old scoundrel in rot-gut for life, but Ezekiel was a stubborn old sod. He spit in Von Herder's face and said he would sell to the devil himself before he'd sell to a damn foreigner." Winthrop took off his hat and wiped his forehead. He finished the whiskey in one long swallow, then made to get up for another refill. I pulled him back into his chair by his coat sleeve.

"So what the hell happened?" I said under my breath. "And go easy on the Latinizing. It's giving me a headache."

Winthrop looked into his empty glass like the rest of the story was to be found there. "Crump was found, two weeks ago, now, laying in front of the church right before Sunday services." The newspaperman shook his head. "He was riddled with arrows and had been scalped. It gave the good ladies of the Society of Jesus a bit of a turn, I heard." The little man weaved his way through the dim barroom to get a refill. He came back with a bottle this time, sat down, and shakily poured some into his glass. He drank half its contents, then refilled it. "Where were we?" he asked. With his eyes unfocused, he seemed to be studying the wall behind me with some interest.

"Ezekiel Crump was found riddled with arrows," I prompted.

"Oh, yes. Didn't take long. Next day, Von Herder filed papers saying Crump had sold him his mine before the Apaches got him."

"The Apache? Here in town?"

"Don't make sense, but the arrows were Chiricahua — and Kaya is rumored to be heading this way. A trapper spotted her near the Silent Sister Mountains, heading right toward us. If you see one Apache, you'll see a whole passel."

I thought about that awhile. Kaya in the area was something to be considered. She and I had been more than friendly a few years back, but she was unpredictable and we hadn't parted on the best of terms. Kaya was an implacable enemy, but if she took a liking to you there was no better friend.

I had lost my source of information. The whiskey had taken its toll. The newspaperman was now face down on the table, snoring loudly. I opened Winthrop's notebook and read what he had been scrawling. I was amazed. Even though he was windward of a landing, as the sailors say, he hadn't missed any of my tale.

I rose to leave, and stopped at the bar to settle Winthrop's and my tab. I knew Mange would be waiting outside. A back-shooter like Mange wouldn't be able to pass up a chance to kill me in the dark.

Life and Marshaling had taught me caution, so I timed my exit with a group of cowhands who were heading out the door. Once outside, I quickly stepped to the side so my silhouette didn't show against the light pouring out around the swinging doors. The three men with me didn't notice my presence and climbed aboard their horses at the hitching rail. By the time Mange and his men realized that four men had exited the saloon and only three were riding out, I was in the deep shadows of the saloon porch.

I figured there was an even chance that Mange had me pegged for heading directly back to my room at the Silver Lode. It was a certainty that he was waiting in the shadows somewhere to gun me down.

A bushwhacker like Mange setting up an ambush, I thought, would put a man across the street in the alley between the Saddler's Shop and the Chinese laundry. And he'd also put a man in the alley just to my right where I'd have to pass to get back to the hotel. Or maybe he'd be waiting in the back of the saloon, in case a man like myself, known for his cautious nature, left by the rear door.

The light from the gibbous moon was bright on the street, and the dirt shone like silver. I'd be an easy target out there, and not much better off in the alley. I had sought refuge in the shadow of the porch, but the moon was dropping in the west and its light was creeping toward my feet. Silence hung over the street like a heavy blanket, disturbed only by the drinking and gambling sounds from inside the saloon.

CHAPTER 13

◘ ◘ ◘

With a start, Kaya recognized the man, and knew her reason for being in this place of witches.

KAYA WAITED UNTIL the moon was already setting, throwing long shadows across most of Disenchantment. Her pony threw back his head when they neared the arroyo of the nearly dry riverbed behind the buildings. The pungent odor of death and decay breathing out of the ditch caused her pony to flare his nostrils and shake his head. Kaya noted the smell too, and she left the pinto behind a rise across the flow, upwind of the scent. Quickly, the woman warrior jumped down the slope of the arroyo, stepped over the water at the bottom of the ditch, and scampered up the side nearest the town. She paused to listen to the noise from the front of the buildings where the main street ran, and fastened a set of tracking moccasins to her feet. These overlarge moccasins were bundles of feathers stuck together with blood. Her special footwear would leave, not human tracks, but just a few lines in the dust. No one but an Apache tracker would know their meaning.

Kaya moved as silently as mist along the back of the buildings. She *paused often to listen and sniff the air for the smell of the sweat of the white-eyes. Her Power had brought her to this town of witches for a reason, and she kept moving to find her mission. From shadow to shadow she drifted, even as the moon settled lower in the sky.*

Her keen senses detected the odor of leather coming from a building near her, but it was the acrid smell of sweat that caused her to melt deep into the shadow at the rear of the building. The sound of a movement of boot against earth, and low voices of white-eyes that came from a space between two buildings just next to where she stood, made Kaya, knife in hand, flatten herself against the wall. Only the shadow of a stairway leading to an overhanging porch gave the woman cover from the light of the moon. Cautiously, she slipped out from the darkness and peered around the corner of the building, into the alley. Two men crouched there, backs to Kaya, as they intently watched the building across the street. One of the men carried a shotgun, and the other held a large knife. The building they were watching looked like one of the lodges where the white-eyes got drunk. Kaya wondered if she was sent here by her Power to kill these two.

The doors of the drunk lodge swung open and four men came out. The man in front of her who carried the shotgun, brought it to his shoulder, but did not shoot. The man with the knife went into a crouch, as if he were about to fight.

Three of the men who had exited mounted ponies tied to the hitching rail. The fourth had stepped into the shadows and stood waiting. Kaya doubted that the two men watching could even see this fourth man. He was completely still, but the moonlight would soon find him.

Suddenly, two gunshots sounded. The watching men burst across the street, raced up the alley next to the drunk lodge, and disappeared behind it. And the man waiting in the darkness sprinted across the street, coming up the alley toward Kaya. She dropped further back into the darkness and watched him run past her along the ditch.

With a start, she recognized the man, and at once knew her reason for being in this place of witches.

CHAPTER 14

◘ ◘ ◘

"Speculation at this stage of the investigation will only lead us in circles. We will end up bending the facts to fit the theory."

J ust as I was about to move, gunshots exploded from behind the saloon, followed by a piercing scream. Mange broke cover and ran across the street from the alley beside the saddler's, carrying a shotgun. He was closely followed by deputy Blade. The two men disappeared up the alley to my right, and around the back of the saloon. I didn't wait to see what the shooting was about, but sprinted across the road, up the alley, and back to the rear of the hotel. I melted into the shadows and waited while I listened for any following footsteps. Gunshots are a common occurrence in Disenchantment and there was little reaction. Off in the distance, a coyote yipped, and I heard a man cough from inside a house nearby. A faint sound behind me brought me around with my revolver drawn. Darkness and silence. I listened hard, but all I could hear was my heart pounding in my ears. The night breeze from the cooling desert sprang up and brought the faint smell of something rotten in the shallow arroyo that housed the Tomorrow riverbed behind the town. I let out my breath and strained all of my senses. Nothing but loose dust was moving with the breeze.

Then the back door of the hotel opened slowly and I was looking down the barrel of a cannon. It was Sherlock Holmes with his strange pistol.

I was barely in the door leading to the hotel kitchen when young Sherlock whispered, "I've made some inquires of my own while you were out."

"Does Miss Kane know you left the hotel?"

"I didn't leave the hotel. I merely spoke to the kitchen staff."

"And exactly what did the kitchen staff have to say about the crime?" At this point I was more interested in getting a night's sleep behind a locked door than speculations from the kitchen help.

Holmes smiled. "The hotel buys its pigs live from Wesson's Butcher Shop, and slaughters them in the adjoining backyard. And, it's of some interest to note, a pig was slaughtered early yesterday, the very morning Mr. Davis was killed. I reason that is the source of the pig blood."

I thought for a moment. "Good work, Lad."

"The killer must have been watching Sergeant Davis' room," the young man continued. "After the policeman left, the pig blood was splashed around. I did not observe any pail in the room, which means either the killer had an accomplice who took it with him, or the killer himself set the scene, then returned the bucket to the back of the hotel."

The boy was thinking hard. I merely nodded.

"I rather think there was an accomplice," said Holmes, his brow furrowed. "Someone who brought the blood to the room, but remained in the hallway. We may find some drips on the hall runner which would further strengthen the case for such a scenario."

Holmes paced back and forth in the confined space of the kitchen, his chin sunk onto his chest. It seemed to me the lad was almost speaking to himself.

"The murderer took off his clothing and painted the room with the blood. He then wrapped the bucket in a towel and handed it to his helper. The killer then waited behind the door holding the hatchet."

"It holds together," I spoke up, "but the reason for the pig blood still doesn't figure."

"I, too, can fathom no reason to use extra gore at a crime scene. It seems completely illogical to me."

"Speculation at this stage of the investigation will only lead us in circles. We will end up bending the facts to fit the theory." I clamped my hand on his shoulder as we left the kitchen. "Now, I suggest you prop a chair under the doorknob of your room, and put that unusual gun of yours within easy reach by your bedside."

CHAPTER 15

🔲 🔳 🔲

My Irish blood didn't like looking down the business end of a 10-gauge held by a skulking killer.

The next day, the sun was just over the mountains when a soft tapping on my door caused me to pull myself from a cloud of dreams and open it to young Sherlock. He announced that he and Miss Kane were about to depart for breakfast. Would I be interested in joining them in the lobby and fill them in on the details of my night on the town? He looked well rested and even graced me with a rare smile.

I hastily dressed in a loose-fitting shirt, grey cloth coat, tan trousers and polished boots. Morning ablutions would wait. When I saw Elspeth, however, I regretted my decision to forego my toilet, for she was the picture of well turned-out gentility. Dressed in a white blouse with billowing sleeves, a full riding skirt of russet hue, and a small yellow bonnet, she brought the sunlight of the desert into the humble lobby of the Silver Lode.

"Miss Kane and I have spent much of the night talking," Holmes said quietly. "The body of Sergeant Davis will be transported to England, but we shall remain here until justice is done."

I opened my mouth to object. My first task was to make sure no harm came to these two, and this town was a dangerous place. The next stagecoach out was five days away. In fact, I had considered sending a telegram to Pinkerton urging him to send an Army escort and coach to take us to the railhead in California, but realized that plan would take at least a week.

"I'm famished," Elspeth said before I could voice my objections. "Shall we be going?"

The discussion the two had had during the night must have been productive, I thought. She seemed to have a glint in her eye I hadn't seen before. It made me a bit uneasy.

"The Blue Cup Restaurant is a block away. It'll be better than the muck served at the café across the street," I volunteered.

I followed Elspeth and Sherlock toward the front door, but had a new thought. "Hold on a minute," I said quietly, as they turned toward me. "I seem to be drawing a rough crowd of late. It may be better if you two go ahead. I'll just stay back awhile and step out alone. We can meet up at the Blue Cup."

"Do think it's safe for us to walk about the streets alone, Mr. Goodfoote?" Elspeth asked.

"Safer than it would be if I accompanied you. And, like the lad here said, we can't find Maldrome by hiding in a hotel room. I'll follow in a few minutes."

With that we went our separate ways. I watched the couple stroll into the sunshine and mingle with the townsfolk. I had another thought, and went to the back door. Something about last night was irritating the mystery nerve in my brain. I entered the yard and examined the ground. Immediately, I saw my footprints in the dust. Curious, I did a quick scout looking for other tracks to see if the sound I heard the night before was my imagination, or something more sinister.

This is strange, I thought. My own tracks, with my clearly defined sole prints, were obvious. But just a few feet from where I had been standing, were faint lines in the dust. Try as I might, the lines brought no notion of what could have made them. A couple of feet further toward the arroyo were more marks, as if something had come from the near-dry river bed and wound up at the back door. It was a mystery, and I put it into my mental 'puzzle box.' Then I hurried back to the lobby, nodding to the robust, youthful clerk who had replaced Pottle at the desk. But rather than step directly out the front door, I took a slight detour.

The Silver Lode has a restaurant on one side connected to the lobby through a double door. The other side is given over to Bell's Emporium, again connected by a double door. I went into the Emporium, purchased a few of their finer cigars, and then stepped out onto the boardwalk. My eyes adjusted to the morning light while I scanned the street. Sheriff Bodkin, Blade and a group of rough-looking deputies were standing across the alley that ran next to the hotel. I stepped off the sidewalk and strolled up the street toward the sheriff.

"Breed!"

I turned facing Mange as he moved out of the alley holding a 10 gauge shotgun pointing in my general direction. He was within spitting distance of the sheriff.

My Indian blood remembered what my uncle, Keeps-the-Lodge of the Blackfoot Nation, told me when I was just a pup. Life and death didn't really matter. It's all the same.

But my Irish blood didn't like looking down the business end of a 10-gauge held by a skulking killer like Mange who had an uncommon hatred of me.

"I'm gonna' kill you, Goodfoote, you half-breed, copper-colored, blood-thirsty son-of-a-bitch. And there ain't nothin' you can do about it, God Damn you."

This was only my third day in Disenchantment. Heat, dust and stink pretty much summed up this town, and, despite current appearances, I wasn't about to die here. Mange, who had been merely a nuisance, was becoming downright annoying.

"You pole-axed one of my friends last night, and you ain't gonna git away with it. This here scattergun will make two of you, so git on your knees and start beggin,' you stinkin' pile of horseshit."

That's almost humorous, I thought, coming from Mange whose stench stung my nose although he was a good ten feet away. He had the pungent smell of someone who sleeps in clothes never touched by soap and water.

But I didn't respond. I didn't think talking would get me out of this. And I didn't get on my knees.

"Say hello to Hell, Breed," Mange said, as he cocked back the hammer.

I drew and killed Mange with two shots. The first hunk of lead exploded his heart, the second his brain. My Irish part had calculated that it takes two heartbeats for a sober man to pull the trigger of a cocked shotgun. A sober man has to see me start to draw, make the decision what to do about it, and jerk back on the trigger. A man with a pickled brain like Mange, and an uncocked shotgun, will take five heartbeats. I had plenty of time, and I'm quicker than a snake. Heat, dust, stink, and blood.

Mange lay face up in the dirt, his left leg jerking spasmodically. His normal acrid smell was now mixed with the pungent odor of blood and brains. My Remington Army pistol chambers a large caliber with a heavy powder kicker so I figured the whole back part of the man's head was gone. I didn't get down to look.

I slipped my revolver into the cross-draw belly holster I fancy, turned on my heel, and continued on my way. Sheriff Bodkin had been standing on the sidewalk not six feet away from Mange when the gunman had stepped from the alley. The Law had been leaning on a post looking like he had enjoyed the show. Now, when he saw me look at him, he spat a chaw into the street. I kept walking. The day had just begun and I was ready for breakfast.

CHAPTER 16

◻ ◻ ◻

Far, far overhead, a Golden Eagle called four times.

TU SAT QUIETLY watching her husband make preparations for his Spirit Walk. She knew that once he had given away his Bear Protection, his time would be short. Yesterday, Dasod had told Neva to gather six warriors. She had heard the Shaman tell the men to help Kaya in her upcoming battle, that she couldn't conquer this enemy alone. Then, Neva and his small band had followed Dasod into the sweat lodge the medicine man had built in the red-walled canyon near the camp of the Aiaha. Later, she saw Neva and his warriors leave the camp, painted and dressed for war.

Tears filled her eyes as Dasod gathered his sacred medicine pouch and a special blanket woven by the People-of-Colored-Robes, the Navaho. Tu followed the old man out the door of their wikiup where he gathered his water bag from the arbor pole. He turned and smiled at his wife.

"Your tears are for the joy to which I go," he said. He reached for her with his free hand. Her tears wet his hand as she pressed it to her face. Then, she began to sing the sacred 'Traveling Song.' Dasod turned away

and walked toward the West, her singing filling his heart with happiness.

"Wa-ho. In a sacred manner, I walk.
In a sacred manner, I walk.
My eyes are clear of pain.
My heart is clear of pain.
My hands are clear of evil.
My feet are on the red road.
In a sacred manner, I walk.
Wa-ho. In a sacred manner I walk.
Ho-wa, Ho-wa, Ho-wa"

Far, far overhead, a Golden Eagle called four times.

CHAPTER 17

◙ ◙ ◙

When I got to the Blue Cup Restaurant, I found Elspeth and Sherlock sitting in a far corner, menus in hand. They had apparently not yet ordered, so I picked up a menu, made sure my back was to the wall, facing the door, and sat down. Both had their heads down as if intently studying the list of daily offerings. Neither spoke after I greeted them.

"What kind of person are you?" Elspeth finally said, laying down her menu. "You just killed a man, and yet you sit here, calmly, about to order breakfast." She paused, her face flushed.

"Pinkerton's doesn't employ Quakers for this type of assignment, Miss," I answered. "And few Baptists."

She stared into my eyes for a moment, then looked away. "This town… these people…" she said, as she looked at Sherlock. She shook her head, then sighed deeply.

"We were outside the restaurant and saw the entire episode. It was shocking to both this young man and myself." She set her jaw in her now-familiar manner. "I suppose you're right. We do have need of a man who can handle a firearm. But have you no remorse for the man's death?"

I continued to scan my menu. "He won't be missed by many, Miss Kane. A good hanging would have been more peaceful, but I was out of rope at the moment." I put down my menu, leaned forward and looked into her pale face. "Remorse won't get the job done, Miss Kane. This is rough country, and this is a murderous crowd. The man I just gunned down was sent to kill me. I suspect his handlers are the same people who ordered Sergeant Davis' death. And they won't stop coming."

"Then it's time for us to stop reacting and rather form our own plan," Master Holmes said in a near whisper. "If we're to survive and find Maldrome, we'll need to keep ahead of his hired killers." For one so young, the lad had a head full of smarts.

Mrs. Nelson took our order and poured me coffee. Silence reigned at the table until our food was served, hot and plentiful. I tucked in and paused when I noted Elspeth was only picking at her food. She had little appetite, either for the local fare or the killing. But Holmes, seemingly unaffected, was engaged in his second egg and slice of ham. He was right, of course, about the need to form a plan, and my brain was already working in that direction.

"This group has made two runs at me in the short time I've been here," I said, as I swallowed the last bit of my toast. "Yet they haven't gone after young Sherlock here, and I'm starting to wonder at that. He would seem to be the natural target of Maldrome."

"What do you mean, two runs at you?" Elspeth's face looked pinched around her eyes, a sign of stress I hadn't seen before. I filled them in on my talk with Winthrop, and the shots and yells at the rear of the Silver Slipper Saloon.

Elspeth pushed her plate from her. "Perhaps they don't know that he can recognize Maldrome, and your troubles may be from your own past," she said.

Sherlock Holmes spoke up. "But that wouldn't explain the attack on Sergeant Davis. We had been in town for only a few days. And we still haven't heard from the two government men who accompanied us." His lips pursed, and his eyes shown with a steely brightness. "The question, Mr. Goodfoote, is who attacked the man behind the saloon? Whoever it was may very well have saved your life."

"I do have a thought on that, Master Sherlock. Mange said the man was poleaxed, not shot. It's mostly a mystery and, for now, I'll just take it as a gift, and let it go."

"I'm beginning to think it's time the boy and I left this pestilent town before they kill us all. Sherlock can't identify Maldrome from the grave," Elspeth said. Her voice had lost all strength, and was barely above a whisper. Seeing a man shot down in the street, even a man like Mange, had, it seemed, forced Miss Kane to change her mind about justice for Davis.

Both Holmes and I looked at her. Sherlock placed his hand over hers on the table, and she didn't pull away. "We can't leave until we find this criminal mastermind," the boy said quietly. "He's responsible for the destruction of too many innocent lives."

"Miss Kane has a valid point," I interjected. "But there is no stagecoach until next week, so we may as well do what we can until then. You have arranged for Sergeant Davis' body to be shipped by the freight carrier, and we can follow later on the Butterfield stage."

Holmes leaned back in his chair. "We have until next week, then, to find Maldrome."

"Five days," I said, nodding. "And it will be a long five days, I wager."

"Do you have any questions for us?" Holmes had ordered tea for himself and Miss Kane and put down his cup as he leaned toward me. The lady sat quietly staring across the room.

"Where did the Sergeant spend his time during his short stay in Disenchantment?" I asked.

Elspeth seemed to snap out of her reverie and picked up her teacup. "Well, he was going to meet with the sheriff again. Then he was to make inquires at the saloons for signs of any recently arrived patrons with large bankrolls."

Sherlock Holmes refilled his cup. He looked at Miss Kane with the teapot raised, but she shook her head. "The Empire Saloon was where he felt he had made a bit of progress," he said, replacing the pot. "The evening before his demise, he mentioned planning to meet someone there in the morning. It would seem a logical place to start our own inquires."

"My inquires, Lad. I plan to move you both to the safety of the mountains. I'll return to town alone, and continue the investigation."

"The mountains, for pity's sake? Among the savages? You do know the heathens are rampaging across this part of the country? We shall be murdered by the end of the first day." Miss Kane stared at me, her eyes wide. "Besides, you'd be unable to identify Maldrome without Sherlock's help, and he's my responsibility, especially now that Mr. Davis is no longer with us."

I leaned back in my chair, watching the door of the restaurant. "When I find a likely prospect, I'll bring the lad in to take a look. But until then…"

The door to the café opened and Sheriff Bodkin stepped in. In his left hand he carried his shotgun. He fastened his eyes on our table, but then stepped to one side of the door.

A corpulent man of middle years made his entrance into the restaurant as if he was stepping before the footlights of the Palace. He was dressed in a long, dark morning coat, shiny silver vest, gray pin-striped trousers, and a broad-brimmed plantation hat. Unless he had a hidden derringer, the big man carried no firearms. His vest sported a gold watch-chain that looked heavy enough to buy the town. A small grey goatee and mustache were dwarfed by his round face, and as he turned to our table, his smile showed small yellowing teeth with one prominent gold incisor. He held a cigarette in a holder in one hand, and swept, more than walked, toward us. The sheriff leaned against the far wall, and I perceived that the twin barrels of his shotgun were pointed in our general direction. I could see Deputy Blade through the window of the restaurant as he lounged against the front of the building, right outside the door.

"Mr. Goodfoote, I'm told," the large man boomed. "My name is

Von Herder."

He said it as if it should be immediately recognizable.

"I'm honored, Sir," I replied, as I stood up. Few can match me in the genteels. I noted the other customers in the restaurant heading out the door.

"Count Henreich Stephone Von Herder, to be precise," he said loudly. The Count gave a little bow, as he swept his hat from his head. I expected a heel click, but none was forthcoming.

When at Harvard, I had spent summers in Europe and had become familiar with a few of the Middle European accents. Von Herder's speech was definitely Viennese, but whether the accent was genuine or not, was open to question.

I looked at Sherlock Holmes to see if he recognized Maldrome in this pompous bullfrog. The boy gave a slight headshake. The Count certainly didn't match the lad's description of the villain seen in London, but William Pinkerton had warned me that the rogue would often use a disguise. However, according to the newspaperman Winthrop, Von Herder had been in Disenchantment when Maldrome was still in England being chased by Scotland Yard, so the timing was wrong for the two men to be the same miscreant.

"Please join us," I said. "Let me introduce Miss Sigerson and her brother, Will."

Von Herder gave another bow to each. I resumed my seat, but the Count remained standing.

"It seems you shot one of my men," Von Herder continued. "Just a few minutes ago, I'm told."

I nodded. "So Mange was on your payroll," I said. "One can only wonder in what capacity."

"I asked the sheriff not to arrest you. He wanted you hanged for murder."

I smiled.

Von Herder now pulled out a chair and sat down. Beads of sweat covered his brow. "Mange was a handy man to have around the ranch, but he liked the town life." The Count waved his cigarette holder in the air making little circles of smoke. "A man of various gifts, although impulsive. I hold no grudge, Sir. Someone would have shot the fool, sooner or later. "

Both Elspeth and Holmes sat silently watching our exchange.

"More importantly, what is your reason for being in my town, Mr. Goodfoote?" The count swept a white handkerchief across his face.

"I'm sure the sheriff has told you. I'm with the Pinkerton Detective Agency. I was hired to protect this family from any depredations while they conduct their business."

Von Herder gave a deep sigh. "A noble endeavor, to be sure. But with the death of the gentleman in the hotel, surely their business here is concluded, and the continued presence of you, the gentlelady, and the boy, is unnecessary." Another wave of his cigarette holder. "To be blunt, Sir, when will you be leaving?"

"We may be enjoying the pastoral scenery of this fair village for some time yet," I said, not to be outdone in the literary verbiage. I leaned back in my chair. This innocent motion did two things. One, it gave me an air of nonchalance. More importantly, it brought my revolver close to my gun-hand, although I would try to avoid gunplay anywhere near either of my charges.

Von Herder stood, still smiling. Another wave of his cigarette holder sent a shower of ashes into the air. "Very well. But this can be a cantankerous town, Sir. Remarkably cantankerous. Especially for ladies and the young, wouldn't you say?"

I nodded, returning the smile. "I'll keep them close," I said. I remained seated, but locked eyes with the man. Von Herder held my scrutiny for only a moment, then swung toward the door. At the threshold, he paused and turned to us as he pulled his hat firmly onto his head.

"*Besser laufen, als faulen,*" he said, then swept out, followed by the Sheriff. Elspeth, Holmes and I sat in silence for a few moments. I finished my coffee. "What was that last remark?" Elspeth asked. "Just as the fop left?"

"It was from Goethe," Holmes answered. He refilled his teacup. " 'Better to run than to rot'."

CHAPTER 18

◩ ◩ ◩

Bedford had earned my trust in a business where trust is a precious commodity.

One of the most enterprising men I have ever had the good fortune to meet is one Jubal Trevelyan Bedford. Mr. Bedford was barely out of his teens when he rode with Jeb Stuart from Chancellorsville to the Battle of Yellow Tavern. A wild and daring cavalry man, he was often at the front of the head-long running attacks favored by Stuart and the Army of Northern Virginia. I first laid eyes on Jubal T. when he lay in a Union field hospital, wounded and captured during the final weeks of the War. A year or two after the end of hostilities, I watched him put down a riot in a Kansas cattle town. He wore a deputy sheriff's badge then, and he displayed the same calmness that others had noted during some of the fiercest fighting of the War. And now, some years later, he worked for the Pinkertons, a valued operative, and a fast friend. Bedford had earned my trust in a business where trust is a precious commodity, and not to be taken lightly.

I had dispatched Jubal T. to Disenchantment before I had left

Chicago. His specialty, along with his skill with a Colt and an unhealthy love of his horse, was an ability to blend in with any populace. The gentleman could change more than his attire. It was the way he moved, spoke, spit, and scratched that made him invisible in any gathering. No one but me, not even William A. Pinkerton himself, knew Jubal T. Bedford was in Disenchantment. He was my hole card that I knew was an Ace.

  Dressed as a worthless drunk, Bedford had drawn my attention in the Silver Slipper when he had thrown up on the floor during my brief discussion with Mange. Now, I needed to know what he had learned in the time he had been trolling for information.

CHAPTER 19

◘ ◘ ◘

*"If I sent someone after you, Mr. Goodfoote,
it wouldn't be a fool like Mange."*

I parted company with Elspeth and Sherlock in front of our hotel and headed down the street toward the Empire Saloon. Jubal T. would find me, or I would find him, most likely in one of the town's drinking holes. The Empire was the first on my list, as it was the one name Holmes had had from Sergeant Davis.

The saloon lived up to its name. Money had been spent, and spent well. The far wall sported a long oak bar, topped with black marble. A full-length gilt-framed mirror, fronted by sparkling bottles of various liquors, was back of the bar. Two barkeeps dressed in white shirts with red vests were serving a few customers, while two Chinese men wearing white smocks carried drinks to the tables. Cut-glass chandeliers hung from a plaster-mould ceiling. The brass spittoons were polished to a golden shine, and the wooden floor looked like it was cleaned and waxed regularly. The roulette table was empty, and the Chuck-a-Luck wheel was still. An air of quiet respectability pervaded the large room, but the day had just begun. A handful of customers were quietly conversing, and a couple of trollops were sitting out of the way, against a wall. They barely looked up when I walked in the open double door. Their business would start in earnest after dark.

Blade sat at a table with two other men. All three had been wearing deputy stars when I had seen them earlier on the street. None had badges on now. They looked at me long and hard as I made my way up to the bar, but they didn't move. Someone was holding their chain, and I suspected it was Von Herder. Blade hated me as much as Mange had, but he didn't have orders to take me on. It said much about the discipline in this gang.

I got a beer and sat at a side table facing the bar. Again, I made sure my back was to the wall. I also had a side view of the door. The table where Blade and his pals sat was in front of me and to my left.

After a few minutes, Blade leaned over and spoke to one of the men, the one the sheriff had called 'Dub.' With a nod, Dub rose and ambled to the staircase that ran up to a balcony running over the bar. He climbed to the second floor and knocked on a door. Minutes later, I was surprised when Von Herder gazed at me over the side of the railing, then followed Dub down to the barroom.

After greeting several customers, Von Herder made his way to my table. He dropped into a chair opposite me, put on his disingenuous smile, and paused to light the cigarette in its holder.

"Mr. Goodfoote. Have you followed me here to continue our discussion? You honor our humble dwelling with your presence."

I looked around the room. "You've done well for yourself. It's a magnificent place."

"Well, it will do."

I glanced at Blade and the deputies. "You seem to keep the sheriff and his minions on a tight leash," I said. "So I wonder if Mange slipped his collar, or if someone gave him orders to kill me."

The smile on his broad face slipped a bit. "If I sent someone after you, Mr. Goodfoote, it wouldn't be a fool like Mange. That, as they say, you can take to the bank."

I smiled back. "Maybe someone armed with a fake Chiricahua hatchet? And a bucket of pig's blood?"

"You are boring me, Mr. Goodfoote." He then paused for a moment. "What do you mean 'fake' Chiricahua hatchet?"

"I know a lot of Apache, but never met one who used a hatchet."

Von Herder's smile weakened. "I'm sure you're incorrect on that point." He blew a stream of smoke toward the ceiling. "Anyway, I think the three of you should heed my advice and leave Disenchantment. The Apache, Chiricahua or otherwise, are getting closer every day, and this can be a rough town for women and children."

"You've shifted your accent," I said with false surprise. "It was Viennese, now it's Prussian."

Von Herder's smile remained plastered in place. He seemed to be sizing me up. Finally, he took a long pull on his cigarette. "I was born in Austria, but spent much time in Prussia." He reached into an inside pocket and produced his white handkerchief which he used to dab his moist brow.

It was time for me to push and see what popped. "No, I read East End London in your speech, probably near the Bow Bells." It was a long shot that caught him between wind and water, as the nautical saying goes.

Von Herder stood, his face red. "Leave this town, Mr. Goodfoote," he said through clenched teeth. "If you can." With that, he turned to go.

"What," I said, "no pithy quote from Goethe? You disappoint me, Sir." A little salt adds spice to the brew.

I watched Blade and his men rise from their chairs, and I did the same. But Von Herder stopped halfway up the staircase, turned, and motioned the rouges to sit down. They did, but their hard stares followed me as I walked to the door and stepped out onto the sidewalk.

I wondered again at the hand that held the reins to these men. Bodkin was a hired gun, plain and simple, but his chain was held by who? Von Herder? The Count was a middle manager, shuffling papers, buying up silver mines and real estate. To what end? The silver, by all accounts, was playing out in this part of the territory and would be gone in a couple of years. According to Winthrop, only low-grade ore was being pulled out of the ground now and mineral rights were going cheap. Why take over a town and buy up worthless property?

Behind it all, I felt sure, was the invisible Mr. Maldrome. Miss Kane and the boy had been in town for several days and I had enough evidence of young Sherlock's powers to feel confident he would have spotted the villain in any disguise. And a nagging feeling that William A. Pinkerton knew a lot more then he had let on during our brief meeting was beginning to haunt me.

My next stop was the Red Garter Saloon back down the street near the hotel. As I paused to light a cigar, and watch to see if anyone exited behind me, I noticed Sherlock Holmes, dressed in his safari outfit, walking along the board sidewalk toward me on the opposite side of the street. As he strolled along, his gaze was moving across the faces of the men he passed. He merely glanced at each passerby, and didn't miss a single person. All came under his brief scrutiny, even as some heads turned to stare at him. I wasn't sure he had seen me, as the intervening dirt street was choked with wagons and teamsters.

I had just stepped off the sidewalk to intercept Sherlock when a rifle shot exploded from an alley between two buildings on my side of the street. I saw Sherlock Holmes fall.

CHAPTER 20

◙ ◙ ◙

*She held a Colt in her hand, her arm outstretched,
aiming right at me.*

The window of the haberdashery Sherlock had been passing shattered. More rifle shots poured lead at the lad as he lay on the sidewalk. Slivers of wood flew from the hitching rail and spouts of water jumped from the horse trough Sherlock had dived behind.

By this time I was running toward the alley, revolver in hand, people in the street scattering like pigeons. A team of walleyed drays bolted out of control, tipped over a wagon, and sent barrels of beer onto the street. Another shot, this time from a pistol, cracked from the alley. A moment later I spun around the corner ready to fire. A man lay face up in the dirt, a shiny new Henry repeating rifle across his hands. Blood soaked the front of his shirt. I kicked his rifle away.

Standing there, not ten feet from the dead man, was Elspeth Kane.

She held a Colt in her hand, her arm outstretched, aiming right at me. Her eyes were fixed and staring. When I spoke her name, she seemed to recover her senses and dropped her arm to her side. The gun fell into the dust. With a slight groan, Elspeth covered her face with her hands.

I ran quickly back to the horse trough where Holmes had sought cover, leaving Elspeth in the alley. Sherlock was on his feet, dusting off his knee breeches and looking for his pith helmet.

"Are you hit?" I asked. I grabbed the lad by his shoulder and examined him quickly.

"No, Mr. Goodfoote," he said calmly. "He fired high."

"It was a close thing, Lad," I said.

"Some of his shots came somewhat close." He pointed to the splintered wood.

"We can be thankful he was a bad shot," I said. The boy seemed incredibly calm for someone who had been shot at and missed by only inches.

"I don't think those we pursue would send a bad shot to eliminate me. They would send their best man."

He picked up his helmet and we hurried toward the alley where a large crowd of gawkers had gathered. Miss Kane was wiping the dust from her pistol which she put into her handbag as Holmes and I approached.

"Are you strong enough to walk to the hotel?" I asked. When she nodded, I took her arm and walked her around the dead man.

She suddenly stopped and looked at Sherlock. "My God. Are you all right?" she cried out. Holmes just nodded.

I had work to do in this alley, so I turned Elspeth over to a couple of upstanding-looking women. Clucking and cooing like hens, the women walked Elspeth out of the alley.

The body of the shooter lay in the dust, head to the street, feet to the opening that ran behind the passageway. His hat had come off and long dark hair flowed past his shoulders. I quickly examined his wound and noted it was a small hole directly in the center of his chest. Death had come instantaneously, the bullet stopping his heart from pumping much blood onto the ground. He must have turned to face the rear of the alley when Elspeth shot him dead. I squatted down and tilted him over so I could see his back. There was no wound coming out. Dark blue work pants, a grey shirt, and a brightly beaded vest completed his outfit. High cheek bones and a prominent nose were his main facial features. I picked up his hat. It had a high crown, black with silver Conchos around the band.

"Do you recognize him?" I asked Holmes, who was standing with his hands behind his back. He shook his head from side to side. I turned to the crowd. Across the street, I saw Blade standing with a smile on his face.

"Does anyone recognize him?" I asked.

"Yeah," a grizzled old prospector grunted. "It's that Kiowa Kid. He's one of Bodkin's deputies, when he ain't rustling cattle or holding up the stagecoach." The old man let loose a stream of brown tobacco juice, as if to punctuate his sentence. There was a general murmur of agreement from the crowd.

"Someone better tell the sheriff," I said. "He can find me at the hotel, if he's looking." Holmes and I turned and headed to the Silver Lode.

"Miss Kane saved your bacon, Lad," I said.

" I thought Miss Kane was asleep."

"She must have come after you — and was able to act decisively when she saw you in danger."

Holmes gave a quick smile. "Miss Kane means well, but she smothers me with her constant shielding. I felt the need to get out and delve into this matter for myself." He gave me a quick glance. "And, as I said, I don't believe I was in real danger. The man was shooting high."

I nodded. "They sent Juan Catena. He seldom misses his first shot, let alone several."

"You knew him, then?"

"Only by reputation. His moniker is the 'Kiowa Kid,' a name he invented for himself. He's neither Kiowa, nor a Kid. I never had call to cross his path when I was Marshalling, but I heard a lot about him." I paused. "He's noted for his skill with a rifle."

"I saw his reflection in the window of the haberdashery shop just before he fired. I was diving behind the horse trough before the rifle went off," Sherlock explained.

I nodded. "That accounts for it, then," I said. We arrived at the hotel and walked into the lobby. "I've seen wanted posters on a couple of Bodkin's deputies, top gunhands all. Well known as brutal killers." I motioned to the wing chairs along the wall. "We can sit here while you tell me what you noticed about the town."

We had just sat down when Elspeth came through the door from the Emporium. I noted her color had returned and she seemed in control of herself once more.

"My Dear God, Sherlock. You could have been killed!" She fluttered around him with endearments that soon gave way to censure and scolding for going off on his own. Holmes, for his part, showed as much emotion as he did when the bullets were flying. "You must promise never to leave my side. You cannot be on the street by yourself. I won't have it!"

Holmes looked at her. "I will investigate the death of Sergeant Davis however I choose, Miss Kane," he said quietly. "Nothing will deter me from this inquiry."

"You are a mere boy," Elspeth Kane burst out. "You will do as you are told!"

Holmes stood and picked up his helmet. "Thank you for your assistance with the gunman," he said to her. Turning, he walked through the double doors of the lobby into the Emporium.

Miss Kane watched him go, then turned to me, her face red with agitation.

"You were sent to protect us," she said. "I expect you to fulfill your duty, as Sergeant Davis would have done. You should see that he follows my orders."

"And I will. It's a marvel you arrived at such a commodious time, just as that killer was lining the boy up in his sights. Very fortunate for the lad."

"Yes," she replied. "I was looking at some hats in the millinery shop when I heard the first shot. I ran out and saw that man pointing a rifle at Sherlock, so I drew my revolver and yelled at him to drop his gun. He turned toward me instead, and I fired."

"An accurate shot it was, indeed," I offered. "And a quick eye to recognize Sherlock behind the horse trough across the street."

"His choice of clothing is unique in Disenchantment, I believe. It makes him a ready target for any gunman."

My thoughts were on the emotions of young Holmes. He was able to handle blood, examine the dead, and face imminent danger without turning a hair. In addition, the entreaties of a beautiful woman seemed to have little effect on him. He was headed for a life of greatness or madness, I concluded. Perhaps both.

I rose and turned to Miss Kane. "Elspeth, you did your duty magnificently. I'll do mine with as much skill and resolve as is humanly possible. Now, if you can persuade Sherlock, you and he should probably stay in the hotel for now. I need to see a man about a horse." With that, I strode through the door and onto the streets of Disenchantment.

The body of the Kiowa Kid had been taken to the busy Swann's mortuary by the time I arrived back at the alley. With the body gone, the crowd had dissipated, the good citizens of Disenchantment returning to their iniquitous lives. I stepped around the few bloodstains in the dirt and walked the length of the alley. My backtrack of the Kiowa Kid's boot prints led directly to a Paint pony tied loosely to a post behind the buildings. I then examined the ground for Elspeth's smaller tracks. Her footprints showed she had come out the side door of the millinery shop into the alley between the store and the Assay Office.

I got down on my hands and knees and read the manuscript in the dust, remembering lessons from my mentor Keeps-the-Lodge. When I was a boy learning at his knee, he often said that the wisdom of life was in the tracks. I have carried his words and his lessons my whole life, and was to apply them once again.

From what I read on the ground, Miss Kane had stepped from the side door of the shop and moved behind the gunman. Her feet were then spread side-by-side, in what some characterize as 'The Ladies Stance,' so-called because the gun is held in two hands for stability. The Kid turned when Miss Kane called out to him. Her tracks showed no hesitation, which can be seen by small waves Keeps-the-Lodge called 'shadowing.'

Just then, I spotted the red face of a broken-down drunk peering around the corner of the building that housed the Assay Office, then it pulled back. I got to my feet and headed over to talk to Jubal T. Bedford.

"You've created quite a sensation, Charles," he said, as he leaned against the back wall of the building. "Killing seems to follow you around. Two bodies in one day. That's a stretch, even for you." While he talked, he pulled the fixings for a cigarette from his shirt pocket. From the battered broad-brimmed hat set atop his pile of greasy hair, to the worn, dusty boots, one with a broken heel, Bedford looked, and smelled, the part of the town drunk. I noted with some interest his coat, for I had seen it recently on one of the cadavers stretched out in Swann's Undertaking Parlour. It covered a dirty work shirt, partially tucked into his broadcloth pants with holes in both knees. He had poured whiskey on the coat to give it an authentic smell, but there was a more pungent odor about him. I recognized it as horse urine. A black eyepatch completed his outfit.

"The second one wasn't mine," I said. "I had help."

"So I heard." Jubal T. offered me his tobacco, and I shook my head. "I was in the Red Garter when I heard the shots," he said. "I circled around, but it was all over by the time I got here."

"Well, Miss Kane was able to drop the Kiowa Kid before he did any real damage."

"How did she take the killing?" he asked.

"She seemed a might shaken at first, but she recovered quickly. I don't know exactly what her original assignment was, but she sees her duty now as protecting the boy, and she stepped up when needed. The beautiful Miss Kane drilled the Kid right through the pump, dead center."

Jubal T. looked puzzled. "How did she do that when he was busy pouring lead onto Compton Street? What made him turn around?"

"She said she called to him to drop his rifle. To a gunman like Juan Catena, that would bring him whirling, ready to shoot whoever was interfering. Miss Kane's footprints show determination, solid tracks with no second thoughts. That's how she was able to put her bullet through his heart. Two handed. Anyway, that's one more of Maldrome's boys out of our way."

Jubal T. smiled as he licked the paper of his cigarette. He touched a flame to the rolled butt, took a deep drag, and exhaled a stream of smoke. "Two down, a hundred to go."

I nodded. "What happened behind the Silver Slipper last night? I heard shots and a yell."

Jubal T. took a drag on his cigarette. "Yeah, that was me. I figured you'd be coming out the back, so I staggered out to relieve myself. There was Zeke, one of Bodkin's men, lurking behind a water barrel. I tapped him over the head, fired his gun in the air, and gave a holler."

"Did anyone spot you?"

"No one sees a drunk pissing in an alley in Disenchantment, Charles. And by the time the rest ran to the alley, I was out the back."

I thought for a minute. "Thanks for the help, Jubal."

"That's my job, old friend."

"Did you happen to follow me back to the hotel?" I was still wondering about the strange marks in the dirt.

"No. I went right back to the livery stable. I'm sleeping in the haybarn there. Next to Triumph."

I smiled. "You still have that bay horse," I said. "You should marry her."

"Why ruin a good friendship?" Jubal T. said with a grin. He then got serious.

"One thing you might be interested in," he said, then paused as he pulled his eyepatch onto his forehead.

"What's that? Anything would help right about now."

He rubbed the eye the patch had covered. "Something I heard the sheriff tell his deputies over in the Empire last night. Bodkin and his gang are leaving town for a couple of days. It sounded like they'll be heading out to Von Herder's fort."

"Fort?"

"Haven't you heard? Von Herder built himself a fort, but he calls it a ranch. His house looks like something from a stately Southern plantation. Only, it's surrounded by adobe walls, gun ports, sentries… built for defending against the Apache, he says. He's even got a Gatling gun and a couple of cannons."

I filed away this information, then asked, "Any idea when Bodkin is leaving?"

"Could be any time, I guess. They must be waiting for something, or somebody, or they would have been out there already."

I thought for a moment. "Maldrome hasn't shown himself around town, so there's a chance he's at the ranch."

Jubal T. pulled the eyepatch back over his eye, crushed out his cigarette butt with the toe of his boot, and turned to go. "I'll keep my eye open," he said, as he flashed his wide grin. "Keep safe, Charles."

On my way out of the alley, I picked up two cartridges. They were forty-four caliber, rim-fire casings, certainly from the shooter's Henry repeater. The rifle, now in the hands of either the sheriff or an enterprising thief, had appeared to be new. Henry repeaters were no longer manufactured, but they had been, and still were, a formidable weapon.

Unless I was mistaken, the chain of command of these murderers went from Maldrome, to Von Herder, to Bodkin. From there it went to a large group of hardriders. So far, all we had run into were the gunmen, with Bodkin and Von Herder as their handlers. But I knew a criminal organization needed more. It needed a source of revenue, like any government, and from Winthrop's information, the silver mines were mostly defunct. It also needed informers among the enemy. Maybe even someone to tell them what Pinkerton's Agency was doing.

CHAPTER 21

◙ ◙ ◙

*"Bodies are as common in this town as
crows at a buffalo jump."*

My thoughts were interrupted by the arrival of Doc Gosling. In addition to being the only physician, dentist, and druggist for two hundred miles around, Doc Gosling was also the local clergy. I had had business with him when I was in town two years past, and we knew each other well.

Doc was a tall man, thin as a hay-stem with a mane of grey hair that hung to his shoulders, a scruffy salt-and-pepper beard in need of trimming, and watery blue eyes that peered through wire-rimmed spectacles. With a long, pointy nose, wearing his black rumpled suit, and bent almost double from his years at bedsides of thousands of patients, Doc Gosling looked like a great wading bird about to peck at a frog. He was by far the smartest man in these parts, and the proud possessor of the only microscope in town, other than my own. In addition to his preaching duties, he delivered babies, prescribed treatments, dug out bullets, pulled teeth, and removed infected arms and legs. When his ministrations didn't work, he gave last rites.

He was also the Coroner.

"Marshal Goodfoote," Doc said, as I stood at the entrance to the alley. "I heard of your return. Is it true you are no longer with the government, but have taken up the calling of a private citizen?"

"More or less, Doc. It's good to see you."

We chatted for several minutes, standing in the shade of the assay office, before the Doc got to the point.

"The Summerset boys, little Cal and Israel, found a couple of bodies in that wash some folks call the Tomorrow River. They told their father, and he told me."

"Bodies are as common in this town as crows at a buffalo jump. What's special about these?"

He pulled a battered pipe from his pocket. "Nothing I was particularly interested in. They had been laying there for a while and the coyotes and pigs had a go at them." He put a flame to the bowl and puffed until he got it going. "They're mostly skeletons, just a little meat left by the varmints. But you being a private citizen now, you probably have other things to occupy your time." He seemed to take an intense interest in the passing scene of wagons, walkers, and horsemen. "Maybe I better tell Sheriff Bodkin. He's the law here."

"You didn't come over here for no reason, Doc," I said. "What did you find?"

"Well, one thing of note. When I examined the men's suits, I made a little discovery. The hogs had chewed some of the fabric, but there was enough left to see that the men had stitched their names and rank into their coats. They were two Army officers, traveling in mufti."

CHAPTER 22

◙ ◙ ◙

*Someone was attempting to insert a key
into the lock of my room.*

The sky had gone from red to purple to black, and I found myself once more in the Silver Lode Hotel. After seeing to my neglected ablutions, I sat for some time in the lobby organizing my thoughts.

From the time of my arrival, I had been faced with murder and bloodshed. Killing Mange wouldn't cause me any loss of sleep, for our final fight had been coming for some years. Miss Kane gunning down the Kiowa Kid was noteworthy. It was rare, even in Disenchantment, for a woman to shoot a known killer like the Kid. This was obviously a formidable woman, despite her vapors after the shooting.

The fate of the two government officers who had traveled with the English group was now known. Ex-military men who still had the habit of stitching their names and old Army units into their civilian clothes, they matched the information provided by Pinkerton. Whether they had been forced to reveal any information, or had given the identities of the English trio away willingly, was something only their killers knew.

I climbed the stairs to my room and began to get undressed, my mind still occupied by the puzzles of this assignment I had been handed.

A sound in the hallway got my attention. Then, a soft rapping at my door brought me quickly to the wall, dressed only in my trousers. My revolver was in my hand, fully cocked, when I asked who was knocking.

"It's me, Elspeth. Please, I must speak with you."

"Wait one moment." Quickly, I buttoned on a shirt, then opened the door carefully. Miss Kane, wrapped in a lounging gown, was standing in the hall. I admitted her into my room, then checked the hallway in both directions. All was quiet, and I closed the door.

I turned to find Elspeth standing in the middle of my room, dressed only in a thin nightdress of a greenish hue. Her shoulders and arms were bare, her outfit held up by thin straps. She threw the robe she had been wearing onto the bed, still made up as I hadn't yet graced its environs. Her gaze met mine directly, and her reason for this visit was clear. She stepped toward me and began to undo my shirt.

I will draw a veil over the ensuing events of that early evening. Some lads may come across this scrawl and be given prurient ideas that would be unhealthy for the innocent young. But I will say, my third day in Disenchantment was remarkable. After an hour, Elspeth left quietly in order that she might return to her own room unobserved.

It is my custom when sleeping in hotels in discommodious towns to place a chair under the doorknob. It assures that I will be awake if someone with murderous intentions comes calling during the hours of darkness. After the engagements with Mange and the Kiowa Kid, I made another concession to safety by placing pillows and blankets on my bed in such a manner as to falsify my sleeping there. In reality, I would be in my bedroll on the floor. If truth be known, I have never felt comfortable in a bed, even when living in the East, so I have often slept beside my bed on a blanket roll.

I curled up under the windows against the wall, and fell immediately into a light sleep. It was sometime between the middle of the night and the first light of dawn that I came awake. The town had finally quieted down, and peace held sway. For a moment I wondered what had wakened me. Then I heard it. A sound of metal scratching at the lock on my door. Someone was attempting to insert a key in the lock, but I had taken a further precaution of locking my door and leaving my key in it. I sat up slowly in the dark, my Remington hammered back. Silence from the hallway.

I had opened the three windows in my room about a foot in the hope of admitting any stray breeze. In the silence that followed the scratching in the hallway, the sound of a creaking loose board on the balcony outside my windows caught my attention. Someone was standing just outside my window, his shadow in the moonlight thrown across my bed. Cut-throats at the door, gunman at the window. This lot was serious about ending my stay here in Disenchantment.

I moved to stand against the wall adjoining my door while keeping my eye on the windows. Slowly, the doorknob turned and I expected the door to come crashing in, but instead, silence returned. Then I heard muffled whispers coming from the hallway.

Tiring of this game, I hit the door hard with my fist, making sure I was out of the line of fire if someone shot through it. This was answered by a gruff exclamation and a clamor from the corridor.

No sound came from the balcony, and I could see nothing moving outside my windows. I removed the chair from under the doorknob, turned the key, and jerked open the door. I ducked low and checked the hallway. Nothing stirred, and laughter from inside one of the frolic rooms was the only sound.

After I relocked the door and replaced the chair, I raised a window enough to see onto the balcony. No sign of anyone there. I pulled my way through the window opening and searched for footprints on the deck. To my surprise, I found some lines in the dust, like the ones I had discovered behind the hotel.

I returned to my bedroll, and while sleep was not immediately forthcoming, I awoke when the first light of dawn made outlines distinct.

CHAPTER 23

◨ ◨ ◨

"I'm not yet fully grown but were I to be so, I would thrash you for ungentlemanly behavior…"

We breakfasted early. This was going to be a busy day. Miss Kane, other than having little appetite, was exceedingly calm. Master Sherlock seemed to be regarding me with heightened interest.

"You have shaved off your mustaches," Elspeth said with a smile. "I'm not sure I like the change."

"It'll grow on you," I said.

"There is a notion in Disenchantment that sleep is not a primary requirement of those who reside here," I said. "Visitors feel free to call at all hours of the night." I smiled at Elspeth who had the good graces to blush prettily. Holmes fixed me with a glare.

"To what do you refer?" he asked in a quiet voice.

"Someone attempted to get into my room during the night. This person had a key, and may have meant me mischief." I related hearing the sounds outside my door and windows.

Although Sherlock said nothing else, he seemed more distracted than usual.

"I'll see to getting us mounts for the trip to the mountains," I said. "But first, we need to outfit ourselves for a few days. Food for a week should hold us. And the desert can get cold at night, so we'll need suitable clothing."

"I believe those are church bells I hear," Elspeth said. "Will the commodity stores be open on the Sabbath?"

"In a town located between Hell and Purgatory, I think we can safely assume the niceties of polite religion are, for the most part, ignored."

Elspeth said nothing, but I noted her jaw was set. She insisted a change of clothing was mandated by our upcoming shopping spree, so Holmes and I retired to the hotel lobby to await her return.

I leaned back on the couch, trying to find a comfortable position. Holmes stood in front of me, his hands clasped behind his back.

"Mr. Goodfoote," he began. I glanced up at him. "The evidence is clear that you and Miss Kane had a rendezvous last night." I smiled at his serious manner.

"We had a lot to discuss," I ventured.

"I'm not yet fully grown but were I to be so, I would thrash you for ungentlemanly behavior. You have taken advantage of an innocent woman who is far from her home and family. She has been thrust into a dangerous wilderness, rendering her vulnerable to your unfettered masculinity."

"Her vulnerability was well hidden when she blew a hole in the Kiowa Kid," I said as I sat up straight. "She may not be quite the innocent flower your portrait of her portrays."

"Nevertheless, I will thank you to remain professional regarding Miss Kane. She is under my protection as much as I am under hers."

I stood and bowed from the waist. "Master Holmes, I will endeavor to obey your wishes, to the best of my ability."

He searched my face for any sign I was not taking him seriously, as indeed, I was not. This time, however, he took me at my word.

"I would have preferred a more resolute concession. However, I accept your affirmation as a gentleman. This matter need never be discussed again," he said, offering his hand. We shook on it, just as Miss Kane descended the stairs.

Making good on my promise to move both Holmes and Elspeth to the mountains proved more difficult than I had thought.

"I agree that Sherlock should be placed in a safe setting," Elspeth said. "I will allow you to move him wherever you think he will be free from danger. My trust in you has grown." She set her jaw in a way that was becoming very familiar. "But I will remain here. As you may have observed, Charles, I am capable of caring for myself."

"You saw what happened to Sergeant Davis," I reminded her. "I'm sure he was an able policeman also."

"My mind is quite made up, Mr. Goodfoote. My duty is to see that the rotters who caused the death of Mr. Davis are brought to justice, and I'll not progress in my investigation by hiding out in the rocks. We are here to identify the mastermind of a vicious organization that nearly brought down the British government. I intend to get on with that assignment."

"Very well, Miss Kane. But my job is keeping you and the boy safe, and splitting you up will make my job doubly difficult." I let my words sink in, but could see they had no effect. I felt the lad was in more danger than Elspeth, and I needed to get him to a place where I could ensure his well-being.

Shopping was uncommonly simple. The boy already had clothing that would work well in the mountains and needed only a couple of additions. We purchased blankets, packs, and a grubstake that would last a good week, or until the next stagecoach came through.

I deposited Elspeth, young Holmes, and our recent purchases at the hotel after which I engaged the owner of Haggis Livery Stable in a hot debate over the choice of horseflesh he proposed to sell us. I don't like to haggle, but the cost he quoted for two horses was double the going price for good mounts, and, even when the money isn't mine, I refuse to pay usurious rates. I had the foresight to fill my pouch with gold coin before leaving Chicago, and gold is always appreciated. Fortunately, we came to a mutual agreement and he threw in well-worn saddles and bridles for a small-enough extra fee.

"This here fine Arabian mix is called Dobs, on account of his gentle nature," Haggis said, as we saddled up the broncs. "That pinto answers to Paintbrush. Both gentle creatures, Mr. Goodfoote." I liked the looks of Dobs. She had good lines and her hooves showed none of the usual chips and cracking seen on so many of the horses in Disenchantment. But, as I approached, she laid back her ears and fixed me with a wall-eyed stare. A lump of sugar and a gentle voice go a long way in a convivial relationship with a horse, and I employed both. Dobs was no more Arabian than I am, but I hadn't expected Haggis to tell the truth. Paintbrush was as gentle as a fawn and made no objection to my presence.

Well enough mounted and outfitted, Sherlock and I made no secret of our departure, riding up the main street and out to the East into the desert at a walking pace. Holmes rode well on the pinto, or 'piebald' as he called it.

The desert was in bloom. Not the full flowering that would happen in a month or so when the storms came, but now it held a beautiful array of early colors. I breathed deeply, glad to be out of the town, back in the wilds where I felt more at home. Spread across the landscape were yellow flowers of the spiny barrel cactus, and the red, orange, and pink blossoms of buckhorn and staghorn cholla. I noticed young Sherlock Holmes seemed engrossed in the dry landscape, and was impressed with the ease with which he rode. Later, he explained that riding is encouraged in the young of the English countryside, and he had had access to some fine stables.

Once around the first outcropping, we changed our pace to a lope that brought us, within a couple of hours, to the canyons and ridges of the Silent Sister Mountains. Taking a side trail that lead up among the boulders, across a rocky table, and into a hidden valley, put us out of sight of even the keenest of observers. After dismounting and unpacking the animals, I returned to wipe out any signs of our passage. As a precaution, I laid a false trail away from our hiding place, in case the valley had been discovered during my absence.

This was as safe a hideout as possible within a couple of hours from Disenchantment, and I was confident Holmes would be secure. We had to forego a fire, but our cold, mid-day meal was no hardship. Mrs. Nelson had taken a liking to the boy, and she had packed enough food for a trail crew. I left the lad with instructions to make camp as comfortable as possible, while I crawled among the rocks to watch our back trail. Within an hour, five riders took the delusive path I had created and disappeared over the ridge. They would follow the false trail directly toward Purgatory. If the riders did as I expected, they would give up and return before night-fall. Riding among the sheer drop-offs and narrow pathways of these Mountains was difficult in the full light of day. At night, it would be downright foolhardy.

I returned to our camp, settled down the horses, and prepared for a long wait. Sherlock rested against a boulder staring off into the distance, lost in his own thoughts. My mind was going over what we had found out, which was two bulls short of a herd.

The death of Sergeant Davis, within such a short time after his arrival in Disenchantment, was surprising. Either the two government men accompanying the English party had been in the pay of Maldrome, or they had been indiscrete in one of the saloons. The efficiency and manner of their deaths suggested the latter.

I dismissed the thought the policeman's death could have been a random murder in a violent town. The dramatic way he was killed, and the elaborate stage-setting of the crime scene, had sprung from the mind of a creative villain, not some hired gunhand. Sheriff Bodkin hadn't the imagination.

Bodkin was dangerous as a killer, but he hadn't the wits to plan ahead. Von Herder was still a puzzle. His ability to quote Goethe accurately gave me pause. Perhaps he was just a well-read, consummate confidence man. Then again, Von Herder may run deeper than appearances, I mused. Deep and dirty.

The Kiowa Kid shooting at Holmes was also strange. Sherlock ducked and spoiled his first shot. But a killer with the reputation that the Kid carried didn't miss a target like the one Sherlock had presented, unless he did it intentionally. But why would a crack-shot purposely miss, unless he was under orders to do so? Sherlock was the only one in the country, according to the British, who had actually seen Maldrome and could identify him. And why spare Elspeth Kane? If it was known that Davis was from Scotland Yard, then why let his partner go free? Despite William Pinkerton referring to Elspeth as "little more than a clerk," from my reading, it would be a tough job for Bodkin and his gang to murder her, for she had shown her mettle when she saw Holmes being fired on. But why hadn't they tried?

CHAPTER 24

◳ ◳ ◳

An Apache warrior stepped out onto the rock outcropping, not forty feet from where we stood.

My mother's people, the Peigan Blackfoot, put a special value on teaching the young the lessons of the land. I had become aware of a change in the sounds of the wilderness around us, and reasoned now was a good opportunity to pass on some of this wisdom to young Sherlock.

"Step over here a minute, Lad," I said, motioning to him. We were speaking in quiet voices, for the towering rock setting and the silent wilderness demanded it.

"Yessir?" he replied. His early coolness was gone. Once again, he was just a lad.

"Listen carefully. Tell me what you hear." I watched a perplexed look cross his face. He looked in several directions, his head cocked to one side.

"I'm afraid I don't hear anything. Do you detect the sound of horses or men?"

"No. Simply tell me what you hear."

"I hear nothing."

Now I had a chance to pass on the lesson old Keeps-the-Lodge had given to me when I was younger than Sherlock.

"Where do you hear nothing?" I asked.

The lad looked at me a trifle perplexed. "I'm afraid, Mr. Goodfoote, that I have no idea to what you are referring."

I smiled. "You hear that coyote, yipping out on the flat? Good," when he nodded. "Do you hear anything else?"

He smiled back. "Oh. Of course." Again, he cocked his head, and this time, closed his eyes. "I hear the breeze blowing over rocks. I hear the chirping of insects. I hear the sound of a bird, but I'm unfamiliar with the species."

"Good Lad. Do you hear the rattlesnake crawling away from us? Over near the camp bag?"

"No," he said, "I don't hear that." He opened his eyes.

"Someday you will. But now, please answer my question. Where do you hear nothing?"

A light seemed to come into his gray eyes. He cupped his ears. "I hear a slight scratching over there," he said, almost to himself. "And I hear an insect over there." He turned his head in a circle. "Nothing there at the rocks where lies my shadow."

"Where do you hear nothing?"

"Among those rocks, to the East. There is no sound."

"You're a fast learner, Lad." I said. "That is the area of silence. So that is the area of danger."

I was facing the up-side of the rocky slope. "Here's a lesson for you, Master Sherlock. It's a lesson taught to the boys of the Blackfoot since time began.

"A predator moves in a bubble of silence. Birds and insects are calling to each other in front of the predator, and birds and insects are calling to each other behind the animal. But where the animal is moving, is silence. It is like a hole in the background symphony of the wild."

Sherlock Holmes shielded his eyes with his hand as he gazed up at the rock pile. "That means that an animal is up in those rocks?"

I pretended not to have much interest. "The size of the bubble gives an idea of the size of the predator. But some animals, like a weasel, cast a concentric ring far larger than their small size. It's because of their hunting nature." I squatted next to my pack and began to untie the rawhide laces that held its cover in place. "A puma, of course, is a large, ferocious hunter, so throws a huge ring. The Blackfoot call it the 'ring of spirit.'"

Master Sherlock had his hand on his gun. I stood, reached out to touch his arm, and shook my head. He let his hand fall to his side.

"The biggest ring of all is that of a human. Well, except for a grizzly bear."

"How big is this ring?" Sherlock asked.

"Just about the size of an Apache checking us out," I said with a smile. "And now because we've been standing looking right at him for several minutes, he knows that we know he's here."

The words were hardly out of my mouth when we heard a voice call out, "Ya Hay," and an Apache warrior stepped out onto the rock outcropping, not forty feet from where we stood.

CHAPTER 25

◙ ◙ ◙

*Her love for him was like that for the brother she had lost.
Perhaps, more than a brother.*

KAYA CRAWLED ALONG the rock outcropping until she reached a flat stone just beneath the top of the ridge. Here she moved into a sitting position, cross-legged, where her gaze could take in the whole valley of the near-dry Tomorrow River. She looked carefully across the flat floor of the basin, searching the near rocks first, then to the middle desert and finally to the San Loco Mountains to the east. Her nose took in the scent of the magenta blossoms of the porcupine cactus. A movement caught her eye and she watched a coyote slink into the cholla forest that covered the desert floor to the west. The small forest was a good place to hide, for its jumping thorns made it impenetrable to the White-eyes. Far to the east, the sun outlined in brilliant white the form of a tall bank of clouds that held no hope of rain. They would be gone as quickly as they had formed.

The rock formation on which Kaya sat was part of an extensive plateau cut by hundreds of dry washes that had sprung to life when the snows in the mountains had melted. The arroyos would roar again briefly with the summer storms, then remain dry for months. The rim of the cup in which she sat was granite, but the sandstone base had long ago eroded from wind and water, breaking free huge boulders that had crashed or slid into the valley below. The holes left were used by the Apache for campsites when on the war trail. The sandy floors of these rooms were reached only by narrow trails between massive blocks of stone where only one horse and rider at a time could pass. A single warrior with a rifle could hold off many enemies. It was in one of these small valleys that Neva and his six warriors now camped. They had found Kaya the day before.

Across the valley to her left lay the town of evil, a distant shadow on the horizon. The trail to the town lay around the cholla and through the gray saltbush. She stretched out her arms, palms facing the town, and closed her eyes. Immediately, Kaya felt a tingling in her hands, then something stronger, as it crept up her arms. She opened her eyes and dropped her hands. Her nostrils flared and her jaw clenched. There lay the enemy, she thought, in great numbers. She closed her eyes and let the warmth of the morning sun relax her. She must visit the town of witches again.

Today she must meet with Travels–Far, for he is again in need of her help. Of all the warriors she knew, only Travels–Far engendered her fierce loyalty. He had earned her respect many summers ago, and her love for him was like that for the brother she had lost. Perhaps, more than a brother. Last night, she was ready to kill to keep him alive, but Travels-Far had moved as quiet as a whisper to safety. Kaya knew that her own spirit was poisoned from going to the village of witches, and later she would construct a sweat lodge and perform the ceremony to protect her from the ghost disease that haunted this town of white devils. The preparation would take two days, and then she would be ready.

The young Apache woman moved from the flat rock to the stones along the ridge line. She took care her silhouette didn't show against the sky. She had encircled perhaps a mile of the rough terrain when she suddenly stopped. A motion below, on a flat spot near a deep crevice in the rocks, caught her eye. She climbed over and around boulders until she was positioned over a small camp, well hidden except from above.

Kaya could make out two people below, both white, but she felt no sense of danger. She crawled closer, slowly, slowly, until she was directly over the camp and the two people below. The man stood facing the rocks where Kaya was hidden behind a scrub pinion, but even an Apache wouldn't have seen her, she thought. This man was familiar to Kaya. He wasn't Apache, but he moved like an Indian, although dressed like a white man. This man called the slim boy over to him and spoke quietly, then bent to unfasten the ties on his pack. Finally, the boy turned, shielding his eyes, and looked directly at Kaya. The man stood and smiled up at the Woman Warrior, and the Apache woman smiled back.

It was good that Travels-Far had returned to the land of the Apache.

CHAPTER 26

◨ ◫ ◧

*Holmes seemed transfixed by this exotic woman,
studying her carefully.*

Holmes and I had our hands at our sides. The lad knew better than to show fear by pulling his sidearm.

This was a young Apache warrior of some local fame. And this warrior was a woman. Her broad smile revealed white teeth set in a sun-darkened face, and her shiny black hair hung straight below her shoulders. Dressed like a man in shirt, breechclout, and high buckskin boots, the warrior woman sported no decorations but a wide band of yellow paint across her eyes. A beaded pouch hung from a strap across her shoulders. In her belt she carried a large sheathed knife, and in her left hand, an old lever-action rifle.

I smiled in return.

Kaya gave young Sherlock a quick look, put down her rifle, then leaped into my arms. Her steel spring legs squeezed around my waist, and her arms encircled my neck. I could smell the sand of the desert and the wind of the mountains in her hair and breath as she peppered my face with kisses. I must admit, I returned a fair share myself, despite the keen gaze of Master Holmes. Finally, I put her down and held her by her shoulders so I could gaze into her eyes.

"Kaya, my sister," I said in the language of the Apache. "It has been many summers since we last met."

"Travels-Far, my brother. It has been long." Travels-Far is a rough approximation of the name the Apache had given me when I had stayed with them as I roamed about the country after various villains.

I turned to young Sherlock. "This woman is Kaya-te-Nse, my sister," I said. "She's come to renew our friendship."

Holmes smiled thinly. "Sister?" he said.

"Well," I said. "Not a blood sister, but a good friend. We became acquainted when I was through here a few years back." I looked at Kaya. "Of course, she was just a young girl then, not more than twenty-one or two."

"Is this your younger brother?" Kaya asked. She pointed with her lips.

"No, the boy is my friend," I responded. "I have a need to protect him from the bad men in the town where evil dwells, so I brought him to this place of hiding."

Kaya nodded. "There are many devils in that town," she said.

"Yes, there are," I replied.

Sherlock spread a blanket from our pack and opened our lunch basket. He watched Kaya carefully, even as he handed the Apache some fruit. Holmes seemed transfixed by this exotic woman, studying her carefully.

After our repast, I approached the subject I had been waiting to discuss with Kaya.

"Will you help me kill the witches?" I asked. Although Kaya spoke English, I made sure to ask her the question in Apache.

The Woman Warrior thought about it. Her right hand rose to clutch a necklace she wore around her neck. I saw it was the claw of a large grizzly hung on a leather thong.

"This town is protected by a cloud of evil," she said quietly. "Killing the demons will not be easy."

"Have you seen the demons?" I asked. Kaya feared nothing on this earth, but her courage didn't extend to taking on all the evil in the Apache spirit world as well.

Kaya looked at me and didn't speak of what she had or hadn't seen. Instead, she glanced around the little valley in which we were camped, and rubbed the bear claw. "Evil pours from that village," she said.

Finally, she turned back to me and said, "I will help you kill the White-eyes who are witches. Then, we burn the town."

That's the problem dealing with Kaya. When her brother was alive, he kept her more or less under control. Now that the Comanche had killed the great war chief, Kaya was pretty free to do what she wanted. And what she wanted was to kill whites and Mexicans. My conundrum was getting her to help, yet protecting the innocent people of Disenchantment, of which there were a number. If I could get her to confine her activities to the 'witches' of the town, we wouldn't have the slaughter of common citizens. This would take fine diplomacy indeed.

"There is a place we need to go," I told Kaya. "There are things we must see together."

CHAPTER 28

*"I need to learn to track men," Holmes said…
"In London, it is men who will be my prey."*

The sun was still a good two fingers above the horizon. Bodkin's hardriders had returned nearly an hour ago, heading back to town. The dust of their passage hung in the windless desert air. Kaya, Sherlock, and I moved out onto their desert trail on foot. Horse tracks of the five riders were in sharp relief on the desert floor, the rays of the sun low enough to give their prints clear outlines.

"One horse is lame," Kaya said. "It is the mare." I looked at her, for it was unusual for Kaya to comment on anything as plain as the tracks of an injured horse.

"I haven't been gone that long," I said, smiling. Kaya nodded. I translated for Sherlock, for Kaya had spoken in the language of the Apache. "Kaya says the mare is lame."

"How does she know the horse is lame?" he asked. The youngster had been studying Kaya for hours like she was a strange plant he had found in the desert. I noticed his eyes brightened when she came near, and he watched her every move.

I took a deep breath, and gazed along the line of hoof prints. "First, look at the tracks of the horses that are not lame." With an effort, Holmes pulled his eyes from Kaya and bent over the horseshoe tracks. "Here," I said, pointing. "This horse is only tired. Study these tracks first." Holmes got down on his knees and pulled a hand lens from one of his many pockets. He crawled along the trail, his nose just inches from the sand.

"The Apache are mountain and desert dwellers," I said. "And that means they require a prodigious sense of orientation. They must forever be reading tracks on the earth, from hoofmarks of a horse, to the trail of a tick across a rock." I pulled my bent briar pipe from my 'possibles bag.' "It's the only way to survive in this country. Tracks tell the Apache who has passed, where they may be going, how many there are, and, often, their intentions." I was about to light the pipe, then recalled that the scent of tobacco smoke would travel for miles in this dry heat. I looked longingly at my filled pipe, then put it away. Time enough for a relaxing smoke when this was over.

Kaya and I had done a quick survey of the trail. Something else had occurred after the riders had passed. I waited for young Sherlock to catch it.

"One of the hoof prints of this horse is sharper than the other three," he said. "That must indicate a new shoe?"

"Excellent," I said. "Now take a look at these tracks. This is the lame horse."

Again Holmes studied the prints. Kaya had drifted off, not interested in teaching tracking to a white boy.

"This track is lighter than the others. The horse must have put less weight on this leg. He therefore puts more weight on the other three, making those deeper," Sherlock said, pointing.

"You're learning fast," I said. "But the horse is a mare, not a 'he.'"

Holmes studied the tracks again. "I can't tell a mare from a stallion by the spoor," he said. "How does a tracker manage to do it?"

I smiled. I hadn't heard tracks called 'spoor' in a long time. "That's a lesson for another time," I said. Kaya came back down the trail as I answered Sherlock. "But now, see the sun haloing the spines of that golden cactus there? That means it's time to return to camp."

"Wait," he said. "Here is a different track that crosses the trail, then disappears on the rocks. It looks like the pugmarks of a large cat."

This time I laughed out loud. "You have an awareness that will take you far, young man. That's the print of a puma. He came just after the riders, crossed their trail, and went down into the canyon. Kaya smelled him before she saw his trail, and she backtracked him while we were engaged in studying the horse tracks."

Holmes looked at the woman warrior with unrestrained awe. "She smelled him?"

"Like I said, she uses all her senses in order to stay alive out here. In a single day she reads and interprets thousands of different signs. Most of them invisible, to all but a few."

"How does Kaya orient herself out here?" Sherlock asked as he looked around him at the landscape. "These mountains are a warren of valleys and canyons."

"This is Kaya's country. Just like you know the names of the streets in London, she knows the spirits of each of these washes, arroyos, canyons, and valleys." I motioned to the trail that led up to our camp. "Our little valley is in what I call Fallen Rock Canyon, one of hundreds in these mountains. The Apache don't really have a name for it, but Kaya knows every side trail running off it, and what's down each of them. The Apache are home in an area twice the size of California, and Kaya can no more get lost in this vast area than you could get lost in Trafalgar Square."

Young Holmes stepped up to me. "Will you teach me how to track like you and Kaya?" he asked. "It's a skill I would like to master." His eyes glowed with intensity.

"What you ask may be beyond my Power," I replied. "It's easier to know how to track, than explaining how I know. Much of it is like trying to explain why one color is red, and another, green. It's something you know perfectly well, but may have difficulty explaining. I was taught in the way of the People, which doesn't translate well to school learning. Some of these lessons are beyond language. They must be experienced, over years of practice."

"I'm a sedulous student," he said.

"That I know, Lad. But tracking is tied to the landscape, the plants, and the movement of the rivers. It has as much to do with the sun and wind as it does with the physical prints on the Earth."

"I am able to learn about the sun and wind…"

I nodded as we moved toward our path between two giant boulders. "I can teach you some things that may help, but the rest is practice. In order to learn about the tracks of the puma, you will need to follow the deer. Where does the deer make her bed, what buds does the deer eat in winter, how does she find a mate, move at night, drink from her watering holes? Tracking knowledge is never complete. It's a 'coming-to-knowing.' By learning the ways of the deer, you learn the ways of the puma."

"I need to learn to track men," Holmes said, as we continued our climb. "In London, it is men who will be my prey."

If this lad is to become a policeman, the criminals of London had better be on their guard, I thought.

Back at camp we at last prepared a simple, cold supper and all three of us ate ravenously.

Holmes and I returned to our discussion while we ate.

"Learning to track man," I said, "is as difficult as learning to track the puma."

Holmes looked puzzled. "I'm not entirely sure of your meaning."

"You must watch as a fat man walks by, and then look at his tracks. How are they different from those of a thinner man? When a man carries a package in his right arm, are his tracks different than when he carries it in his left? How do a man's tracks change when he goes from a slow walk, to a brisk walk, to a run? You need to watch and learn."

"I understand. I will do my utmost to learn," he vowed.

I scratched my head. "London is sidewalks and cobblestones, but I reckon there's plenty of open space in England where you can study tracking. Just remember the sun and the wind. When the tracks are laid in different parts of the country, the sun and wind will change with the landscape. You must take these changes into account at all times, in all places."

Holmes moved to sit next to me. His face was aglow with interest. "How do you track over bare rock? I saw the prints of that puma in the soil of the trail, but you followed them onto the stone. It seemed like a conjurer's trick."

Again, I thought quietly for several minutes.

"All rocks that haven't been rained on recently have a thin coat of dust on them. When a man steps on the dust, his boots take it away, leaving a print. It's no different for a puma. Even mice will disturb dust on rocks. Are we clear on that, Lad?"

Holmes nodded. He produced a notebook and pencil and began scribbling. When he paused and looked at me expectantly, I continued.

"Sometimes, a footprint is formed when a paw or boot is pressed into soil or snow. That's what you saw in the dirt on the path. Other times, like I said, a print is formed when something is taken away. On rock or hard soil, it'll be dust, and you need to look closely."

The boy stood to go, while pulling a hand lens from his pocket.

I caught his arm. "No, not tonight. Now we sleep and wait to see what tomorrow brings. The tracks will be there for days in this dry weather." I smiled. "Always keep a weather-eye out. In the city you have a barometer, but out here you have the sky and your senses."

I noticed that Kaya had made up sleeping pads for herself and Sherlock. "Are you sure Maldrome's riders won't be returning?" Holmes asked. Again he looked at Kaya, who sat on a folded blanket nearby, sharpening her knife with a sliver of stone.

"We couldn't be safer if we were at an English inn in Coventry," I replied. "Time now to sleep. Kaya and I will be leaving early tomorrow. Neva will be keeping an eye on the camp, but you'll need to keep yourself busy while we're gone."

Sherlock glanced around. "Who is Neva? I haven't seen anyone with Kaya."

I smiled. "Neva is a warrior who rides with Kaya. He and his warriors are just around. You won't see him, or his men, unless they want to be seen, but they'll be here for you if you need anything."

"Thank you," Holmes said. "I'll be fine. One more thing, Mr. Goodfoote. Did you remove your mustache because the Apache favor a clean face?"

"Most Indians think hair is better left on animals, not humans."

During our talk on tracking, the sun had dropped behind the ridge. The large moon had risen a short time ago and stars were just beginning to make their presence known. It wouldn't be until hours from now that the sky would be ablaze with its nightly show of twinkling lights. Some Indians called them the campfires of those who had passed over.

I was having trouble sleeping. My mind kept going back to Keeps-The-Lodge. He had taught me to track by having me watch and listen. Little was actually said. Often, Keeps would put me out to watch a spring fill with water. It taught me patience. Other times, I would watch a mouse family for days. How the mouse found a mate, built its nest, raised its young. How the tracks changed when a weasel was hunting nearby.

Keeps once told me that all the wisdom of the animal was in the tracks. So he put me to watching weasels and foxes. Their tracks became part of me, not just a body of knowledge. From foxes to wolves, to deer to puma, to buffalo, they resided in me still. Finally, I tracked humans.

"The track is the sign that each man leaves to tell of his passage. For the tracker, it is the place the spirit of the man being tracked can be touched, and his thoughts, good or evil, can be known." Keeps had told me that when I was younger than Sherlock.

How do you tell an English lad about the years it takes to master even some beginning sense of the marks? And he wanted to track humans. The tracks of men are sometimes the easiest to find, but the most difficult to fathom. Animals usually have solid reasons related to physical survival for being in certain places and doing certain things, but men may be driven by love, hate, greed, or some obscure thought. To read tracks of men is a study of mankind itself.

CHAPTER 29

🔳 🔳 🔳

From this vantage point, the entire fortress lay below us in the clear, desert moonlight.

When the moon was riding the sky at its peak, I rolled from my sleeping mat and found Kaya sitting on a rock with her back to the camp. In silence we mounted up and rode down the slim path, and out onto the desert floor. With the large moon to guide us, we made good time. We quickly covered the distance to Von Herder's ranch, and crept close enough to view the sprawling fortress.

From our outside vantage point, we could see little but high walls that appeared to enclose the ranch proper. In size, it rivaled an army compound, but was made more substantial by the use of adobe battlements, rather than a log stockade. Bartizans at the corners of the front wall provided a crossfire against attack on the front gate. All-in-all, it was an impressive sight, made more so by its massive, iron, double-door gate. Little sound escaped from behind the fortifications.

Kaya and I took the better part of the night circling the compound. The guards we could observe seemed vigilant, peering over the wall, constantly checking the surrounding country. I desperately needed to see inside, to get a total layout of the place, time the guards' rotations, and look for weaknesses.

Kaya found the crack in the stronghold. The rear wall of the compound was basically unguarded. The reason for this lack of caution was simple. This back fortification, much higher than the others, overlooked a deep canyon with a sheer drop into a black abyss. In order to scale the wall, an attacker would need to climb a vertical rock wall of several hundred feet, then mount this outer adobe battlement.

Near the northeast corner of the fort at the back of the compound, Kaya discovered a narrow ledge running horizontally across the rock face, deep in the shadow of the looming fort wall. I was doubtful of its usefulness, for it seemed too narrow for a human foot, but Kaya wasn't waiting for my opinion. Using small imperfections in the rock face, Kaya slipped onto the ledge and inched her way along. A crack in the canyon side ran up to the outer adobe fortress wall, and in a matter of minutes, I heard a hiss. I had already moved onto the ledge, going along by feel more than sight. Her hand touched my shoulder and I was able to climb behind Kaya up to the top of the unguarded parapet.

From this vantage point, the entire fortress lay below us in the clear, desert moonlight. There were several small buildings, a large stable, and what looked like army barracks. The center of the compound was dominated by a large white house, straight off a Georgia plantation. We moved slowly along the wall until we were able to conceal ourselves in a dark corner where the two outer walls met. From here, we viewed the front of the great house. A sweeping drive led up to a sprawling portico, complete with fluted Corinthian columns, and a double front door. We saw no lights coming from within. Two field cannons protected the afore-mentioned front gate, and I noted a Gatling gun covering the front of the house. A frontal raid was out of the question.

After I pointed out a few of my serious concerns to Kaya regarding the enclosure, we slithered to the back wall and moved carefully back down along the ledge. Unseen, we made our way back toward camp before the moon had set behind the western peaks.

Kaya stopped her pony a short distance before the mountain trail that led to our sleeping camp. She gave a sign with her hand to follow, so we trotted to a spot behind a large boulder. The small stream that ran near the camp emerged onto a flat plain surrounded by large stones. Two withered cottonwood trees grew along the banks of the trickle of water, making a pleasant oasis. Kaya dismounted and spread her horse blanket on the ground between the trees.

"It has been long," she said, as I joined her.

CHAPTER 30

🔲 🔲 🔲

"His is a face I've seen in my nightmares ever since."

The next day Kaya disappeared to make her own arrangements. I chanced a small fire of dry twigs to heat water for tea. A good deal of the food Mrs. Nelson had prepared still remained and made for a sound breakfast. The tea seemed to help brighten Sherlock's mood and I noticed the young man was studying his notes on tracking. He moved up the trail to a crack in the hard ground where a trickle of water flowed. A few tracks from kangaroo rats and lizards could be seen along the soft earth that bordered the little stream. Holmes got busy drawing the marks.

I spent the rest of the day reflecting on my plan. I went over it several times in my mind, looking for places where Coyote the Trickster could cause us grief. Holmes and I retired to our blanket rolls as the sun dropped behind the mountains and quiet lay across the land. Kaya was nowhere to be seen.

I noticed a figure rise from the sleeping area and move toward the open space near our dead campfire. I got up and followed.

The night chill of the desert was settling in, and Holmes was wrapped in a blanket, only his head and hat sticking out of his cocoon.

"Can't sleep, Lad?" I asked quietly. He shook his head. I sat down and pulled my capote closer around me. The earlier strong breeze had dropped with the sun, but there was still a bite to the air.

Sherlock looked up at the stars. "Unbidden memories come when I close my eyes," he said. "The memories are not pleasant." This time, I nodded.

"Maybe it's time you told me what happened in England to bring you chasing Maldrome all the way to America," I said. "It may help to figure out what he plans to do next."

Holmes pulled his blanket closer around him, looked at me, and nodded his consent.

"Right from the beginning," I said, "if you don't mind. Don't leave anything out."

"First, I had better tell you about my friend Potty," Holmes began. "His full name was Popsam Smyth Thackeray. I believe he was the third Earl of Thackeray, but we all called him Potty. He and I were in the same form and shared a room in Easton Hall at Westerly."

"So Potty was your best friend?"

"Really, the only bloke I befriended. He was of a serious nature, seldom smiled, and had a first-rate brain. His specialty was solving puzzles, from cross-words to ciphers. He dearly loved his puzzles. I think that's why we hit it off from the start, me with my deductive reasoning, and he with his puzzles." Holmes gazed at the span of stars overhead. He seemed lost in the memory of his friend. "He was the kindest of people, never spoke ill of anyone."

I handed Master Sherlock a piece of dried jerky. It's tasty, but tough, even when beaten with berries.

"For much of the year, Potty and I had been reading the *Agony Column* in the newspapers, and breaking the simple codes that lovers used in their correspondence. Most were simple codes which offered little challenge. We would then sneak out after the porter had retired, and check to see if we had been correct in our conclusions. If we were caught, we faced a brushing by the Prefect, but the bedder for our hall was a good egg and left the door on the latch so we could get back in. Once out, it was but a matter of doubling through the streets to the rendezvous place and beaking on the young romantic couples."

I noted that Holmes' manner of speech had dropped into the slang of his public school as his story unfolded.

"Bedder?" I asked.

He shrugged. "I apologize. A bedder is a charwoman. She makes the beds and cleans the rooms." Holmes pulled his blanket closer around him. "We would snicker into our sleeves when the lovers we saw were obviously married to other people."

I pulled a chaw of jerky and asked, "So what went wrong?"

"There was a code running for months that we had been unable to break. Finally, I stumbled upon an article about a Polish Army Officer who had broken a code that was considered unbreakable — the notorious Vigenere Cipher."

The Vigenere Cipher. It had been developed in the Middle Ages, if I remembered correctly, and had never been solved. I hadn't heard of a Polish Officer breaking it.

Holmes went on. "Maybe the messages in the Agony Column were written in this cipher, we reasoned. If they were, we could use the method described in the article to break them." Sherlock watched the ridgeline for a moment. "It was a purely mathematical problem, and Potty and I worked on it feverishly."

A sound from high on the ridge caught our attention. As we gazed at the rock ridge, a lone coyote was silhouetted briefly against the starry sky. Then he was gone.

"Potty's father had asked that I spend a month of the mid-summer holiday at Thackeray Hall, and my parents agreed. The second month was spent at my family home. The summer went by with Potty and I working to unravel our difficult conundrum.

"By the time school resumed, we had worked out a method for

solving the cipher, but it was October before we were finally able to read the first message. It was cryptic, even when rendered into English. But what set our minds whirling were the signatures. The one apparently giving orders signed the message, 'Victor.' The other respondent signed, 'Alberta.' Potty and I thought the names might indicate a clandestine affair between Queen Victoria and a suitor who used the name of the late consort, Prince Albert. If not the Queen herself, then perhaps some members of the royal family were engaged in a love affair, and probably meeting outside the palace walls."

The moon had risen and cast long shadows among the rocks. Far off, a lone Burrow owl hooted to its mate. Young Sherlock sat quietly.

"You suspected royal involvement because of the names used, or did you have other evidence?" I asked.

Holmes sighed. "No, just the names and our own imaginations."

"What happened next?" This story was important, I reasoned. It might help me understand the driving force behind Sherlock Holmes' determination to find Maldrome.

"The last message in the Agony Column indicated a meeting. It was to occur in two nights time, right at midnight, in Coltonwood Park in London. Not a half mile from our school."

"Were there any other meetings, or was this the first?"

"There had been several, but they all had taken place before we had broken the code. We were able to go back and read the earlier messages, but were too late for the meetings. And some had been too far from our school. This one was nearby, and we were determined to discover who the lovers were. Because of my father's position in the government, I had seen most of the royals in various ceremonies and felt certain I'd be able to recognize the writers of the cipher."

"So you went to the meeting place?"

"I remember that a wind had been blowing all day, and the ground was covered with dry leaves as we left the school hall. But the wind had now stopped, and the short run to the park took only minutes. We had to duck into a doorway once to avoid a constable patrolling the street near the park. We were unseen by anyone. The park has a iron fence surrounding it, with a large ornate wrought-iron gate, which was locked at this hour. We were able to squeeze though a gap in the fence that had been caused sometime in the past, perhaps by a toppled tree. The moon was hidden by fast moving clouds when we took up our position near the gate, ready to see who would enter."

"You're sure the gate was locked?"

"Yes. We had tried it ourselves. The gate had a large lock that only a huge key would open. We wondered who kept the key, and how these lovers were to gain access to the park. But when one is of the ruling family of England, obtaining a key would offer no impediment, we reasoned.

"We had waited but a short time, hidden in the bushes, when a Brougham drawn by two coal-black horses arrived at the gate. The teamster jumped from his box and unlocked the gate with a key that was several inches long. He pulled the carriage onto the road that runs through the wooded area, and then stopped. The door to the coach was not thirty feet from where we crouched.

"And could you see into the coach, see who the passenger was?"

"We couldn't at first, although there was a gaslight a few feet away. But, within minutes, a second coach pulled in behind the first. The first driver then ran back and re-locked the gate.

"At this time, the passenger in the forward carriage stepped out directly under the gaslight and we saw him clearly. I almost gasped out loud when I recognized the man who was my father's superior in the Cabinet. This was a man beyond reproach, a man who held the financial well-being of the entire kingdom in his hands.

"It was Sir Rodney Brighton Hudson, the Chancellor of the Exchequer of England, Scotland, Wales and Ireland. He held one of the highest offices in the government, second only to the Prime Minister. He walked back to the second coach and climbed in.

"And who was in the second coach?" I knew little of British politics, but Sir Hudson was obviously a man of some influence.

"That was our difficulty. We couldn't see into the second coach from our position in the bushes. I motioned to Potty for us to sneak closer, but he shook his head.

"'Potty,' I whispered. 'I must see who's in the second coach.' But Potty shook his head again. His eyes behind his thick glasses were large and frightened. 'Right,' I said. 'Don't move, don't rustle any leaves. Don't cough, and don't sneeze.' Both drivers had walked back to the gate, beyond hearing range of any conversation between Lord Hudson and the unknown passenger. This gave me the opportunity to cross the road around the next curve and work my way back to the far side of the second coach. I lay flat behind a wisteria bush, waiting for an opportunity to crawl closer to the window and peer inside. I became aware of two male voices inside the coach, but was surprised to hear a third voice, briefly. It was the voice of a woman. That's when the horror happened."

"They found Potty?" I offered.

Sherlock Holmes hung his head. He took a deep breath. "Yes. One of the drivers had come back to the second coach. Potty had moved, and the crunch of dried leaves alerted the villain. He thrashed out of the bushes holding Potty by the back of his neck. Potty had lost his glasses, and I knew he had trouble seeing without them. It was then Lord Hudson jumped from the second coach and ran back to his own. His driver bounded into the box, turned the coach back towards the gate, and Lord Hudson was gone. I heard the creaking of the gate, even as I watched Potty struggle in the grasp of the footman. I was frozen by indecision, when a man leaned out of the coach. His is a face I've seen in my nightmares ever since. A face I see in crystal clear detail every time I close my eyes. A black mole on his left cheek, and a wine-colored birthmark on his forehead."

"Maldrome," I whispered.

Holmes nodded. "He nodded to the thug holding Potty, and the man cut Potty's throat in one brutal slash."

We sat quietly for several minutes, Holmes re-living this terrible moment of his friend's violent death.

After a while, I asked softly, "What happened next, Sherlock?"

Young Holmes looked up at me, for I had stood during his narrative. "I don't know. For the first, and only, time in my life, I passed out. When I awoke, I found myself on a cot in the police station. A doctor was putting smelling salts under my nose, and I was surrounded by detectives.

"As soon as I mentioned Lord Hudson, the detectives left. I sat on the cot sipping tea until my father and brother arrived. With them were two officials from the office of the Prime Minister. And Potty's father. I won't relate what that scene was like, but all my bravado disappeared at the sight of Sir Thackeray's red-rimmed eyes and trembling lip.

"I soon learned that Lord Hudson had been found hanging in the gun room of his manor house. Later, a package arrived at Scotland Yard from Lord Hudson, sent shortly before his death. He outlined an entire plot, with Maldrome as its mastermind, to assassinate the Queen and bring down the financial structure of the government. Maldrome apparently had assembled a large group of criminals and was planning on various bombings and murders in an effort to create turmoil and chaos while he stripped the treasury of its contents. He and his band would escape in the ensuing confusion. He had been blackmailing Lord Hudson for some indiscretions of a prurient nature. The whole thing came undone when Lord Hudson, perhaps driven by a guilty conscience, revealed the details of the scheme."

"And they traced Maldrome to this country?"

Young Sherlock stood up and shrugged out of his blanket. He nodded.

"Yes. He left a difficult trail, but the Prime Minister was now involved and his reach is substantial. Scotland Yard was able to turn one of Maldrome's henchmen. He told them much of what the detectives had suspected, including the villain's plan to flee to America.

"Apparently, no one, other than I, has ever seen this evil mastermind. Even his own rabble have never seen him in full light, just a voice and a shadow, and a pile of hundred pound notes. Shortly after we arrived in New York I spotted a man dressed as an Indian rajah. I'm sure it was Maldrome, but he slipped away in the crowd, shedding his exotic garb as he went."

"Where did the name 'Maldrome' come from?"

"Lord Hudson wrote it in the letter he sent to Scotland Yard. The only other name to surface during the investigation was that of Maldrome's carriage driver, the man who killed Potty. He is a brutal criminal named Frederick Putnam. But he has also disappeared."

I put my hand on Sherlock Holmes' shoulder. "This was a difficult tale for you to tell, and you're to be complimented for telling it. Know that it helps me reason out Maldrome's next move."

Holmes again nodded. Now it was time to crawl into our blankets and get some rest. It was uncertain what new devilments the dawn would bring.

CHAPTER 31

◙ ◙ ◙

"He was wanted in Kansas for bank robbery, murder, rape, and forgery. But I can't touch him."

Dawn in the desert comes in three phases. First, just before the sun comes up, a deep purple covers the sky, and this is when outlines are first seen. To the Indians who live in this vast expanse, it's the mystery time. Then, the light of the sun, a pale yellow from just below the horizon, is visible. The Apache call this the time when the breath of man can be seen. Finally, the red sky of the sunrise breaks over the land.

Sherlock Holmes and I sat on a boulder overlooking the desert below. We sipped our tea as I briefly explained to him the meaning of dawn to the desert dwellers. The rising orb cast the mountains along the rim of the valley in moving shadows, and bathed the desert in a rosy glow.

Kaya had returned, and we were joined by Neva for a simple breakfast. Once again, I was leaving Sherlock Holmes in the care of the Apache, for I needed to go into town alone.

I saddled up Dobs and loped into Disenchantment in the rising heat. Along Compton Street I noted a peculiar peace. It had the air of a normal town, rather than its usual swirl of rascals. A few horses were hitched outside a saloon, an industrious citizen was sweeping the wooden sidewalk, and four trollops were languidly taking their morning coffee on the balcony of the Red Garter Saloon. It was early for the usual mayhem of this metropolis, but not that early, I thought. Two small birds flew along the street and I saw a crow perched on the roof of the feed store. No one shot at it. I took a deep breath and discovered that even the stink from the offal of the town, while not that of a flowery bouquet, was less pronounced. I slowed Dobs to a walk, and stopped in front of the Empire.

I pushed open the swinging doors and peered around the dim room. After coming in from the sun, it took my eyes several seconds to adjust. A Chinaman was sweeping the floor, and a lone barkeep in a red vest was working behind the bar. There was a slight smell of stale beer, but my impression was one of general cleanliness. Other than three or four drovers at the bar, the place was nearly empty. A lone figure sat at a table away from the door. I walked over to extend my greetings to the real law in this part of the territory, Marshal Sam Thompson.

The Marshal was tipped back in his chair against the paneled wall of the saloon, dressed for the trail in a long pale duster and a brown cattleman's Stetson with a flat, wide brim. His wind-blasted face looked like it had been cut from pipestone. Once you got past Thompson's waxed and trimmed handlebar mustache, it was his ice blue eyes that captured your attention. They were as cold as the prairie in winter.

"Charles," Thompson racked his chair forward and unwound his tall frame. I shook his large hand.

"Sam," I answered.

"Grab a chair, Charles. We got some jawboning to do."

I sat down next to Thompson and we both tipped our chairs back. Remembering what I drank from my last visit, the barkeep brought me a beer.

I opened the conversation as the waiter left. "What brings the

Federal Marshal to this Paradise on the Tomorrow?" I asked.

Sam picked up his glass and took a sip that wouldn't have wet the whistle of a cricket. He put it down as his eyes continually swept the room.

"Been hearing some things down in Tucson," he answered. "Troubling things about Disenchantment."

I smiled. "Trouble in Disenchantment? You surprise me, Sam."

He turned to face me. "I heard you were with the Pinkerton's now, Charles. Maybe you better explain what you're doing back here in Arizona."

So I did. I didn't hold anything back from the Marshal, although the *Science of Detection* was not foremost among his many gifts. He was known for quick, violent, decisive action when he was sure of his lawbreaker. But I related why I had been sent here, the death of Sergeant Davis before my arrival, my shooting Mange, and the threat of Von Herder. I gave a brief account of the attempt on young Holmes and the quick action of Elspeth Kane. I finished with the thwarted attempt of some unknown miscreants to enter my own room at the Silver Lode Hotel.

"And we still haven't found Maldrome, the British mastermind we're looking for."

"Okay," Marshal Thompson said after a lengthy pause. "Maybe we can help each other."

I waited. The barkeep was wiping the top of the counter and the cowboys had drifted out. A drummer came in carrying his display case. He moved up to the bar.

"What do you know about this Sheriff Bodkin?" Sam asked.

I shrugged. "Met him a couple of days ago. Why, Sam? What's he done?"

Marshal Thompson focused on me. "You killed Mange, who was one of his deputies, Charles. Don't tell me you don't know him."

"I didn't say I didn't know him. I said I had just met him. If you want my opinion of him, he's a gunslinger who got hired on to take over this town. He and his deputies are run by Von Herder, who takes orders from Maldrome. But that's just my take on it."

Thompson went back to watching the saloon. I waited until he spoke again.

"Bodkin is not the sheriff. The elected sheriff of Disenchantment was Jake Platt. His body was found over by Timber Creek, full of Apache arrows. But I've never known Apaches to leave their arrows behind like that. Them arrows are too damn hard to come by. I think he was shot first, then filled with arrows by someone who wanted him out of the way, and the Apache blamed for it. I think that someone is Michael Bodkin, also known as Cody Winters."

"Winters? That name doesn't ring a bell."

"He's also known as Frank Ogle.

"Nope."

"Lester Beach?"

I shook my head.

"How about Charlie Tuttle?"

I sat up and looked Sam in the eyes. "Bodkin is Charlie Tuttle?"

"Maybe yes, maybe no."

"You got a warrant for Charlie Tuttle?" I asked.

"Nope. He was wanted in Kansas for bank robbery, murder, rape, and forgery. But I can't touch him."

I just looked at him.

"No witnesses. The juries in Kansas set him free. As far as the law is concerned, Tuttle is as free of sin as you or me. But maybe I can arrest Bodkin because he's posing as a sheriff without being elected."

A town drunk staggered into the saloon, spotted the Marshal and me, then spun around and weaved his way out again.

I watched him go, then turned to Sam. "That won't get him hung," I said. "But it'll get him out of town for awhile."

Thompson put his head back and laughed. "You got a short memory, Charles. Remember what happened when you drug Mange in front of a jury in Tucson? He was out before you could stable your horse."

"Step outside with me a minute, Sam," I said as I stood. "I want you to meet someone."

We walked outside to the alley that runs along the side of the Empire. Halfway up the alley, we stopped while I packed tobacco into my pipe. The town drunk was hunched behind a large box. He looked like he had fallen asleep.

"Marshal Sam Thompson, I want you to meet Jubal T. Bedford of the Pinkerton Detective Agency."

Jubal T. didn't stand, but his head came up. "Pleased to meet you, Marshal."

Sam nodded a greeting. He said nothing, but his eyes squinted as he took in Jubal T.'s disguise.

"You've done yourself proud, Mr. Bedford," I said. "That weeklong beard is your *piece de resistance*."

"Why, thank you, Mr. Goodfoote," he said with a grin. "That's high praise coming from a man who has no hair at all on his face."

"You've been keeping an eye on Elspeth Kane, like I asked?"

"Yes I have. So far, she's been out of her room only twice. She dined alone at the Blue Cup, bought a few things at the General Store, including some cartridges for a Colt. Last night, she took her evening meal alone in the hotel's restaurant."

I nodded, then looked around. "Why's this town so quiet?" I asked.

"Kaya," he replied. "Talk is, she and her band are headed this way, and the way she feels about this town, most folks have either headed for Fort Crawford, or are too scared to come out."

Marshal Thompson, who had been watching the front of the alley, spun to face Jubal T. "Anyone say where she was spotted?"

"A rider rode in all in a huff. It was still dark out, maybe an hour before dawn. Yelled that the army had chased Kaya all the way from Mesquite Canyon. Said she was definitely headed this way."

"Did you recognize the rider?" Sam asked.

"Oh, I sure did. It was Stone, one of Bodkin's deputies. He damned near broke his neck, riding up and down Main Street, shooting his gun in the air, and screaming at the top of his lungs. Sheriff Bodkin came out and added to the confusion by calling for volunteers to run get their rifles. Then he changed his mind and told the posse to 'go home and see to your womenfolk.' Then he ordered the Empire to open and serve a round on the house that he paid for in cash." It was plain Bedford had enjoyed the show. "And you know what the courageous sheriff did next? He and all his deputies mounted up and rode out to meet Kaya, only they went in the opposite direction. He left the volunteers in the saloon, discussing the looming massacre." Bedford's chuckle turned into a belly laugh.

This was the news I had been expecting. I figured Bodkin and company would be meeting with Maldrome later today or tomorrow. So most of the gang would be out at Von Herder's ranch.

"What about Von Herder? Did you see him?"

"Yes I did," Jubal said. "He, his clerk, and his bully boys all rode out together last night. They went real quiet-like, so I mounted up and followed 'em all the way to his ranch."

"You've seen the ranch, then?" I asked.

"Oh yeah," he said. "Thought it would be good to take a look. The ranch is huge, with several mines, cattle range land. He's bought up several ranches in the area, not all connected, and in a crazy pattern. And Von Herder's fort, as the locals call it, is secure. A few men could hold off an army, unless the army had cannon. Even then, it would be difficult to breach the outer walls."

"I know," I said. "I spent some time looking it over. It looks nearly impregnable." I smiled grimly. "But not quite."

"I've been past the ranch myself," Marshal Thompson said. "If Bodkin is hiding out there, it'll be hard to dig him out."

Sam thought for a long minute. "I don't think the Apache will be attacking this, or any other town. There just ain't enough of 'em. Juh and the main band are over near the Peccary River. That's nearly three hundred miles. I got that from the Army only three days ago. They got a column that should be here in another two days to get after Kaya."

"It seems like a long shot," I agreed. "Maybe it's just whiskey talk."

The Marshal nodded and smoothed his large mustache. "Kaya is alone out there. Or maybe she picked up one or two bucks. Not enough to take on this town, or even a ranch."

"I have some folks I need to see," I said to Thompson. "But I'll be back in town tomorrow with the British lad I've been keeping an eye on. I'll look you up."

"That suits me," Thompson said. "If Bodkin comes back, maybe I'll arrest him and take him to the Territorial Seat for trial. Impersonating a peace officer can be a right serious offence."

"That's a long ride," I ventured. "It's about four days across some rough country."

The Marshal nodded. "Yep," he said, "it is that." He turned and walked out to Compton Street.

"Jubal T.," I said, "keep watching Elspeth. I'll be back tomorrow early."

CHAPTER 31

◙ ◙ ◙

The boy smiled. "The game, Sir, is afoot."

I rode hard back to camp, and only slowed to let Dobs catch his wind. The sun was directly overhead and the noonday heat was becoming intense. Halfway up the trail to the hidden camp, Kaya stepped from behind a boulder, holding her rifle in her hand.

"We need to talk," I said as I dismounted. "Where is the boy?"

"The boy is in the desert below. He is with Neva." Kaya pointed down the trail with her chin.

"Then we talk. Alone." We moved off the trail and squatted with our backs to large rocks. "The Army is coming. In two suns, they will be on the trail of Kaya and her band."

Kaya smiled. "The bluecoats are two suns behind Kaya for many seasons."

"Well, we need to move quickly, before they arrive." I further outlined what I wanted her to do. We had laid in a plan earlier that we would now put into action. "Now, I must talk to the boy," I said.

I found Sherlock Holmes sitting on the hot sand, book in hand, studying a shrub. Nearby, Neva squatted atop a boulder, his rifle cradled in his arms.

"This is an ocotillo shrub," Sherlock said, after I had dismounted. "Unheard of in Europe, but plentiful here." He gestured with his book. "That plant is yucca. Kaya said the Apache wash their hair with a soap made from it."

I marveled at his ability to dismiss our looming mission from his mind and give rein instead to his curiosity about the plant people of the desert.

"She seems a remarkable woman," Holmes said.

"Yes, Kaya is that."

He gazed up at me, and I observed he was beginning to develop a brown complexion. "And her name, Kaya. Does that mean something in her native tongue?"

"It's a shortened form of a longer name," I said. "Kind of like a nickname. It has to do with a lot of courage."

Young Sherlock considered this. "She seems to know a great deal about desert flora. I would very much like to have her teach me more."

"We'll need to postpone your botany lesson until later," I said. "I'm going to need you to perform an unpleasant task."

"More unpleasant than examining the body of Sergeant Davis?"

"Maybe. We'll see. But we must keep Miss Kane in the dark, even if it means lying to her. She's far too concerned about your safety to allow you to do what I have in mind. We'll be heading back into town tomorrow morning." I looked into his grey eyes. "We need to end this Maldrome problem. There will be some danger involved."

The boy smiled. "The game, Sir, is afoot."

CHAPTER 32

◙ ◙ ◙

"There's trouble waiting to happen," Winthrop said.

Our ride to town the next morning was uneventful. With the sun high in the sky, Sherlock Holmes and I rode up the main street. Since Von Herder, the Sheriff, and their gang of hardriders were out at Von Herder's ranch, I felt Sherlock would be safe. He and I stopped at the Records Office, which doubled as the Assay Office, the Post Office, and the Telegraph Office. We spent an hour studying the geological maps of the area around Disenchantment. Then I put several questions to Silas who ran the place.

After we joined Elspeth for a light luncheon in the hotel restaurant, I left the two of them and made my way alone to the Empire. It was filled at this comparatively early hour by miners and drovers who sought hard liquor and safety in numbers after the tale had spread about the upcoming Apache raid. No one, I noticed, had bothered to set up barricades, or organize any resistance. Leaders of the town had been systematically removed by Sheriff Bodkin, which now left a vacuum. Marshal Sam Thompson was nowhere to be seen.

I elbowed up to the bar and ordered a beer, pushing my way past a clot of patrons who grumbled and swore. I took my beer and headed for a back table where I had spotted the editor, Winthrop. He waved me over to sit with him and stood as I approached.

"*Salve*," he shouted. "*Salve*, my good friend." A shot glass of red-eye whiskey was sitting on his table, along with a full bottle. It appeared he hadn't begun his serious drinking yet.

"The rats have left the ship," he announced.

"Most of them, anyway," I said. He offered me the chair next to him so we both could watch the room.

"From talk I hear, some Apache are headed this way to burn the town to the ground," I said.

"You think anyone would miss it?" Winthrop replied.

"No, but I'm surprised you locals haven't set up some kind of defense." We sat in silence for several minutes, watching the patrons come and go. "Have you seen Marshal Thompson this morning?"

"No. Last night, he was sitting right where you're sitting, but he hasn't put in an appearance yet today. The telegraph line is still open so he may have sent for the Army." He took a sip of his whiskey. "*Cur ante tubam tremor occupant artus*," Winthrop continued, after carefully checking out a group of loud miners at the bar. "Why should fear seize the limbs before the trumpet has sounded."

"You'll be doing me a large favor, Mr. Winthrop," I said, "if you'll hold the Latinizing for awhile."

The journalist was watching a young blond man who stood near the door. Dressed in baggy trousers, a soiled shirt and flop hat, the slim youngster was scanning the room. I noticed he wore his wheelgun low on his leg, his holster tied down. The only clean and shiny part of his dress was his revolver. Setting his hat more firmly on his head, the youth headed for the bar, and pushed himself between two buffalo skinners. The large men looked him over, saw the anger in his eyes, and moved aside.

"There's trouble waiting to happen," Winthrop said. "That kid is on the prod and he'll either kill someone or get himself killed." The newsman finished his drink in one swig. "Probably right off a dirt ranch and thinks he's mighty fast." He opened his mouth as if to pop out another Latin phrase, but my look made him swallow it.

"I have bigger fish to fry," I said. "Here's a question for you. Was Crump's the only mine Von Herder was set on buying, or were there others?" I knew the answer to this question, but it was an introduction to others I needed to ask.

"The munificent Count Von Herder? He was buying up ranches, Marshal, mostly. Oh, several had defunct silver mines on them, but those small holdings are common enough in this area."

"Were the ranches he purchased viable? Did he buy up the cattle as well?"

Winthrop looked into his empty glass. "No, not as far as I know. Most of the ranchers hereabouts have been run off by the Apache. They were glad enough to sell, even at a loss. A lot of their cattle had been killed or stolen by the hostiles."

The young cowboy had started arguing loudly with an older man at the bar. I recognized the older man from my days as a Marshal. He was fast with a gun, and had no objection to killing. The kid was biting off more than he could handle.

Winthrop filled his glass from the bottle on the table. He nodded. "We may see some gunplay here soon, Marshal. Perhaps you should step in."

I leaned closer to the scribbler. "I'm no longer a Marshal, Mr. Winthrop." I took a sip of beer. "I'm looking for an Englishman."

"I haven't seen any English around here, other than the late gentleman and his family," Winthrop said. He pulled his ink pot from his pocket, along with his pen and a pad of paper. "This little fray could be of some interest to my readers, if the Apache don't burn me out before the paper goes to press."

I could see I wasn't going to get any information from him while he was watching the little drama at the bar unfold. With a sigh, I stood and walked over to the bar and stepped behind the young man. As the youngster started to turn, I grabbed the gun from the kid's holster and smacked him over his head with it. He crumbled to the floor.

I unloaded his Colt and tossed it to the barkeep. "Keep it until he wakes up," I told the man behind the bar.

I came back to the table. "That won't hold him for long," Winthrop said. "I have a choice Latin phase to cover the subject of fools, but I'll spare you the education." He finished his drink. "How about a little repast? The Purple Dragon puts out a passable spread."

When we sat down at a table in the restaurant, a Chinaman came over, a smile on his face, and handed us cardboard listings of the available, exotic-sounding dishes. Nothing on the menu resembled anything American, so I ordered a vegetable dish and hot tea. Winthrop simply handed back the menu.

"The menu is from a restaurant in San Francisco," Winthrop explained. "And the waiter doesn't understand a word of English." Winthrop, probably as sober as he ever got, looked around the room. "They make one dish a day and that's what we'll get, regardless of what we order."

The meal came and resembled ground beef with vegetables and was surprisingly tasty. After eating, we had a cup of tea each.

"What can you tell me about Von Herder?" I asked. "How did he get Bodkin to be his lap dog?"

"Not much to tell, Marshal. Bodkin came in and he and his gang took over the town. It seemed to me, he was tilling the soil for someone by eliminating any competitors for power. So when the Count arrived, he had an open field to buy up ranches and old silver mines, as well as half the buildings in town. Then he started building his fort, wagon loads of goods, mule trains of materials. He even dragged some of the rock from somewhere in the mountains. It was a big project and took a full year, even with scores of men working on it. I don't know if it's finished yet, because no one is allowed near it."

"You must have looked into it, reported on its progress."

"Oh I did, until one night when my office was trashed and the presses smashed. It was Bodkin's men, but I knew the Count was behind it. They made sure I knew what would happen if I wrote anything more about their business."

I thought for a moment, sipping my tea. "Someone must be putting money in the bank. Maybe that's a starting point for understanding what's happening."

Winthrop pushed his tea away. "Let's get something with a little more body, Mr. Goodfoote. I really need a drink."

As we were leaving, Winthrop turned to me and said, "As for the bank, Von Herder bought it shortly after he arrived. It's his bank now!"

CHAPTER 33

"What river of silver?" Holmes asked.

It was getting on toward dark when Sheriff Bodkin, Blade, and two deputies rode into town and up Compton Street. I kept an eye on them from my perch on the porch of the Empire. Winthrop had gone back to *The Dispatch* to write up the news of the day, or to drink himself into a fog. A handful of town residents stopped to watch the four men tie up their horses at the hitching rail outside the Sheriff's Office. After they entered their lair, I walked up the street to the hotel to find Sherlock. He was in the lobby, sitting on a small couch along the back wall of the deep room, a heavy volume open on his lap. Elspeth was not in sight. I pulled a stuffed chair over and plopped in front of him.

"Bodkin is back in Disenchantment," I said, as he raised his eyes to me. "It may be wise to stay out of sight."

Holmes stared at me for a few moments. "Thank you, Mr. Goodfoote. And I perceive the man who just came in the door is wearing a badge that denotes he's a Federal Marshal," he said, looking past me.

And so it was. Sam came over and I made the introductions.

"This lad has an idea how the Scotland Yard man was murdered," I began, when we were all seated. "And I can vouch for his smarts."

Thompson leaned forward and clasped his hands together, his elbows resting on his knees. "Let's hear it, young man," he said. "I'd be interested in any idea right now, no matter how half-baked."

Holmes didn't seem to take offence. "It's a simple matter, although I wasn't able to confirm my theory." He looked directly at me. "I was forced to abandon my observations at a critical moment." He leaned forward, dropped his voice, and told the Marshal his idea of how the murderer escaped from the locked room.

"But you didn't have the door of the room under your eye the whole time?" Sam asked softly.

"No Sir, I did not." Again, Holmes looked accusingly at me. "But there were other signs that the murderer was in the room at the time Sheriff Bodkin obscured our view. He was quite effective in doing so, first with a cloud of smoke from his shotgun, and then with the cluster of his three deputies."

Sherlock Holmes held up his hand and began ticking off items on his fingers.

"One, Blade has been in the Sheriff's shadow since my colleagues and I arrived in Disenchantment. The only time I didn't see Blade immediately behind the Sheriff was when Mr. Bodkin arrived and fired his large bore firearm into the door."

"There may be a rational explanation for his absence," Sam said reasonably.

"Two, we found evidence in the room that someone with a unique cut on the sole of his boot had been in the room. The shoe pattern is entirely different than those found on Sergeant Davis' shoes. According to Mr. Goodfoote's calculations, this man would be six feet three inches in height. I believe you will find Mr. Blade is exactly that tall, if you care to measure him."

Sam nodded.

"Three, the sheriff called our attention to the large amount of blood, then he and his deputies obstructed the doorway so that it was difficult to see anything other than the body and blood. Our view of the entire room was carefully orchestrated so no one was able to look behind the damaged door, or, indeed, into the wardrobe." Holmes leaned back and put his fingers together in a steeple. "It's a trick all magicians use, distracting our attention from what they don't want us to see. It's also called sleight-of-hand, or legerdemain."

I spoke up. "We believe the bed sheet had been used to wipe the blood off the killer after the murder. Or could have been to shield him from the spray when he struck the Sergeant from behind."

Sam sat back in his chair with a perplexed look on his face. "You're saying you believe Blade did the killing and Bodkin covered it up. Is that what you're telling me, Lad?"

Holmes nodded and Sam turned to me.

"So you're backing his play on this, Goodfoote?"

"Yes I am. And Blade has a cut on the sole of his left boot. I've seen his tracks. My measurements make him as tall as the boy here says."

Marshal Thompson just shook his head. "It's a lot of spitting in the wind as far as real solid evidence. I trust your trackin' skills, Charles, but the jury down in Tucson won't hang a man with this many 'maybes.' Maybe Blade was somewhere drunk. Maybe he was in that room sometime last week and left his bootprint there. Maybe the sheriff wanted to keep the mob from looting the room so he blocked the door."

"But if we eliminate the unlikely, whatever remains is probably the truth," I said. "Do you have a better explanation for that locked door and what we found in the room?"

"No I don't," Sam said, as he rose to go. "No, I don't. But I need a motive. Why would Bodkin and Von Herder go to all that trouble? You said yourself that this Maldrome isn't even in Disenchantment, maybe not in the territory. Maybe he plain don't exist and this whole damn thing is just Bodkin or Von Herder pulling the strings."

"Bodkin is a man of so little imagination that someone else must be setting up this entire business," I said as I stood. "He would just shoot down his enemies in the street. He's done it before."

"How about Von Herder? He seems a man with ideas." Sam pushed his hat back on his head, then put his hands on his hips.

I shook my head. "I just don't see either of them that bright. We checked the land survey map for the way Von Herder is buying up land in this part of the territory. All his properties are co-joined. If you put them all together, they form a line that covers over a hundred miles of dry desert. Why would a man do that if he had any brains?"

"I don't know, Goodfoote, damn it. But you can't hang him for wasting his money on worthless land." Sam sat back down, a pensive look on his face.

"Wait a minute, Goodfoote. Where did you say this line of mines was located?"

"It runs from about ten miles from El Canon de Muerto to just east of Purgatory. Why, Sam? What are you thinking?" At this, young Holmes leaned forward.

"Well, I'll be damned," Thompson said. "That fool is buying the land where the *Rio de la Plata* is supposed to run."

"What river of silver?" Holmes asked.

I, too, sat down. "I first heard about a river of silver years back. It's about as believable as the City of Gold," I explained. "There's been a rumor of a wide river of pure silver somewhere under the desert out west of town. It's been searched for by prospectors, miners, and dreamers for a hundred years, but all anyone found was mostly low-grade ore. Once in a while a claim paid off, and the rumor was resurrected, but the giant mother lode has never been found."

Sam finished the story: "The mines and ranches that Von Herder is buying up are right over the area where the rumor says the *Rio de la Plata* is buried. He must have lost his mind. That rumor has been disproved a thousand times."

Holmes spoke up. "But it would give Sheriff Bodkin a motive for murdering Sergeant Davis. When we arrived, we told the sheriff we were interested in buying mining property in this area. And, I remember, he became visibly upset. It's possible the Sheriff reported to Von Herder who then told him to kill the Sergeant, thinking he was a threat to their scheme."

The look on the face of Marshal Thompson went from thoughtful to angry. He nodded slowly. "If we can prove that's the case, I can arrest Bodkin and Blade. Maybe even Von Herder. We'll need to find those connections."

Once again, Sam Thompson stood to go. "You've given me something to chew on. We'll see how it plays out." With that, the Federal lawman left the hotel.

CHAPTER 34

🔲 🔲 🔲

"Sherlock is missing…"

Elspeth Kane came down the stairs into the lobby just after the Marshal left. Neither Holmes nor I felt obligated to share our speculations with the lady. Instead, we all went to Delmonico's Restaurant for supper, followed by a brief shopping trip at the General Store. We then returned to the hotel and our own rooms.

I lay in my bed pondering the various angles and relationships of the people involved with this mystery man named Maldrome. He remained hidden, but his presence seemed to hover over the town like the smell from the arroyo behind it.

I had fallen asleep when a pounding on my door cut through my fog and awakened me. I hammered back my revolver and opened the door to a distraught Elspeth.

"Sherlock is missing," she said. "He's not in his room and I can't find him anywhere in the hotel. I'm afraid he's gone out alone again."

I buckled on my gunbelt and grabbed my hat. "Stay here in the hotel. I'll find him," I said.

As we left my room, I nearly bumped into an elderly man in the hall. Miss Kane moved closer to me. The old man was bent nearly double, and wore a long, stained coat, battered shoes, and a soft flop hat that nearly covered his face. He came so close I was forced to put my hand on his chest to stop his advance. There was the odor of horse urine on his coat. Then he raised his head and gave a laugh. Under a layer of grime was the face of Sherlock Holmes. He put his finger to his lips and motioned us back into my room.

"Blade is afoot again," he said in a whisper after we were inside. "I followed him as far as the back door of this hotel."

"Sherlock, what are you doing dressed like that," Elspeth said. "How did you get so wrinkled and dirty?"

"It would have been foolhardy to attempt to follow around a man like Blade dressed as a British Lord," Holmes whispered. "And please, keep your voice down, Miss Kane. As to the wrinkles, I used beeswax. I got it from the dressmaker's shop. But that's not important now."

He turned his attention to me.

"Mr. Goodfoote. We've seen you in action with a firearm. If I'm correct, you may have an opportunity to again use your skill."

"Continue," I said. Nothing this lad did or said would take me by surprise again, or so I thought.

"I believe Mr. Blade is here to kill me, as he did Sergeant Davis. He may at this moment be hiding in my room with a weapon intended to produce the maximum amount of horror."

Elspeth grabbed the boy by the shoulders and spun him around. "What have you done, you fool?" Her voice was strained. "What in God's name have you done?"

Holmes looked at me, turning himself away from the lady. "Before I assumed my disguise, I let it be known around town that I was interested in buying up any available silver mine, for top dollar."

"You fool," Elspeth repeated. "You arrogant fool." She turned away and sat on the bed.

"I'm not without resources," Sherlock said. "Marshal Thompson will be joining us shortly. The two of you can certainly arrest Mr. Blade without much bother. When Sheriff Bodkin arrives and discharges his shotgun into the door, the Marshal can arrest him as well. His actions will show a guilty mind. That's *mens rea* in law."

It was a weak plan, in my estimation. When Marshal Thompson came aboard he had a less dramatic idea.

"We simply wait to see if Bodkin shows up," the Marshal said. "If he does, I'll arrest him for impersonating a sheriff when he goes to the boy's door. I can arrest Blade for trespassing in the boy's room after I have Bodkin in custody." Sam Thompson stared me hard in the eye and I could read his intent. "I'll hide out in the room across the hall so I can get a clear view when Bodkin comes up the stairs. You folks stay clear. He may object to being detained in such a manner."

The Marshal stepped into the hall and I saw he had obtained a key to the room directly opposite mine. It was a good half hour before we heard someone slowly climb the steps and move past our door. I waited a moment, then silently opened my door a crack so I could watch as Bodkin approached Holmes' room, his shotgun in hand. Elspeth stood at the windows, her back to the door, her arms folded. She stared silently out at the main street of Disenchantment, seemingly lost in her own thoughts.

Despite my wishes to keep young Sherlock away from the door, he pushed his way to the opening.

Bodkin paused at Holmes' door and searched the area of the floor directly in front of it. Then he knocked quietly and the door was opened by Blade who had his big knife in hand. I glanced at Holmes to see his reaction to the fate that had awaited him had he gone into his room, but the lad could have been watching a mildly interesting stage play in Drury Lane for all the emotion he showed.

The Marshal stepped into the hall and shouted, "Throw up your hands, Tuttle, and drop that scattergun." When Tuttle/Bodkin turned, Marshal Thompson fired twice. Bodkin stumbled backward as the heavy slugs slammed into his chest. Before the man hit the floor, the Marshal fired again, this time into Blade's open mouth. The outlaw spun around sending a spew of blood along the door to the room, and the hallway wall. The shot was remarkable, but then Sam Thompson is a remarkable man.

I glanced at Miss Kane who had not moved from the window. She stood as still as stone, and then dropped her head as if in prayer. Sherlock fully opened the door and bounded into the hallway in front of me. We reached the Marshal just as the he nudged Bodkin with his toe.

"One through the heart, one through the left lung," he said. He then looked at Blade who had fallen half out of Sherlock's door. "That is one ugly son-of-a-bitch," he eulogized.

"He was no oil painting when he was healthier," I added.

After Mr. Swann and his helpers arrived to remove the bodies, and the Marshal retired to the now-vacant Sheriff's Office to prepare his report, Holmes was able to clean up and change into a white shirt, grey pants and his good boots. He and I then went down to the hotel restaurant for a late cup of tea.

Elspeth didn't accompany us. She retired to her room to check on her belongings. She said she wanted to make sure Blade hadn't had access to her adjoining room during his wait.

"You knew the Marshal was going to kill those two men, Mr. Goodfoote," Sherlock said, as we sat on cushioned chairs in the restaurant of the hotel. He sipped his tea, sweetened with brown sugar this time.

"I know Sam Thompson as a man with the bark still on," I answered. "I admit it's not an elegant conclusion."

"Inelegant and vulgar," he said. "But it's apparent the American West knows no method of solving problems other than with a pistol." He took another sip of tea. "There was no pig blood in my room. They obviously meant to use my blood this time to shock the citizenry."

I didn't respond, but watched the lad closely.

"You realize this shooting of Sheriff Bodkin simply creates an employment opportunity for some other gunman," he continued. "Von Herder won't waste any time replacing the two dead men."

"Four, if you count Mange and the Kiowa Kid," I added.

Elspeth joined us then, looking a trifle pale. She refused to take any tea, but did accept a glass of white wine from the waiter. "Nothing was touched in my room," she informed us. "I had locked the adjoining door last night, and it was still locked."

We spent the rest of the evening planning our next move. With the death of Bodkin and Blade, only Von Herder and Maldrome comprised any major menace. While the town itself was dangerous, most of the real threat would come later when more competent gunmen arrived. After a short time, we retired to our rooms.

The next morning, Miss Kane, young Holmes, and I were having breakfast in the hotel restaurant when we heard a commotion in the lobby. Someone was shouting, and men who had been reading their newspapers began talking with loud voices. The doors to the restaurant swung open and a bare-headed man dressed in a suit and vest burst in.

"The Apaches are coming!" he shouted. "We need all able-bodied men to man the streets!"

CHAPTER 35

◙ ◙ ◙

"Marshal, you've got to organize a defense or we'll be murdered right here in the street."

We filed out to the street and saw that pandemonium had seized the town. The good citizens of Disenchantment were dashing in and out of the saloons and gunsmiths, arming themselves with rifles and shotguns. Horses snorted and bucked, dogs barked, and several children ran and jumped as if at play. I caught a glimpse of Leviticus Winthrop bounding down the street, his ink-stained coat open and flapping. He stopped abruptly when he spotted me, then scampered over to us, thrust his face close to mine, and grabbed the lapels of my coat. "Marshal, you've got to organize a defense or we'll be murdered right here in the street."

His breath, even at this early hour, would have given the cobble-wobbles to a Clydesdale.

"Winthrop, damn it. I'm not the Marshal," I said, as I pried his hands from my coat. "Find Marshal Thompson. He's over at the Sheriff's Office." I knew Kaya wasn't about to raid Disenchantment, and Juh was on the other side of the territory.

"Winthrop," I grabbed his sleeve as he was about to take to running again, "who says the Apache are coming?"

"It's all over town," he shouted. "I got it first from the bartender at the Silver Spur, then Doc Gosling. Everybody knows about it."

"You're a newspaper man, Winthrop. Who started the story?"

"Doc Gosling said Jedidiah Dawson came running into town yelling his head off. He came by Von Herder's ranch and saw it burning. The Apache were raping and murdering everyone in it." With that, he fled to find the Marshal.

"I know Dawson," I said. "He's an old sourdough who comes to town twice a year to get drunk. He's always on foot, leading a mule. It's a good four hours by foot to Von Herder's ranch, even if he ran the whole way, which I'm sure he didn't."

"Given that information," Sherlock said, "we can assume the raid took place sometime during the night."

I glanced at Elspeth and noted that her eyes were narrowed and her lower lip was between her teeth. She seemed to be nodding slightly. It was an unaccustomed look for the lady. I'd seen her look of concern before, but this intense expression held a tinge of bafflement. "The hotel will be safe, Miss Kane," I said. I took her arm and steered her to the door of the Silver Lode. "I'm convinced there will be no Apache coming into town." To my surprise, she acquiesced without her usual protestations regarding Sherlock's safety, even giving me a wide smile.

"I've seen much in the last few months, Mr. Goodfoote," Sherlock said when I rejoined him. He gazed at the surrounding bedlam. "But I can't believe Kaya is capable of murdering women and children. She is far too gentle a creature."

I just looked at the boy. He had seen much, but he had much to learn about humans, white or red. Just then, Marshal Thompson came striding up the sidewalk.

"People are going crazy," he said. "You and I both know this is nonsense."

"Maybe we should ride out to Von Herder's and see for ourselves," I suggested. "I feel it's safe enough to take the lad with us, if young Sherlock would like to go."

"Of course," Sherlock said.

"No point in disturbing Miss Kane about this," I added.

CHAPTER 36

◨ ◨ ◨

"This saves the government a lot of money in bounties."

Marshal Thompson organized a well-armed posse and we started for Von Herder's Ranch. We rode into the desert at a gentle trot, for we saw no reason to get our horses winded. Winthrop insisted on riding out in his buggy which bucked along on the rutted road. Young Holmes, again in his British safari clothes, rode next to me on his pinto.

We stopped atop a slight rise and saw smoke drifting sideways from the ranch, spreading like a dirty grey blanket over the desert. There was no sign of the Apache hostiles, but we could see a lot of activity around the open gate of the fort. As we rode closer, we saw that the ranch and surrounding landscape were now under the authority of the U.S. Army. A mounted lieutenant with six troopers met us. Leaving the rest of the posse sitting in the shade of the wall outside the gate, the cavalry escorted U.S. Marshal Thompson and me inside. Winthrop was sputtering like a tea kettle when we left him, but the lieutenant brooked no nonsense. Sherlock made himself comfortable in the shade of the wall.

We dismounted in front of Von Herder's columned mansion. An Army Major and his officers were poring over a large map spread out on a table.

"Major Caulfield," the lieutenant announced, coming to attention. "This is Federal Marshal Thompson and Mr. Charles Goodfoote of the Pinkerton Detective Agency."

The major, a tall, well-proportioned man with a rough beard and mustache, pulled the stump of a cigar from his mouth as he turned to us. "What in hell do you want?"

"Little enough, Major," I said. "A quick word to start."

The officer thought for a moment, examining first the lawman, then me, from head to toe.

"I'm in the middle of a military operation, gentlemen. Make it brief."

"We rode over from Disenchantment. I have a young man whose father is missing," I said. "I'd like him to look over the dead and see if he can recognize his poor pa." Marshal Thompson swung his head toward me and gave me a hard look. Deception was not one of his practiced traits.

The cigar went back into the major's mouth. "This is the site of an Apache depravity," he said. "It ain't pretty. How old is the lad?"

"Sixteen," I lied.

"Is that what brought a Pinkerton man and a Federal Marshal out here? To identify a boy's father?"

"Not quite all, Major. We got word of an Apache raid and came to help," I answered. "We have twenty able-bodied men and a newspaperman with us."

The major gave a sigh. "Civilian help is the last thing I need. I don't want a bunch of store clerks and saloon keepers tripping over their rifles when the shooting starts. But, if it'll get you and your bunch out of my hair, bring the young man along. We've got the bodies stretched out over by the burned-out stable. The lieutenant here will escort you." He returned to his map.

I rode back to the gate and got young Sherlock. Winthrop had a lunch basket that must have contained some liquid libation, for he was snoring like an elk in rut. One of the gamblers from town had produced a deck of cards and a bottle of liquor, and had started up a poker game. The town blacksmith, who had accompanied us, had been pressed into duty tending to the soldiers' ponies.

"This may be difficult for you, Sherlock, but it's necessary. Take a careful look," I said quietly, as we walked toward the bodies. "If Maldrome is here, we can consider our job finished." We were accompanied by Marshal Thompson and the army lieutenant.

Bodies were laid out on blankets, in a line, face up. I counted eleven, some with wounds from arrows, but a few had gaping gunshot holes in their chests. Six had their throats cut. I assumed they had been sentries.

While Holmes was examining the bodies, I turned to the lieutenant.

"I don't see any women here, Lieutenant. Weren't there any in the compound?"

"That's a strange thing about this raid," the lieutenant answered. "The women and children were rounded up and put in that big meeting house over there." He pointed to an untouched, low-lying building. "The Apache gave them water and food and let 'em be. Damndest thing I ever saw."

I nodded. "Maybe they were Mormon Apaches," I offered.

"And none of the bodies were mutilated."

The Marshal bent over one of the corpses. "This one here didn't die of the influenza," he observed. "He looks like he was in a full-out razor fight without a razor."

"Yeah," the soldier said. "He has about ten knife wounds. He was found in the house with his hand still holding a bloody sword. But the rest were either shot with arrows, bullets, or just had their throats cut."

I had a sudden, unbidden vision of Kaya and knew the blood on the sword was hers. I shook my head to chase the thought away. What happened had already happened, and there was nothing I could do about it.

Holmes came back to where we were standing.

"Did you recognize your pa, Son?" the lieutenant asked.

Holmes shook his head. "He's not here."

The officer smiled. "Well, that's good news. Did you ever see any of these men before? We're trying to put names to faces."

Young Sherlock looked at me, and I nodded. He turned to the soldier.

"Over there, the fat man with the stab wounds, was Count Von Herder. This was his ranch."

"The Count," the officer said. "I've heard of him. I better get Major Caulfield. Recognize anyone else?"

Sam Thompson spoke up. "Damn near the whole bunch are wanted in different parts of the country. I got warrants and posters coming by post. This saves the government a lot of money in bounties. Unless those Apache renegades come in to claim them."

As the lieutenant went off to report to the major, I spoke quietly to both Sherlock and Thompson.

"Maldrome slipped out," I said. "If he ever was here."

"The coach driver who killed Potty is over there. I'd recognize him anywhere," Holmes said. "We had his name in London as Frederick Putnam. I was told to look for him, too."

"Are you sure?" Thompson asked.

Holmes didn't answer. I turned away to study the bodies once more. "We'll need to get into that pile of a house," I said. "I'd like to see what we can find there." The major arrived on foot, accompanied by the lieutenant and four troopers at port arms.

"We have a real Count, dead?" Major Caulfield said. "Is that a fact?"

"It's a fact," Marshal Thompson responded. "And his men are wanted by the law. They're all dead as well."

"Well, this is a damn smelly pot," the army man said. He stepped close to me. "And you seem to be right in the middle of it, Mr. Pinkerton Man. What in the hell is happening here? What do you know?"

I spread my hands. "I'm in the dark, too, Major. An old sourdough rode into Disenchantment this morning yelling that the Apache had attacked the fort. We rode out to help."

The cigar went back into his mouth. "This whole raid stinks to high heaven," he said. "None of the bodies were scalped or mutilated. Only the outbuildings and barracks were burned. The mansion was left standing. You tell me this, Mr. Pinkerton Agent, why wasn't it put to the torch?" I shook my head.

"Like I told the lieutenant, maybe they were Mormon Indians."

Major Caulfield scowled, chewing on his cigar. "This place was crawling with sentries, armaments, and serious battlements. How in hell did them savages get in here in the first place?"

A sergeant rode up on a lathered horse, jumped off and saluted the major.

"Sir," the sergeant said. "we've just discovered a cache of Henry repeating rifles in a silver mine, not a mile distant. There must be hundreds, along with boxes of ammunition."

The major took his cigar out of his mouth and studied it for a moment before he stuck it back in. "Well, now, ain't that something. And here we just happen to have a real, badge-carrying Federal Marshal and a Pinkerton Detective who dropped from nowhere into the middle of what looks like a gunrunning case." He stared at the Marshal, then shook his head. "Thank God the Apache didn't find 'em," he said. "We'd have a real war on our hands. What can you tell me about all this, gentlemen?"

When I hesitated, Marshal Thompson stepped forward. "Maybe you and I can have a little confabulation, Major. Some place where we can smoke a good cigar in peace, and mull this over."

"While you're doing that, Major," I said. "I'd like to take a look inside that palace there. Might be something the Marshal or I could use."

The army officer looked from me to Thompson, sighed, and waved his hand. "Go ahead, Mr. Goodfoote. But I'll need to know what you find." Both men walked toward a somewhat scrawny shade tree in the wide yard. I noticed the Major hand Thompson a cigar as they walked. The four soldiers went with them, leaving Sherlock Holmes and me to walk up to the mansion alone.

CHAPTER 37

◘ ◘ ◘

"It's obviously a code or cipher of some sort," I commented.

The house Von Herder had built was a reflection of his massive ego. He had successfully created a modified Greek Revival plantation villa in the middle of the desert. The mansion's center appeared to be a finely made structure from which a wide portico projected. From this central edifice, two wings sprawled to each side, festooned with floor-to-ceiling windows. A second story with mullioned panes rose above. A cupola topped off the roof and housed a Gatling gun just partially visible from the ground.

"We have only a short time," I said to Holmes, "but we'll need to do a complete job of it. The answers to Maldrome and his plans may lie somewhere inside this pile."

The thick oaken door, covered with carvings that suggested the Black Forest of Europe, swung open on well oiled hinges. The door was intact, not damaged as one would expect from a hostile raid. The entrance hall was huge, with a balcony that ran along its far wall, reached by a sweeping staircase. This gallery, I observed, was more for defense than any other function, for it contained several gunports that covered the entrance. Blackened beams shot across above our heads, with a dark ceiling beyond them. Our only illumination came from small, round ports high up in the wall, for heavy drapes covered the tall windows.

I pulled open the window coverings while young Sherlock climbed the stairs to the upper reaches. I started down a long corridor that ran past the stairway to the rear of the house. This hallway led to the kitchen, and a series of doors along its length were open. These were small rooms, each simply furnished with a bed, chair, and wardrobe. Rifles and revolvers hung on all the walls. This was indeed a fortress, and I wondered briefly at the ability of Kaya and her small Apache band to take it. It was apparently designed to hold off an organized army, but was obviously unsuccessful against a silent, unseen enemy.

A large paneled room with double doors was just off the foyer. It resembled a museum of the Southwest Indian tribes, with woven Navajo rugs on the floor, Pueblo jars and bowls, and a wall display of ancient Apache weapons. I had begun to examine the collection when I heard Sherlock cry out.

"Mr. Goodfoote, I've found something of great interest." I took the stairs two at a time and Sherlock led me into a chamber that had been used as an office. Holmes knelt before the stone fireplace, and pointed to grey ashes.

"A large number of papers were burned here," he said. "This grey ash is burned foolscap, but there is other ash more typical of the paper on which telegraphs are written. I've collected most of the burned debris and saved them in this box."

"We're too late, then," I lamented. "The evidence has been destroyed."

Holmes smiled. "Not quite. I found this scrap behind the grate in the fireplace. It's singed, but legible."

I looked at the paper Holmes handed me. It was covered with numbers and letters.

"It's obviously a code or cipher of some sort," I commented.

A smile lit the lad's face. "I can break it, Mr. Goodfoote. I'm confident, if it is not arbitrary, or in an unknown foreign language, I can force this cipher to reveal its message. As I indicated to you earlier, it was secret writing that led to the death of Potty, and set me on the path to this very house. It is only right that I use my brain to bring justice to him."

I had nothing to say to that. Reading sign is my gift, and logical reasoning is young Sherlock's. I handed the paper to him. "Go to it, Lad, as soon as we return to town." I glanced around at the disordered room with tipped over furniture and papers scattered around the floor. A large amount of blood was sprayed on the walls and carpet, with a large, still-wet stain in the center of the rug. This, then, was the site of Von Herder's battle with Kaya. Again, I feared for the woman warrior, and fought to put my earlier vision out of my mind.

We rode back with the posse and left Marshal Thompson to make arrangements for the bodies to be transported to town for burial. The long trek across the desert to the territorial capitol would have rendered the corpses unidentifiable. It was Sam Thompson's' duty to try to establish the names of the dead men from the posters, and make due notification to the next of kin, if any could be found.

CHAPTER 38

◫ ◫ ◫

*"With you along, there's a whole bunch of
people bound to get shot."*

The sun was still above the horizon when Jubal T. took the horses back to the livery. After I filled Elspeth in on some of the recent events at the fort, she and Sherlock retired to their respective rooms. We planned to meet in the lobby in an hour.

I walked out of the hotel onto Compton Street. Despite the absence of an organized outlaw gang, Disenchantment was not, even at a stretch, a peaceful New England village. The whole town was celebrating the news that the Army was afield after Kaya. Staggering drunks fired their guns in the air and cowboys rode their horses onto the sidewalks, and, occasionally, into the saloons. A bevy of street urchins wove their way in and out among the flashing hooves. With the screaming and yelling, gunshots, and curses, the town had returned to its normal state, pure Bedlam. The Army had sent a small detachment to use the telegraph and bivouac in the town. The soldiers would be spending their government wages in the Silver Slipper or Red Garter. I, however, had several strings to pull together that I hoped would take no more than a day, and was anxious to get to them. The stagecoach came through heading west one day a week only, and I didn't want to miss our ride out of town.

My secondary mission from William Pinkerton, as I understood it, was to determine if the confederation of outriders swarming the environs of Disenchantment were a real threat to the peace and well-being of the nation as a whole, or just a gaggle of miscreants intent on mischief of a provincial nature. Between Marshal Sam Thompson and Kaya, the matter had been partly concluded in a manner both 'inelegant and vulgar,' to quote Mr. Holmes.

That left only the identification and capture of the brains behind the crime, the mysterious Maldrome. My thoughts on that score were buzzing like horseflies on a colt. I knew I was forgetting something important, but, try as I might, it remained just beyond my recall.

An hour later I walked into the Silver Lode and found Elspeth sitting on the edge of her seat, while Jubal T. Bedford, cleaned up, shaven, and smelling of Bay Rum, was in a chair reading the latest copy of the *Weekly Dispatch* and chewing on a toothpick.

"Where's Sherlock?" I asked, after introducing Miss Kane to Jubal T. I knew they had not met before, as Bedford's disguise as the town drunk had kept him invisible.

Elspeth said in a quiet voice, "He's upstairs scribbling away. He's doing mathematical problems, which seem to relax him. He's a rather strange boy."

"Jubal T., will you get the lad? I have some things to say and I don't want to repeat myself."

When they came downstairs, we quickly reconvened in a corner. I explained that we no longer were looking for Maldrome in Disenchantment.

"We may have missed him, or he may never have been here," I said. "But it's no good risking the boy on a fool's errand. This town will always be a dangerous place and I can't chance a stray shot from a drunken miner doing mischief." Elspeth seemed distant, and remained silent.

"With the death of Bodkin, Von Herder, and the rest of that gang, we have little reason to stay in Disenchantment," I continued. "The only possible evidence we have of Maldrome ever gracing this town with his residency, is that his coach driver is laying dead up at Von Herder's."

"What's our next play, Charles?" Jubal T. asked. "Not that it makes any difference. With you along, there's a whole bunch of people bound to get shot."

"I admit, we've had some vexatious times," I responded. "But the stagecoach leaves tomorrow and I plan to have these folks, and myself, aboard. Our destination is Chicago. You're welcome to come along, Jubal T."

Bedford shook his head. "You won't get me on a stagecoach and you know it, Charles. I came out on Triumph and I'll ride back on him."

I nodded. "Good enough. Ride with the stage as far as the railhead. We may need an extra gun through the mountain passes. Then you can either come with us back to Chicago, or follow the wind. Pinkerton now knows you're here, so he may have some other assignment for you."

Jubal T. stood, pulling the toothpick from his mouth. "I better go make sure Triumph gets some oats. That liveryman skimps a little when he's not watched."

I also rose. "We have a day to pack and be ready for our long journey."

"Nothing we haven't done before, Mr. Goodfoote," young Sherlock said.

I nodded. "I have one or two matters that need some attention. I'll call on you for supper when I'm finished, if you're both willing."

Holmes stood and stretched. "I believe I'll take a nap. It will be the first chance I've had to sleep with both eyes closed." I suspected he wanted more time with his cipher-solving.

Elspeth said nothing, but turned and walked slowly to the stairs leading to the second floor. She was followed closely by young Mister Holmes.

I rode Dobs out of town to an area not far distant and sheltered from view on three sides. It was a small blind canyon I had discovered years ago. Kaya was waiting for me, cradling a shiny new Henry Repeater. Her neck was wrapped in a bandage of leaves, covered by a piece of brain-tanned deer hide.

"It was a hard battle," I said, motioning to her wound. Kaya just looked at me, her eyes dark and unblinking, then smiled. "The fat one had a long knife, but he was slow."

I nodded. "I brought some dressings from the white medicine man. They will help heal your wound."

She shook her head. "Neva dressed my wound. It will heal."

We sat on her blanket in the shade of a large boulder. "Were any of your warriors killed?" I asked. There had been a lot of blood in the fort, some trailing outside the gate.

"Two were injured. Cantanka was shot in the leg, but he will heal. Magna was struck by a rifle butt. He says his head hurts and his eyes are not right."

Kaya took a long drink from her water-skin, then handed it to me. I swallowed briefly before giving it back to her.

"We climbed over the back wall, then killed the guards. I saw a light in the upstairs of the big lodge and ran through the fighting to it, into the room with books. The fat man was there. He was putting papers in a fire, but he saw me and ran at me with his long knife. He cut me here," she motioned to her neck wound. "I cut him many times before he grew weak. Then I put my knife in his belly…and held it there until his spirit left his body."

Again, I could only nod. "You did not burn the big lodge or hurt the women and children. You did as I asked. I am grateful."

Kaya grasped the bear claw around her neck. "My Power told me to do as Travels-Far asks. The women and children are not witches."

I smiled and opened my shoulder bag. I presented her with a gift wrapped in soft buckskin. It was Blade's Bowie knife.

And this remarkable woman had a gift for me. From her woven bag, Kaya pulled out a pair of slipper-like shoes made of thin strips of bark covered with colorful bird feathers.

"When you wear them, you will leave no tracks," she said. I smiled, and now understood the strange marks outside the rear door of the hotel. I had been protected by my own Apache warrior.

We sat together among the flowering desert plants, and I mused about how the fragrant blossoms and bright colors contrasted with the harshness of the rock outcroppings around us. Looking at Kaya, I felt again how alike we were.

It was a longer goodbye than I had planned.

That evening, just as the sun disappeared behind the western hills beyond the desert, I invited Elspeth and Sherlock to dinner. I was even able to persuade Jubal T. to leave his horse long enough to join us. We feasted on beef, pork, and a variety of side dishes. I drank coffee, Holmes drank tea, and Miss Kane settled for a glass of red wine. Jubal T. had a glass of brandy.

Elspeth's mood had lifted along with our festivities, and Holmes and she chatted about the sights of London. I added several engaging stories of my adventures with various pirates I had encountered off the coasts of Morocco and Algiers.

Before we retired to our separate rooms, I took Sherlock aside and clapped him on the shoulder. "It was a brave thing you did, viewing the bodies of Von Herder's men. We wouldn't have known about Maldrome's coach driver being here if you hadn't done what I asked. There are still conundrums to solve, but we made progress today, and much is owed to your courage."

Holmes nodded, and his eyes sparkled. "Vengeance is not one of the more noble character traits of an Englishman," he said. "But I admit to feeling a sense of satisfaction on seeing the body of the man who so callously murdered my friend."

With that, we retired to our rooms and I propped a chair beneath my doorknob.

CHAPTER 39

◧ ◧ ◧

"My trials proved to me that simple substitution ciphers weren't used."

The day was just dawning when a knock on my door brought me upright in bed. I jumped into my trousers, drew back the hammer on my revolver, and slipped to one side of the door.

"It's me, Mr. Goodfoote. I have something that may be of interest." It was the voice of young Holmes, and I swung wide the door. He was dressed in shirtsleeves and rumpled pants, a far cry from his usual crisp attire. In his arms, he carried a sheaf of loose papers covered in scrawls and numbers.

"Your red eyes tell me you've been up all night," I said as he entered. "And your wardrobe testifies to the priority of your message."

"Not my message, Mr. Goodfoote. The message in the cipher."

"You broke the code, then," I reasoned.

"Yes. It has to do with prime number factorization. The solution dawned on me at the same time as the sun."

"What does the message say?" I asked.

"I said I broke the code, but the numbers are too large for simple calculations. It would be easy to encode, but difficult to decode. Here, consider this."

The lad dumped his papers on the dresser top, then thumbed through them until he found the one he wanted. "Remember the sequence of numbers? This is the sheet on which I copied the numbers from the paper we found in Von Herder's house." He smoothed out a piece of foolscap. It read:

T128Y2B4096D32X16384X2N

F1024Z2097152S4096W33554432K4G

"It looks like an impossible puzzle," I said. The combination of numbers and letters appeared to be too complex to yield to a normal attack. "How did you crack it?"

"First, I tried the usual number/letter substitution combination. For the 'one,' I tried A, for 'two,' B, and so on. This led to real difficulty, for the first word would then be TABH. I tried other numbers, but they were just as discouraging. I reasoned the letters could stand for 'nulls,' simply, spaces between words. Then the first word would be ABH, still nothing of value." Young Holmes began to pace, his hands clasped behind his back. "I tried the alphabet backwards, but that, too, didn't work. I noted the number combination '4096' repeated itself in the second line. I thought this might be a simple word like 'they' or 'that' and then the number 'nine' would be the letter E. As you are no doubt aware, E is the most common letter in any English text, and it occurs so frequently that one would expect to find it, even in a brief sentence. Generally speaking, T, A, O or N follow in number, but are so close in usage that it would be endlessly complex to try each combination. My trials proved to me that simple substitution ciphers weren't used." Holmes walked to the dresser and pulled out another sheet covered in numbers.

"At about midnight, the enlightened thought that the numbers themselves could be attacked, occurred to me, but I wasn't too hopeful. If the message was for Bodkin or Von Herder, or any of the criminals we had met, a number cipher would simply be beyond their capabilities. But what if Maldrome had sent a numerical message to someone else, some agent with whom we are unfamiliar, a lucifugous presence, someone learned in mathematics? Then the message would be undecipherable to the lower ranking outlaws, but sensible to the agent. Perhaps he is right under Maldrome himself in order of importance." Holmes handed me the sheet of numbers. "And perhaps he is here in Disenchantment. Bodkin or Von Herder may have been his conduit. They could have received his messages and passed them on." He put his hands on his hips and nodded at the sheet of paper in my hand.

"Did the coach driver, Putnam, have that kind of ability? Was he the agent sent to oversee this operation?" I asked.

Sherlock shook his head. "Scotland Yard had a complete file on Mr. Putnam. He was a bullyboy, a low-life ruffian who was used for brutal work. He most likely would have been sent here as an aide to someone else, someone with the necessary intelligence."

"Has anyone in this town shown this kind of mathematical ability?" I wondered out loud.

"You mentioned the coroner is knowledgeable in science. It's not a stretch to conclude he would also have a mathematical background."

I shook my head. I'd known Doc Gosling and his work for years, and was sure he had had no part in Maldrome's vile machinations. I studied the sheet of paper Sherlock had handed me.

The sheet showed a column of the letters of the alphabet with their number next to them. It was A next to 'one,' B next to 'two,' C next to 'three,' until completion with Z next to 'twenty-six.'

"Mostly out of frustration," Sherlock continued, I tried at first to do simple factoring of prime numbers of the text of the cipher, and that gave me a start. The first number is '128' with the T and the Y each representing a 'null.'"

I hadn't won any awards at Harvard for mathematics, but I was able to follow his thinking. "The letters, then, are placed simply to separate each group of numbers. They have no independent meaning," I added.

"Exactly," Sherlock said. "And factoring 128 gives us 'two to the seventh power' as its prime. So I wrote 'seven' down as representing the letter G, without, at this point, any great expectations. The next number found between two letters was 'two.' Two is already a prime number, and its exponent would be 'one.' So I wrote down the letter A, for it's the first letter of the alphabet." In his excitement, Sherlock was starting to speak faster and his accent became more pronounced. "The third number is '4096,' the number that repeats in the second line of the cipher. The number is a perfect factor of 'two to the twelfth,' representing the letter L, the twelfth letter of the alphabet. I was starting to see a pattern emerge. But many of the numbers that follow are too long for easy factoring. It will take me days to finish."

I glanced at the early morning light peeking through the windows. "I think I know someone who can help us. Do you have any pennies on your person?"

Abel Slade, as I had hoped, was sweeping the sidewalk in front of the saloon. I pulled a shiny new penny out of my pocket and flipped it causally in the air.

"What are the factors of the number thirty-two?" Holmes asked. We started with an easy one to which we already knew the answer.

"Two to the fifth," Abel said, without pause. I handed him the penny.

We went through a list of simple numbers until we were confident Abel knew what we were after. Then we hit him with a harder one.

"16384," Sherlock said.

"Two to the fourteenth," was Slade's immediate answer.

"33554432."

"Two to the twenty-fifth." For that, he earned two pennies.

In minutes, for the price of a few coppers, we had the message.

"Galena July Fourth," Sherlock Holmes read.

"Galena," I said, "a city in Illinois." I pondered the meaning of so simple a message, but soon realized its wicked possibilities. "President Grant entered the Union Army from Galena, and he returns there often. This message may be of great national importance."

We returned to my room. I sat in a chair to think while Holmes gathered his papers. More information was needed, but I felt our time was running short.

"Have you told anyone you were working on this message?" I asked. "Anyone at all?"

"No. I came straight to you. I expect Miss Kane is very likely still asleep, and she would be the only one in whom I would confide."

I stood and began making plans. "Let's keep this to ourselves for now. We can fill Miss Kane and Jubal T. in later. Right now, we'll burn everything but the original message. Leave no evidence anywhere that you have broken the code.

"Use the stove in the hotel's kitchen, then return to your room and crawl back into bed. That's where you're expected to be found. No one need know about the cipher. Is that clear?"

"Of course. We'll be the only two who know about Galena."

"For now," I said, "for now, we tell no one."

CHAPTER 40

◳ ◳ ◳

"Pinkerton says he has proof that this is our man."

After Sherlock left, I bathed and dressed for travel. I strode over to Haggis Livery where Jubal T. had been sleeping next to his horse. It's one of the habits of these horse men, and I knew of more than one Blackfoot who kept his favorite buffalo runner tethered to his wrist at night. I found Bedford brushing down Triumph, and a few moments later we left the stable.

"I'll ride with you as far as the railhead, then I'm heading up the coast to San Francisco," he said, as we stood outside in the sun. He showed me a telegram he had received the day before. "I've a little Agency business there that needs attending to."

"Fair enough," I said, handing him back the wire message. "An agent was killed up there. It stands to reason Maldrome had a hand in it, but it probably also involved some local talent. The other operatives will need your services to see justice carried out."

"If Maldrome skipped out of here, he may have gone to San Francisco."

I nodded. "My sense is that he was never in Disenchantment. After the gang was routed in London, Maldrome sent his lackey Putnam to get Von Herder and Bodkin organized. This was a nascent operation, but well laid out long before the English adventure went bust on them."

Jubal T. shook his head. "This Maldrome is something. What the hell is this all about?"

"I'm beginning to suspect Maldrome is made of straw, Jubal. All we have is a name and description that make him sound like a dime novel villain. The man is reported to be all over the country, and we keep chasing him, but it's like trying to catch smoke. And Bodkin and Von Herder were sent out here to get all the silver mines they could grab," I added.

"The silver ore is all played out, from what I'm hearing," Jubal T. said. "They went to a lot of trouble to get some worthless desert."

"It's just another part of this whole affair that doesn't make sense. I'm hoping a clue to his plans may be in the way he orchestrated his affairs in England."

"Maybe he's made a big mistake. Thought there was silver where there isn't any. But maybe he just wanted some caves to hide rifles in."

"Maldrome is a madman, not a fool. If he's spending money and time on getting the deeds to the silver in this area, he knows something we don't."

"Well," Jubal T. said reasonably, "it's all water over the dam now. Between Marshal Thompson and Kaya, that problem has been solved. Maldrome's gang is no more, at least in these parts. Whatever Von Herder had planned for those worthless mines died with him. And we have no evidence that there even is a Maldrome. Not a bad day's work, Charles. Not bad at all."

We leaned on the top rail of the corral outside the stable. Jubal stuck a piece of hay in his mouth, then said in a quiet voice. "I'm not asking any questions, Charles. But that raid on Von Herder's fort was awfully convenient for Pinkerton's."

I said nothing.

"The women and children were spared, the bodies weren't mutilated," Jubal continued. "That made it mighty easy for Sherlock to take a look at them. I've never known such obliging Apaches, and Kaya isn't known for her gentle ways."

"What's on your mind, Jubal T?" I said.

"Nothing, Charles," Jubal grinned. "Nothing at all."

I was about to suggest breakfast when a boy ran up. "Message for Mr. Goodfoote," the lad said. I gave him a coin and opened the envelope. The telegram was from the Pinkerton Agency headquarters, and I read it quickly.

"Anything I should know about, Charles?"

"It's from William Pinkerton. He wants me back in Chicago pronto. They have a man in a Chicago jail who matches the description of Maldrome given by young Holmes to a surprising degree. And Pinkerton says he has proof that this is our man."

CHAPTER 41

◘ ◘ ◘

Sherlock's eyes lit up. "Sort of a consulting detective? Of course."

We had been traveling for two days and nights aboard the stagecoach bound for California when I happened to gaze out the window just at sunset, and thought I saw a figure on horseback silhouetted against the far-off skyline. I immediately thought of Kaya, but knew she had left with her band days before. However, the sight of that horseman brought forth a longing for the company of that incredible woman that I hadn't admitted to myself before, and I determined to return to Apache country as soon as life permitted.

The journey to the train depot in Pueblo de Las Cruces was not without incident. We indeed welcomed the hard riding Jubal T. Bedford and his blazing Colts, as a determined effort was made by some local outlaws to impede our travel. However, it was done with such clumsiness and ineptitude that I dismissed the idea it had been planned by a criminal mastermind.

We arrived at the railhead in California and were delighted to find that a private coach with an attached private dining car awaited us, courtesy of the Pinkerton Detective Agency. Elspeth gave Jubal T. a quick buss and a brief smile before she climbed aboard. After a hearty handshake with Bedford, Sherlock watched while I grasped my friend's hand.

"Watch your back, Charles," Jubal T. said, his face split with his wide grin.

"Watch your'n," I responded, as the train whistle sounded our departure.

Train travel can be tedious, but it's more comfortable than the Butterfield coach. It's also a quicker way to cross the wide expanse of the Great Plains, and time was now an important consideration.

The heat in our private car was the same as in the public coach, but, because we were at the end of the train, we avoided sparks from the smokestack pocking our clothing. We had a lounge with several seats covered in plush velvet that included a dining area, and two sleeper quarters. A cook and cook's helper came with the package. All in all, it was a commodious way to travel.

As the train rolled out of the foothills of the California mountains and onto the great plains, Holmes and I shared a pot of tea. Miss Kane had retired for a nap.

"I regard Miss Kane as a dear sister," young Sherlock said, as we moved to the comfortable lounge seating.

"Of course," I said. "A dear sister." Although a good ten years his senior, it was clear Elspeth had won the heart of this young English gentleman. There is no stronger passion than youthful love. And no greater disappointment when that love is unrequited.

Sherlock gazed out the window. I thought he might be thinking of Miss Kane, but I was wrong. After a moment, he looked directly at me. "I calculate the town of Disenchantment has a population of some two thousand people, although that varies considerably with the peripatetic nature of its citizens."

I nodded. I hadn't counted the citizenry, but it seemed an accurate number.

"While we were there, we witnessed numerous deaths, most of them felonious."

Again, I nodded. "Yes," I said. "Most of them, certainly. Probably all of them."

"Indeed. There were an average of two murders a week. That translates to a rate of 5.2 for each one hundred members of the population per year. If we take the current population of London, and apply the same murder rate, the result would be about two hundred thousand killings a year."

"It's a querulous town, Disenchantment."

"I believe the entire country of England had less than two hundred murders last year. An infinitesimal rate, considering its population."

Where was this going, I wondered?

"Even New York, a large American city, had about eight hundred felonious deaths last year."

I said nothing.

Holmes again gazed out the window for several seconds. He said, mostly to himself, "London is a barren city for those with special interests in capturing major criminals. A detective practice would consist mostly of property thefts and the occasional blackmail case." He sighed.

"If you're thinking of becoming an independent detective, you could work on only those cases you found challenging," I offered.

Sherlock's eyes lit up. "Sort of a consulting detective? Of course. That would allow me to select the clients and their problems that offer me the intellectual stimulus I desire."

We sat in silence for a time until Holmes again spoke. "May I intrude on your thoughts once again, Mr. Goodfoote?"

I nodded, giving him my full attention.

"You have referred often to your uncle, or grandfather, Keeps-The-Lodge. May I inquire as to the origin of his name, and what it means?"

I pulled my briar pipe from my jacket pocket and began to stuff it with tobacco. "First, you need to understand something of the language of The People. In the Blackfoot tongue, nouns are used sparingly."

"Fewer nouns? Then what does one use to name objects?"

"Verbs, Lad. To the Blackfoot, the world is one of transformation and change. The People don't deal with objects as you do, but see form and movement in all things."

"I don't quite understand," Sherlock said.

I was silent for a long moment. "This is difficult to put into English. A language is like a river, flowing along with its many parts. A noun is like a brief eddy in the river, just there for a few moments." I stopped, thinking intensely.

"Wait. Let me try again," I continued. "Words reflect the way an Indian sees his world, just as your language expresses your history, and your view of the world you call home." I paused to let that sink in.

"The name Keeps-The-Lodge means much more in Blackfoot than in English. It means, roughly translated, 'Here is a man who keeps his home in order with no disputes with his wife or children. His balance extends out into the Great Lodge of the Earth, and he knows how to maintain peace and harmony in this world and the spirit world.'

"So, as you can see, to a Blackfoot, Keeps-The-Lodge is the name of a powerful and wise man. But his name, except in translation, is an action word, and doesn't have the pronoun 'he' in it. Or 'man' for that matter."

"Was Keeps-The-Lodge your uncle or your grandfather?" Holmes asked. His European mind was after specifics.

I put a match to my pipe and puffed aromatic smoke around us and waved the match to extinguish the flame. "In truth, I don't really know. My birth mother was only one of several women who raised me until I was old enough to be turned over to the men. Her father was Stands-In-Thunder, a revered leader among The People. Several men had the task of teaching me skills I would need as one of The People. They were all my uncles. Keeps-The-Lodge was simply an older uncle, or Grandfather. Both are terms of respect. When he taught me tracking, I called him 'Grandfather.' That was the highest praise I could give him."

"So he was your first teacher?"

"One of many. I had seven 'uncles' who also took me under their wings. And I learned about the plants from my mother and many 'aunties.' In truth, the wind, the mountains, the buffalo, and all The People were my teachers."

He thought about this for awhile before he asked, "I believe I asked you before, but your answer was vague. What does 'Kaya' mean in the Apache language?"

"Well," I said. I leaned forward in my chair. "It's a shortened form of a word that means 'fights without weapons,' which means she has shown great courage in battle." I sat back and thought about what I knew about Kaya. She had the ability to tell where the enemy was, and how many.. Her brother, Lupan, had praised her to the whole village. It was the start of her career as a warrior. Later, she killed a Comanche with his own knife. As an unmarried female, her position as a fighter was unusual, and required her brother, and the people of the tribe, to give her their permission.

I sat quietly puffing on my pipe. To my surprise, Sherlock pulled a bent briar pipe from his pocket and began stuffing it with dark tobacco. The pipe looked brand new, as did his tobacco pouch. I made no comment, but offered him a match when he had finished his preliminary task. We sat in a compatible silence, blowing smoke into the air. Within minutes, Sherlock stood up and opened a side window, stuck his head out and let the breeze from the motion of the train blow onto his face.

He looked pale when he resumed his seat. "So you were tracking from a young age," he said, after awhile. Color was returning to his face. He had emptied his pipe and put it away. "The 'Wisdom of the Marks,' as I believe you referred to it."

"I started tracking as a pup, but never stopped, even when I went East after the Army nearly wiped out my band. Tracking, and a view of the world that is rooted in the land and sky, is still my strongest link to the heart of The People."

Again I lapsed into memories from my childhood. It had been a great time and place for a boy to grow, until the day when my world was destroyed. Keeps-The-Lodge had been my cherished grandfather, uncle, and teacher. My mind went back to the time we had studied the tracks of a black bear that had moved toward a berry patch. I had read the prints correctly, and Keeps had smiled and nodded, a rare outpouring of praise from the old man. In my youthful enthusiasm, I told Keeps I was going to be the greatest tracker of all the tribes. "Tracking wisdom belongs to all The People," Keeps had said. "And The People belong to all the tracking wisdom."

Sherlock interrupted my reverie. "Mr. Goodfoote. Perhaps you can enlighten me on several other points."

My pipe had gone out. I patted down the remaining tobacco. "Of course." I put a match to the bowl and puffed it back into life.

"You were raised an Indian, but you were also raised as a white man. Moving between the two worlds must have been difficult."

I thought deeply for a moment. "It's like my eyes. You noted that one is dark, the other light. My blood is the same. I have Indian blood and white blood. It's as if I have two brains, one that lets me do numbers and writing, and the other that lets me read a trail and put the patterns together without thought."

"The patterns of the tracks," Holmes said.

"Yes," I responded. "I can reason out the toes and claws in the print on the ground, or the type of sole on the human bootprint. For that, I use my blue eye." Here I demonstrated by closing my left eye. "But to read the pattern, and what it means, I use my brown eye, and see only with my Indian sight. Then I know what the marks on the ground mean." I smiled. "But to know the history of the maker of the track, be it animal or man, and to peer into his spirit, I need both eyes." I blinked several times. "Being raised Indian and white has given me gifts from two worlds."

We sat in silence for some time as I puffed on my pipe. The door to the lounge opened and Elspeth entered, dressed in a white, high collar shirt, and a lavender skirt that brushed the carpet as she walked.

Holmes and I rose, but she waved us back to our chairs with a smile. When we had resumed out seats, Miss Kane put her hand on young Sherlock's shoulder. He didn't turn red, but his face could have lit up a coal yard at midnight.

The late afternoon sun was casting long shadows across the floor of the car and we watched it turn the sky red, gold, and purple. Elspeth began to light the oil lamps in the sconces. Holmes rose and helped her.

"I'm ready to eat," Miss Kane said. At that moment the lounge door opened, revealing our Chinese cook and his helper. Unlike lunch, which had been bread, marmalade, and tea, the two men had now prepared a feast of quail in sweet sauce, new potatoes with herbs, and various condiments. A bottle of wine, of a reasonable year, completed our meal. The scent of the entree made me ravenous, and it seemed to have the same effect on my dinner companions. We devoured the entire banquet like wolves at a buffalo carcass.

Afterward, sitting comfortably satiated, I asked the lady's permission to smoke, and, it being granted, soon put flame to my pipe.

"Mr. Goodfoote was explaining to me some of the Indian ways," Holmes said. I noticed his pipe did not make a second appearance.

"Yes, Mr. Goodfoote," Elspeth said. "Tell us how you came to be raised an Indian, but schooled at Harvard."

When I didn't reply immediately, she continued. "When were you born, Mr. Goodfoote? Let's start there."

After a few puffs, I answered. "As near as I can figure, I was born in the Moon of the Flowers, three summers after The Taking of the Robes."

"That's hardly an answer, Mr. Goodfoote. Come now, after what we've been through, surely you can be more forthcoming."

I smiled. "My tale is as simple and common as rust on a plow. But you, Miss Kane. The first of your gender to be employed as a detective at Scotland Yard. There's a story that would interest everyone, I'm sure."

Elspeth glanced at Sherlock sitting at the table next to her, then fixed her eyes on mine. "I'm with the Admiralty, Mr. Goodfoote. I'm sure I told you that before. It was the unfortunate Sergeant Davis who was the detective from Scotland Yard. I'm merely a woman sent to fill out the 'family' persona." She again glanced at young Holmes. "More a clerk than anything," she said.

Both Holmes and I stared at Elspeth. For a clerk, she had a wicked eye with a revolver, I thought. Holmes gave me a puzzled look.

"Miss Kane," Sherlock said. "your entire demeanor is one of a competent police officer. I find it difficult to understand why the Prime Minister would send a clerk to oversee my well-being."

"Well, perhaps not a clerk," Elspeth said. "But certainly not as skilled as Mr. Goodfoote here, and not as capable as Sergeant Davis."

"I would like to hear your story, then," I said.

"As would I," Sherlock followed.

Elspeth sighed. "Very well. If you insist." She smiled at each of us in turn. "I was, truly, once a clerk in the Topographical and Statistical Division of the War Department in Whitehall. As I was skilled in foreign languages, I was put to the task of translating communiqués from embassies and agents overseas. Soon I was sent to embassies around the world, and met with a host of diplomats and clandestine agents. This travel allowed me to quickly translate important documents *in situ*. Later, I become an *agent provocateur* with my own little band of spies."

"And you are now with the Admiralty?" I asked.

"Last year, the Admiralty took over the clandestine services of the War Department, and I was transferred." Elspeth rose from the table. "Now, Gentlemen, if you will excuse me, I'm going to retire to my room to finish my report on our successes…and failures."

"Then you know Captain Mayfield," Holmes said, as he and I stood.

"The name means nothing to me, Sherlock. I report to Captain Charles W. Wilson." She smiled, drew up a corner of her skirt to step around the table, and exited the car.

Holmes and I sat in silence for awhile, each with his own thoughts. Then we moved to the more comfortable lounge seating.

"Do you know a Captain Mayfield in the Admiralty?" I asked.

"Yes. He's a friend of my father, and holds a post in Whitehall."

"And there's no Captain Charles Wilson?"

"There definitely is a Captain Wilson. He's the current head of the Topographical and Statistical Section. She was right on point about that."

I again put a match to my pipe. "We've seen her skill with a revolver. Now we know her other qualifications. It puts my mind at ease, knowing she has had a career with the Admiralty."

Holmes sat back in his chair, his eyes on the ceiling. "She certainly has an engaging smile."

I chuckled. "I agree. Her smile could melt the heart of a money-lender."

My mind had been working on my memory lapse, and I finally recalled what had been hidden in the tangle of my recollections. It gave me pause. We were about to finally meet the elusive Maldrome, if Pinkerton was right, and experience has taught me the most dangerous part of a hunt is when the tracking is over and the prey is cornered. It's then a poor time to find out one of your bullets is without powder.

CHAPTER 42

◘ ◘ ◘

Her warrior days were behind her.

KAYA WATCHED THE stagecoach that carried Travels-Far disappear over a hill that lead to a mountain pass. She had been trailing Travels-Far for two days, and now it was time to let him go. The sun was dropping behind the ridge at her back, and she had let herself be seen against the fading light. The man astride the large horse who rode a long distance behind Travels-Far, out of the dust of the coach, had seen her and slowed, pulling his rifle from its boot. Kaya turned her pony's head back toward the land of the Apache.

The Bluecoats were chasing Neva and his band, far to the place where Holos brings the day. It was time for Kaya, alone, to do the ceremonies to rid herself of the ghost disease that she felt would come. The protection medicine that Dasod had given her had served her well in the fight inside the fort. She had suffered only a minor wound and was nearly healed. But she must cleanse her spirit of the blood she had shed.

That night, when the moon bathed the world in grey shadows, Kaya camped in a valley she knew well from memory and experience. It was *where she and Travels-Far had been together on a night much like tonight. The woman warrior wondered if Travels-Far would return someday to the land of the Apache, and, if he did, would he come to her? Her longing for him surprised her and, for the first time, she wondered if he longed for her. Kaya's sense of loneliness and longing confused her, for the desert and mountains had always filled her spirit.*

But now, even the peace of the valley in the moonlight failed to fill the emptiness in her heart. Her thoughts drifted to Dasod, and she grasped the bear claw on the thong around her neck. The old Shaman was gone, and she felt his absence keenly.

Kaya laid on her blanket and watched the moon until it settled behind the mountains. The night sky, ablaze with stars that seemed to come down to the ground and surround her, helped her make a decision, one that had been coming for some time. Her warrior days were behind her. Now, she would help bring new life into the Apache camp, and heal those who were sick and hurt. And she would seek out a helper to teach her the 'coming together' ceremony to bring Travels-Far back to her.

CHAPTER 43

◘ ◘ ◘

"This whole thing smells worse than a coyote's lunch."

We pulled into the Chicago train depot and Mr. Stanislaus Stack, the deputy director of Pinkerton's, was there to greet us. He was short, stout, and well-dressed in a light brown suit, yellow vest, and Bowler hat. A full brown beard graced his round face.

"We got him, Goodfoote," he said without preamble. "While you were chasing your tail around out in the desert, we got him."

"Where is he being held?" I asked.

"In the local hoosegow," Stack replied. "The Agency and the police worked together once we confirmed he was hiding out in a men's boarding house. We threw him into the pokey two weeks ago. I had the honor of slapping the handcuffs on him myself."

"Has he said anything?" Elspeth asked. She lifted her skirt and daintily stepped into the coach Pinkerton's had provided.

"Not a word," Stack grunted as he hauled himself aboard. "We've been going at the rogue day and night, but he won't crack."

Within minutes, the four of us were rattling along a rutted street into the heart of the city.

"As you know, the police and the Agency have been on a tireless lookout for this crook. A snitch told us where to find him," Stack said. "And he had a load of documents on him that gave away his game." Here he raised his eyebrows and paused as he looked at each of us. "Including… a detailed plan of President Grant's hotel…right here in Chicago."

"And you're sure it's Maldrome?" I asked.

"Fits the lad's description to a tee. Right down to the mole on his cheek, and the wine colored birthmark on his forehead. We are very modern here, Goodfoote. We took his photograph, but of course had none to compare it to. However, a bag in his room still had a receipt from the steam/sail ship *Lyceum*, the very one that had brought him to America. The dates match perfectly with the boy's sighting of him in New York. Of course, he was using an alias, the made-up name of Prendergast."

Holmes, who had been lounging back in his seat, sat up. "That doesn't sound like Maldrome. He would have no documents with him, let alone those which would incriminate him."

"I agree," I said. "This whole thing smells worse than a coyote's lunch."

Stack, who I had met briefly months ago in Denver, had an annoying habit of pursing his lips when challenged. "Well, Mr. Pinkerton doesn't agree. Neither do the Chicago police. And neither do I." He puckered and turned, staring out the window.

We all sat quietly for some time, watching the city pass by. The town was growing. Scores of people flooded the sidewalks, and construction was in full swing. Three and four storied buildings were going up wherever we looked. But in the muggy heat, the stench of the stockyards hung heavily over the city.

"It's a great, booming place," Stack said at last, turning from the window. "Railroads from the East end in the city. Trains bring hogs and cattle in from the West. Lumber from Wisconsin is brought down Lake Michigan, and the Illinois-Michigan canal runs all the way to the

Mississippi." He paused for a breath. "We are now the second largest city in America. Some ninety thousand souls call this place home..."

"Are we on the way to the jail?" Sherlock interrupted. "I need to see Maldrome for myself."

Stack eyed the boy. "No, Son. I'll get you settled at your hotel first."

"That's not acceptable," Holmes said. "I need to confirm Maldrome's identity. That must take precedence over all else."

Stack's lips were getting their workout as he glared at the young man. He was apparently unaccustomed to a mere lad speaking to him with such authority.

"I agree," I added quickly. "And I'd appreciate it if you would set up a meeting with the Chief."

Stack smiled broadly, but his face had turned crimson. He sucked on his teeth.

"You see, Mr. Pinkerton is very busy right now. I'm in charge, Goodfoote. I'll thank you to remember that I stand in for Mr. Pinkerton."

"You can take Miss Kane to the hotel," I said with authority, "and the boy and I will go to the police station." I'm not an equanimous man when dealing with officious popinjays.

"Well, Goodfoote. We are sure it's him, so the boy's identification is merely a matter of form. Besides, we're already at the hotel where you'll be staying. The Mercantile is one of the newest, and finest, in all of Chicago."

"We insist, Mr. Stack," I said. "This is a matter of some importance." Stack jumped from the carriage and I followed him out. My patience was wearing thin. The carriage driver had unloaded our luggage and four bellhops were in the process of taking it inside. I loomed over Stack and was about to elevate the discussion when young Sherlock spoke from the carriage window.

"Mr. Stack. Perhaps you could inform us as to the police station in which Mr. Maldrome is being held?"

Stack looked from Holmes to me, then made up his mind. "Well, Mr. Pinkerton gave me orders to drop you here, but, if you go on your own, it's not my fault. He's in the only jail that could hold him. The Harrison Street Police Station."

It took only minutes, once Stack was out of the picture, to hire a cab to take us to the jail, which was not more than three minutes by carriage from the hotel. Miss Kane had insisted on accompanying us, although dark circles had appeared around her eyes revealing her fatigue.

The building was massive, on the corner of Harrison and LaSalle in downtown Chicago. It boasted two full upper stories with tall windows for admitting copious light. The sidewalk level windows, however, were small and barred. The cell that held Maldrome would be in the basement.

There was some initial difficulty getting past the front desk, but my Pinkerton badge opened the necessary doors. A police sergeant with a mustache that obscured the lower part of his face led us down a hallway, then through a locked, barred door that opened into an enclosed stairwell. At the bottom of these stairs, we faced another locked door, this one solid metal with a small open space placed at eye height, which held a sliding cover. Through this door was the jail proper, a narrow room holding a long row of cells with more barred doors. A lockup keeper was sitting halfway down the room in a rocking chair, facing the cells. He was engaged in a shouting match with one of the prisoners when we entered, but got to his feet quickly and nodded to the sergeant.

"Maldrome," the sergeant said.

"Right here, Sarge. He's the quiet one." He walked to the end of the room and pointed through some bars. "But he's the dirtiest rat in this jail."

"Dirty?" I asked.

"Yessir. He never bathes completely and it's all we can do to make him wash his hands. His face is black as a chimneysweep's."

Holmes stepped up to the cage door. A small man lay on the cot inside, his hands behind his head, staring at the ceiling.

"Maldrome, get up here to the bars," the lockup keeper barked. The man swung his feet to the floor, walked up to the bars, and stared at Sherlock.

"That's not Maldrome," Holmes said. The man grinned. "He has a slight resemblance to the man I saw that night. But he is not Maldrome." The man in the cell put his head back and laughed out loud.

I turned to the jailer. "Get me a bucket of water and a sponge." When they arrived, I ordered the keeper to unlock the cell and let me inside. The prisoner scrambled to the far back of the cell, but two burly guards grabbed him and pulled him toward me. I wet the sponge and rubbed it across the prisoner's face. The red-wine birthmark and black mole disappeared.

For the first time in his two weeks of captivity, the man in the cell spoke in a complete sentence. "My name is Billy Prendergast, you miserable flatfoot," he sneered at the jailer. "Let me the hell out of here."

CHAPTER 44

回 回 回

"We've gained nothing from our weeks of hardships."

I handed the pail and sponge to one of the guards and exited the cell. Elspeth took Sherlock's arm and walked away. I turned to the sergeant, who had stood speechless during our encounter. "What you do with this man is up to you, but I want to see all the materials he had in his pockets, and in his hotel room."

"Come upstairs, Sir," the sergeant said. "The detectives have it all in their room."

In short order we were shown the papers, the official ones obviously forged, and a ticket for the *Lyceum*. It was made out to a "Mr. William Prendergast."

The sergeant left the room to return the papers. "When you were in New York, Sherlock," I asked, as the door closed behind the policeman, "and when you saw the man in New York, are you sure it was Maldrome, and not Prendergast, in disguise?"

Holmes studied the floor for a long moment as he contemplated my question. "I had only a brief glimpse of him before he disappeared."

The youth raised his head slightly. "It could have been either."

"This is maddening," Elspeth said. "We've gained nothing from our weeks of hardships."

In silence we rode back to the Mercantile. The doorman helped Elspeth from the carriage, and Sherlock and I followed. Inside the spacious lobby, I paused.

"We'll meet back here in an hour," I said. "The hotel restaurant is probably as good a place to confabulate as any."

I didn't go to my room, but, after watching Sherlock and Elspeth disappear up the sweeping staircase, turned and left the hotel. I had a solitary undertaking to perform.

An hour later I returned to the hotel. Sherlock was sitting on a leather couch in the lobby and rose when I came through the door.

"Elspeth is already at our table in The Golden Grain Restaurant," Holmes said. "And there are two gentlemen with her. One is Mr. Stack and the other is unknown to me."

We entered the spacious dining room, a sea of crisp white tablecloths and glittering crystal. Wine-red plush carpet covered the floor, and enormous crystal chandeliers hung from a high lacunae ceiling. One wall was given over to wide, floor-to-ceiling windows, while another held a long table groaning under the weight of a tantalizing smorgasbord. Silent waiters dressed in black suits and bright white shirts floated between the tables. Filled close to capacity with well-dressed men and women, the low buzz of voices sounded like a genteel hornet's nest. The hum was punctuated only by the clink of heavy silverware on fine china.

Miss Kane and her party occupied a table in a deep corner of the room, opposite the swinging doors to the kitchen area. Stanislaw Stack sat with his back to us, and, next to Elspeth, was William A. Pinkerton himself.

The men rose to shake my hand. Young Holmes, not to my surprise, stepped forward and grasped Mr. Pinkerton's hand when I made my introductions. Stack received only a slight bow from the lad.

"I thought we had Maldrome," Pinkerton said, when we had all taken our seats. "This is a major setback. But why all this subterfuge? What does he gain?"

"That's what we must discuss," I responded. "What does it get him, for he doesn't do anything on a whim. His activities in England have shown us that. He plots and plans, and leaves nothing to chance."

"He doesn't seem to," the Chief agreed. "My concern is the presence of this impostor in Chicago just two days before the arrival of the President. Knowing what Maldrome had attempted in England keeps me awake at night."

"So the President will be in Chicago on July Second," I said. "Will he be officiating at the Fourth of July celebration here?"

"No," the Chief answered. "His plans call for him to arrive in Chicago on the Second, then take the train to Galena on the Third. He'll stay overnight, and officiate at the celebrations there on the Fourth, and be on the train the next day, heading back to Washington."

At this point a waiter, presenting us with large menus, interrupted the Chief's discourse. It took some time before we all had ordered. When the attendant departed, Mr. Pinkerton turned to Elspeth.

"You've had a hard journey, Miss Kane," Pinkerton said.

Elspeth took a sip from her water glass and bestowed a dazzling smile his way. "It had its difficult moments, Sir," she said. "But wasn't entirely lacking in charm."

"Yes, well. This can be a rough country, but we progress," Pinkerton answered. "How does our fair city compare to London, Master Holmes?"

"I've seen little of Chicago," Holmes replied diplomatically. "The City Jail is splendid. Regrettably, Maldrome isn't in it."

"We are men of action and will get this crook, never fear," Stack said with a smile. "Not for us, sitting around sipping tea. No sir. It will take some energy, but we Americans have plenty of that."

Sherlock's eyes narrowed as he considered Stack. "Really, Mr. Stack? The shiny right elbow on your jacket, and the callus on the middle finger of your right hand, indicate you spend a great deal of your day sitting at a desk writing. Shortness of breath when climbing into the carriage this morning, and your red complexion, may very well be due to a lack of strenuous exercise in your daily habits. If it is energy that's required, I doubt you could supply it."

Miss Kane gave Holmes a sharp look. "Sherlock! Don't be cheeky. Apologize at once to Mr. Stark."

"No, Miss Kane. I will not." His assertion could have frozen a campfire. "This man has been sitting here in Chicago while we have been subjected to a wide range of assaults by some of the worst villains on earth. He took it upon himself to insult the British Empire at this table in front of you, a representative of the British government. His behavior since we arrived has been boorish and condescending. He deserves no apology."

This exchange was followed by an uncomfortable silence while Stack's face flushed a deeper red, and his mouth looked like he had kissed a lemon. Fortunately, our food, served by four waiters, arrived at that moment. However, despite the enticing aromas and delicate flavors of our colorful entrées, we barely touched our food. The conversation, what there was of it, was trivial and subdued. After refusing the dessert menu, Pinkerton folded his napkin, put it on the table, and took a sip of coffee.

"This Maldrome continues to escape from us," he said, as he leaned back in his chair. "Somehow, we must penetrate his scheme in order to stop him."

"Why would Maldrome have Von Herder build a fort in Arizona?" Elspeth asked. "I'm able to understand having vast holdings of land, but a fort? It seems a bit extravagant, even for a villain such as he."

Pinkerton looked at me. "I understand the Army found a cache of rifles near the ranch, Charles? Was he supplying his own army, or were they meant to stir up trouble with the Apache?"

"To supply his own army, by my reckoning. He apparently thought the Apache were no trouble and not worth the bother." A waiter filled my coffee cup from a silver carafe. I waited until he left before continuing. "The number of weapons gives some idea of the broad scope of his plans."

"And that Apache raid put an end to the fort and several of his gang," the Chief said. "The Army says it was Kaya. If it was, she saved us a lot of trouble. But until the real Maldrome is either in the earth or in a strong lockup, he'll…"

Elspeth interrupted. "That man in jail had plans on his person for the hotel where your President Grant will be staying. Don't you think we should focus on protecting Grant there? Or get him to change hotels?"

"I think the plans were a subterfuge, Miss Kane. I don't think there will be an attempt on President Grant's life in this city," Holmes said.

I gave Sherlock a sharp look which he caught. Stanislaw Stack snorted. "So, young man. That's what you think?"

Sherlock held his tongue, and I studied him closely before I addressed Pinkerton. "Chief, you and the rest of the Agency have the protection of our Chief Executive in hand here in Chicago. Why don't Sherlock, Miss Kane, and I travel to Galena? It's the last stop on Grant's trip, and we can keep an eye out for Maldrome while there."

Pinkerton thought for a long moment. "Yes, we have over fifty agents guarding him here, but only a couple in Galena. That's a good idea, Charles, seeing as we don't know anything about his overall plan. I'd feel better if we covered both cities more completely. You three travel to Galena. I'll wire the agents there so they'll be prepared to work with you. But you'll only have a short time to get set up and be ready."

The rest of the conversation had to do with our trip out West, the details of the attack on the fort, the deaths of Von Herder and Bodkin, and finding the body of Frederick Putnam. Soon, we rose to go. Pinkerton and I dropped back as the others exited.

"Goodfoote," he said quietly, "we'll go through the motions here in Chicago, but I'll be going to Galena with adequate forces. We need to put your plan into action, and that will take a day or two. Stack can see to the arrangements here, then follow later."

I simply nodded, and, after catching up with the others in the lobby, Pinkerton and Stack said their goodbyes and left.

Miss Kane, who looked tired and pale, excused herself and went upstairs to her room. After she was out of sight, Master Holmes turned to me.

"I have something to show you in my room, Mr. Goodfoote. I believe it may be of some importance."

CHAPTER 45

◉ ◉ ◉

"The book is, in reality, a code book, Mr. Goodfoote."

The generosity of the Pinkerton National Detective Agency had provided each of us with a suite of rooms. The sitting room in Sherlock's suite contained a large table and a variety of upholstered armchairs. Holmes spread a sheet of paper on the table and then pulled a box from his luggage. He dumped its contents onto the paper.

"These are some of the ashes I saved from the fireplace in Von Herder's fort. I've been attempting to determine the type of paper that was burned. In fact," he said, looking at me, "several years ago, I started a collection of cigarette and cigar ashes. Only recently have I begun adding various other forms of ashes to it."

I must have looked at him with a puzzled expression. Here was a boy barely into his teens who had already studied the drying time of blood, and was now telling me he collected ashes of various sorts. With the addition of his newly acquired footprint and bloodstain pattern lessons, he was building a formidable base of knowledge for future use as a detective.

"It's a hobby," he said, with a shrug.

"You're a remarkable lad, young Sherlock."

Holmes poked at the pile of gray material with a pencil. "These ashes are of special interest." He indicated some dark pieces of hard material. "It's the cover of a book. I was able to raise some of its letters, enough of which to reveal that it's *Dante's Inferno*, in fact, the Wainwright edition of 1850."

"Why would Von Herder be burning *Dante's Inferno* when the Apache are coming through the door?"

Holmes grey eyes lit up. "I asked myself that very question and arrived at only one reasonable conclusion. All other possibilities were lacking in logic."

"And what answer did you arrive at, Mr. Holmes?"

"Remember when we broke the code we found at the fort? We wondered how someone like Bodkin or Von Herder, persons with no mathematical background, could read so complex a cipher."

I nodded. "And *Dante's Inferno* is a clue?"

"The book is, in reality, a code book, Mr. Goodfoote. It was disguised as *Dante's Inferno* so it would be unnoticed in Von Herder's library. Just as in Edgar Allen Poe's *Purloined Letter*, one hides one's secrets in plain sight. Von Herder was under orders to burn the book if it looked as if it might be discovered."

"So the number between the letters could be looked up in the code book, and that number would refer to a letter," I offered.

"Exactly," said Sherlock. "For example, remember the first number? 128? In the codebook, 128 would always be G. We had to factor the numbers because we didn't have the book as a reference, but with it, the message could be read in seconds."

I sat down. "Let me fit your new discovery into what we suspect. We had postulated that there was an unknown agent who had some mathematical background, probably living right in Disenchantment. But, with the discovery of the codebook, the mathematically astute agent vanishes, for Von Herder himself could read any message."

"Perhaps, but I think not," Holmes said. "Only some of the messages were sent by wire, according to the records Silas gave us. So others must have been delivered by alternative means. Someone in town sent messages to both Bodkin and Von Herder requiring their attendance at the meeting held at the fort. But according to Silas' records, there had been no such telegram received. Whether it was a spoken message, or one hand-delivered, is something we may never know. But such circumstances do place an agent in the town."

I spoke up. "It seems probable that the rapidly changing events that began to occur after you and your escort arrived on the scene would have required someone close at hand to the situation. Someone with independent authority to issue rapid orders to Bodkin and Von Herder. Maldrome would not use the telegraph, even with a code, to communicate on a minute-by-minute basis. He would either be on site himself, or have a trusted colleague nearby."

Young Sherlock was pacing, hands behind his back like a captain on a command deck. "It would require a confederate highly placed in Maldrome's criminal organization. Someone intensely loyal and trustworthy."

I stood up. "Perhaps the role of Putnam," I said. I walked to the door. "More mysteries and puzzles for us to solve. We leave for Galena tomorrow at sunrise, my boy. And now, we need our sleep."

CHAPTER 46

◘ ◘ ◘

"Maldrome is right now in Galena plotting the assassination of President Grant."

The Illinois Central pulled into the Galena station at noon. After we had gathered our luggage, I stood on the sidewalk and gazed across the Galena River, a tributary of the Mississippi, at the city. Built in the hill region of the Great River, Galena had once been the most prosperous city in the upper Midwest due to lead mining, and was still a thriving community, although the need for vast amounts of lead ended with the close of fighting in the Civil War. A full nine generals in the Union army called Galena their home, including the current President, Ulysses S. Grant. His house on Bouthiller Street, given to him by a grateful citizenry, was where he was to reside during the upcoming Independence Day celebrations.

Two Pinkerton Agents who I knew by sight met our party of three at the train depot. They had hired a carriage that dropped us at the DeSoto House Hotel, a substantial five story structure containing some two hundred and fifty rooms. The DeSoto is only a few blocks from the Galena River, and near a footbridge that crosses it, close to Grant's residence. It fronts onto the busy Main Street, crammed with carriages, wagons, and bicycles at this hour, the sidewalks a flowing river of pedestrians. The town was getting ready for the Presidential visit and people were pouring in from all over the area. We were well met at its front entrance by a uniformed doorman dressed in the garb of a Northern soldier from the late War, and Miss Kane was escorted to the Women's entrance. The lobby, while not huge, was elegant without being ostentatious. A large curved staircase swept upward, a hallway past it led to dining rooms, and a billiards parlor stood across from the front desk. Holmes and I registered for the three of us and had our bags sent to our rooms. The hotel, while elegant, was undergoing some refurbishing since a boiler in the basement had blown up the previous year.

After the three of us strolled around the town in order to orient ourselves, we retired to our rooms, then met together an hour later in the lobby. From there we were directed to where lunch was being served. Since the President and his party were due in two days, I was hoping we could formulate our plans while we ate.

Like the lobby, this dining room was not large. Perhaps ten tables, half occupied, were arranged in the center of the space, and long counters holding fresh flowers and other plants lined two of the walls. The far wall featured large windows admitting bright sunlight.

We were shown to a table near the windows, far enough away from the other guests that we had no fear of being overheard. After we ordered, Elspeth opened the conversation.

"If the threat to your President lies in Chicago," she said, "why are we wasting time in Galena? It seems we would be better used staying near Mr. Grant, and searching for Maldrome."

"There are over fifty agents guarding the President in Chicago, as well as army troops," I replied. "They'll be with him from his arrival there, until he boards the train on his way here. If Maldrome is thwarted in that city, we need to be ready to protect Grant in Galena."

Miss Kane sighed. "It seems like we're to be away from the center of action, Charles. After all, we have no information Maldrome is even coming to Galena."

"There is another reason, Elspeth. And this is of some secrecy." I glanced over my shoulder, then leaned across the table. "Only a select few know of the change of plans I'm about to disclose. President Grant is coming to Galena tomorrow, secretly, a full day early. He'll be stopping in Chicago only briefly, and plans to spend his extra day relaxing at home. During his visit here, the President wishes to meet with, and congratulate us, on our handling of the affair in Disenchantment." I went on, "We're invited to a party given tomorrow evening at the home of his friend, Congressman and Minister to France, Elihu Washburn."

"We still haven't found Maldrome," Holmes said. "And, as such, it seems any such praise would be premature."

Elspeth just stared at me. "Just when did you plan to tell me this? When I was walking up the path to the house?"

"No, I was going…"

"You've done me a grave disservice, and acted unprofessionally, by withholding your President's plans. It shows a complete lack of trust in my discretion."

"It just seemed that the time…"

"I need to go shopping immediately. I brought no attire for such a meeting. It shall be full-dress, I presume?"

"Well, not full dress, no, Perhaps well-turned out for a presidential reception is a better description," I said. Her discomfiture made me smile. As disciplined as she was, Miss Kane still produced a pretty blush when flustered. "Couldn't you delay your trip to the ladies' clothing shops until we finish eating?" I asked. "The reception isn't until tomorrow evening, giving you plenty of time to shop for finery."

Elspeth rose to go and Sherlock and I came to our feet. "Don't wait for me." With that, Miss Kane hurried from the room.

Young Holmes and I sat down. I called the waiter over and told him of the change of plans. Two meals now, instead of three. When he left, Sherlock and I sipped our water.

"The coded message gave us a date and place," Holmes said. "It didn't say anything about an attack on your President."

"Look at Maldrome's history, Lad," I responded. "He wanted to throw Britain into chaos with the murder of Queen Victoria. You thwarted that yourself. Is it too much of a stretch to think he wouldn't attempt something similar here in America?"

Sherlock took another sip of water. "Why would General Grant want to meet us before we have captured Maldrome?"

"By the time we meet the President, Maldrome will be in chains."

"How can you be certain of that, Mr. Goodfoote? The man has proven to be extremely elusive."

I signaled to the waiter and ordered a carafe of coffee. When he left, I leaned forward, and said in a low voice, "I had a lengthy talk with William Pinkerton in Chicago before our dinner last night. His meeting us at the hotel restaurant was not simply for introductions. It's part of our scheme to trap the villain who has evaded us up to now. This whole business is coming to a head, and, unless I'm badly mistaken, the final chapter will be played out right here in Galena."

Sherlock Holmes sat quietly for several minutes, his gaze just above my head. "There is much you've been holding back, Mr. Goodfoote," he said, quietly, bringing his eyes down to look directly into mine. "I fear your trust in me is not complete."

After a pause, I made up my mind. "You're right, Sherlock. There is much I haven't told you. But it's not a lack of trust, my boy. My first duty has been to keep you from harm. Now it's apparent the capture, or death, of Maldrome is required to fulfill that duty. I must rely on your absolute silence about all of this."

"Is there anything you wish to confide in me at this time?"

"Yes, Sherlock. Maldrome is right now in Galena, plotting the assassination of President Grant."

CHAPTER 47

It was Miss Kane's beauty that held their attention.

The next evening, the party was held. Elspeth Kane was a vision of feminine beauty. She had chosen a light green satin gown, several layers of it, trimmed in white satin, worn in an off-the-shoulder fashion. A black choker encircled her throat. Her gloves were white lace and she sported a matching white Battenberg fan. Despite my close scrutiny, I could see no sign of her revolver.

Young Sherlock was attired in a black suit with grey vest. I, too, wore a black suit, but my vest was gold satin. I had left my Remington in the hotel safe, and satisfied myself with a small revolver concealed in an inside pocket I had the tailor fashion to my design.

The reception party for President Grant was held at the Washburn residence, and we arrived in an elegant Brougham, pulled by matching black stallions, the driver splendid in red and gold livery. The home was befitting a former Congressman, designed in the Greek Revival style: two story red brick, temple-like front portico, large fluted Doric pillars. Not my *Modus Vivendi*, but for a lawyer and politician, it seemed appropriate. Torches held by young men dressed in Colonial garb lined the front porch, and a wigged servant manned the front door. The porches were occupied by a few well-dressed men smoking cigars. Most of the men, young and old, wore full beards. The owner of the mansion was in Paris at the time of the reception, having been recently appointed Minister to France.

We were shown into the narrow entry-way which was more a hallway with a long staircase to one side. The parlor, sitting room, and library were served by a door to the right, all occupied mainly by military officers in dress uniforms. The front of the residence was properly separated into formal and informal sections, and the kitchen was in the back. Elihu Washburn was raising a gaggle of children in this house, but no signs of the little ones were in evidence. Civilian men were present in smaller numbers than the military officers, and were dressed somberly in either black or grey dinner jackets. There were women of various ages in formal ballroom wear. The men were standing, as were many of the women. When we entered, all eyes turned toward us, and it was Miss Kane's beauty that held their attention. For a woman who could, by her own admission, shoot the eyes out of a crow in full flight, she cut quite the eye-catching figure in this elegant crowd.

An officer wearing the insignia of a Colonel in an infantry regiment approached us. He was younger than many of the other men in the room, and his full mustache without a beard gave him an even younger appearance. He was resplendent in a dark blue frock coat, light blue trousers with white stripe down the side, and gold epaulets on his shoulders. His sword belt was worn over a crimson sash, but his sword was not present. I noted that the officers in the library, although in full dress, also wore no swords.

The smiling Colonel bowed low over Miss Kane's proffered gloved hand.

"Allow me to introduce myself, Miss Kane. I am Colonel John Baynor, of President Grant's staff." Then to me, "And you must be the redoubtable Charles Goodfoote." To Holmes, "Surely, this is the brave lad who has been traveling in dangerous territory to aid our cause."

"Master Sherlock Holmes, Colonel Baynor," I said. "And a brave lad he is."

"Honored," the officer said, bending from the waist to Sherlock.

The hum of conversation in the room increased as more people arrived. The crowd had spilled into the dining area, parlor, and drawing room.

"We've come at President Grant's invitation," I said. "Perhaps he'll be joining us."

Colonel Baynor compressed his lips and gave a slight shake of his head. "Oh, I'm so sorry, but the President has been called away. I'm afraid he'll have to deny himself the pleasure of your company this evening. A little matter of the European question, you understand. Prussia seems intent on invading Austria-Hungary."

William Pinkerton appeared beside the Colonel. "Thank you for your attention, Colonel. Now, if you'll be kind enough to excuse us, I have some information for Miss Kane and her party." He lead us to the library off the sitting room and closed the door behind us. The room was furnished with bookcases, a desk, a writing table, and various upholstered chairs in the French style. An interrupted chess game occupied a central table and fanciful paintings of Indians by Catlin adorned the walls. One was of old Bull Back Fat, a Blackfoot warrior who I knew well in his declining years.

"Chief," I said, "Your presence is most welcome. It seems the President has been called away."

"Not completely, Goodfoote," Pinkerton said. He bowed to Elspeth. "The President is in an important meeting with cabinet members at the DeSoto House Hotel. He has requested your company in his private room. We must leave immediately."

CHAPTER 48

◘ ◘ ◘

I found myself looking down the barrel of a Springfield rifle...

Within minutes, our carriage had deposited us at the hotel. Pinkerton bade us wait in the lobby while he 'cleared the way,' as he put it. Elspeth smiled and made small talk, but young Holmes seemed distracted, paying scant attention when we attempted conversation with him. Presently, the Chief returned.

"Come this way, please," he said, motioning to the staircase.

We climbed the stairs to the third floor. Two uniformed soldiers stood at port arms outside a closed door halfway down the long hallway. Our footsteps made no sound on the soft carpet, and Pinkerton spoke softly when we arrived at the closed door. "In here, please," he said. He didn't knock.

Holmes stopped to stare at the sentries before following us.

William Pinkerton swung the door open to permit Miss Kane and myself to enter, and Sherlock slowly followed. The Chief came last, then closed the door and stood with his back to it. The room was empty, but for some furniture. No President, no meeting of cabinet ministers, no other people at all.

"It's time we had a talk," the Chief said. Sherlock glanced at the door that had just closed, and seemed about to speak, but Elspeth gazed at Pinkerton before she spoke.

"What is happening here, Sir?" she challenged. "Where is the President?"

In response, Pinkerton pulled his watch from a vest pocket, studied it for a moment, then replied. "Right now, he is in Chicago, under the protection of fifty agents." He put his watch away. "He'll arrive in Galena tomorrow, as originally planned."

"Then what is the meaning of this charade?" Elspeth had walked to the window, then turned to face the Chief. She began to fan herself, one hand on her hip. Her soft green dress set off the high color in her cheeks. The very picture of an infuriated lady.

"Please," Pinkerton said, indicating a settee to Elspeth. "Master Sherlock, if you will be kind enough to wait in the adjoining room." He motioned to a door in the side wall. "There is no need for you to hear this, Lad." Reluctantly, I thought, young Holmes seemed to comply, and moved to the adjoining door, as Elspeth sat down. The Chief and I kept our eyes fastened on the lady.

"Now, Miss Kane," the Chief started, when we heard the door close. "Or should I say, Miss Maldrome?"

"What bloody nonsense is this?" she said, drawing herself up straighter. Even in the lamp light, I could see her eyes glare with a cold flame. "Have you gone mad?"

Pinkerton put his hands behind his back and addressed the lady. "No, no, Miss Kane. That won't do. We have known of your subterfuge for some time. You, Miss Kane, are the Master-villain Maldrome."

In response, Kane simply looked at us. I could see her mental wheels spinning. Finally she put back her head and gave a loud laugh that sounded a mite strained.

"Where did I go wrong?" she asked. She sat back. "Please enlighten me."

"For that," the Chief said, "I'll yield the floor to Goodfoote."

I stepped forward and bowed slightly to Elspeth.

"Perhaps," I said. "We should start with your real name."

"My real name? I've changed it so many times, I find it hard to remember." She sat demurely, her hands clasped in her lap, and gave a Gallic shrug.

"At your trial, we will be telling the judge how much or how little you cooperated. He may lighten your sentence."

Again, more loud laughter. "You mean, he'll use a new rope?"

Pinkerton's face had gone red. His mustache bristled. "You're a hard woman, and a treacherous..."

I interrupted the Chief. "Please," I said, motioning him to sit down. "There are questions that we need answering. Allow me to continue." I was a bit surprised when he sat without argument.

"Let's start with the overall plan, Miss Kane," I said as I moved around the room. "If you don't mind, I'll continue to call you that, even though it's not your real name."

Elspeth simply smiled and waved her hand.

"This whole sorry scheme was set up long before you arrived in America," I went on. "So who is the real Maldrome? Who is the real brains and means behind your plot to seize this government?"

William Pinkerton stared at me, but said nothing. I had kept some of my suspicions to myself, even from the Chief.

Miss Kane again sighed and casually straightened her skirts. She remained silent, and covered a yawn with her gloved hand.

"All right," I said. "I'll tell you what I think, and perhaps you can confirm my ideas."

"Perhaps, Clod," she said with a hard smile.

"The pig's blood and the hatchet. Smoke and mirrors to keep the crowd from looking too closely?"

Elspeth again laughed, then shrugged. "*Epater la bourgeoisie*, I suppose. It seemed a rather silly idea in a town of murderers, but it worked."

"What did she say?" Pinkerton said, still steaming. "My French is a little rusty."

"She was using the blood and hatchet as shocking distractions," I answered. "It usually refers to a stodgy middle class, but…"

"Bodkin and Von Herder never knew your real identity," I continued. "They knew someone in town was giving orders, but otherwise were completely in the dark."

"The blundering fools nearly killed the boy despite my directions not to," she said. "They would probably have murdered me as well, although I had given them direct orders to kill only the policeman, Davis. The government men who escorted us were overheard in one of the saloons talking about the rich British investors looking for silver and they were summarily shot by the deputies the very night they rode into town. Of course, all this took place before you arrived." She gave a small shake of her head. "In truth, I wasn't heartbroken when the Marshal eradicated both Bodkin and his maniac deputy with the scar, although it did disrupt our plans somewhat."

"How did you get messages to Bodkin and Von Herder? You were watched closely."

"You think I didn't spot the town drunk lounging outside the hotel, then showing up everywhere I happened to be? How arrogant you are, especially for a half-breed. I wasn't surprised when he turned out to be your friend, Bedford."

I began to walk around the room, impressed that she had recognized Jubal T. and yet had given no sign of it in Disenchantment. "Still, you must have gotten the coded papers to your cohorts some way. I suspect it was a clerk in the hotel itself."

Again, Miss Kane gave out with a sound somewhere between a laugh and a bray.

"I did notice," I said, mostly to myself, "that Pottle used the town boys to run messages. They could travel unnoticed."

Pinkerton, his complexion now normal, asked, "Who is the man the lad thought was Maldrome in London?"

"That man was a marvelous actor and dancer," she said. "He was also a garrotter of the first order, trained in Persia by the followers of Hassan-al-Sabbah."

"The Assassins," I said. It was probably Elspeth's voice Sherlock had heard in the carriage in London, I reasoned.

She studied her fingernails. "Do you know something amusing? He was fearful of blood. The least little cut would send him into the wozzies." She looked up. "I had to leave him in England in case we had further use of him there."

"Why did..." the Chief started.

"Why, why, why," Elspeth flashed. "Why are men such fools? How did I persuade your government, and the British government, to give me a ringside seat to all your sorry plans attempting to find and stop me? That's the question you should be asking. How was I able to make fools of you and your whole Pinkerton Agency for so long?"

"So that's why Holmes was safe," I reasoned. "He was your ticket to the inside of our investigation. If something had happened to him, you would have been shipped back to England and cut off from knowing what we were up to, or how close we were to unraveling your grand scheme."

"How smart you think you are," she said with a tight smile. "How clever is the heathen savage. Without that boy, you would have been sitting in the dark."

"Without that boy," I fired back, "you would have cleaned out the Bank of England, murdered the Queen, and sailed to America to continue your reign of terror. You and the real Maldrome were stopped by a mere child."

Pinkerton looked hard at me. "The real Maldrome...?"

Elspeth again smiled. "My first mistake was trusting in fools. My second mistake was to let the boy live." She gave a sigh. "I'm getting bored with all this. No more questions, please. Just get on with whatever you think you're going to do."

"Why a fort in the desert?" I pressed. "The Army could simply surround it, isolate it, and wait for the food and water to run out."

"I'll let you figure that one out, Charles. You and that boy are so smart," Elspeth sneered.

"If your plans had worked, there would have been no United States Army worthy of the name. Is that right?"

Elspeth said nothing. Then Pinkerton spoke up. "We know about the gang in Atlanta," he said. "And the one in San Francisco. Your henchmen were arrested this morning."

That got Miss Kane's attention. A look of fear flashed across her face, but was quickly replaced by a smile.

"You have been busy boys, haven't you?"

"Your gang in New York has been rolled up and put out of commission as well."

She shot an angry glance at the Chief.

"Was the assassination of the President the signal to start your movement?" I asked. When she didn't answer, I went on. "With Grant gone, Shuyler Colfax would move into the White House. Is he part of this scheme?"

Pinkerton watched Elspeth closely. He leaned forward in his chair. "Colfax has strong ties to the Credit Mobilier of America," he said. "Is that where you're getting the financing for this little drama?"

I looked at the Chief. "I'm afraid I've been out of touch," I said. "What is the Credit Mobilier?"

Pinkerton never took his eyes off Elspeth. "The Credit Mobilier is a group of politicians, including Senators and Representatives, railroad people, and other businessmen. They set up a sham business to bilk the government out of one hundred million dollars that had been intended to finance the building of the Union Pacific Rail Line. The Vice President is one of its 'investors.'"

Miss Kane's fanning became more rapid. "You fool. That money hardly filled my petty cash box. I didn't need it."

"But is Colfax involved in this plot?" I asked.

"I see no reason to remain here playing this tiresome game. Mr.

Goodfoote, it has been a mixed pleasure knowing you and Master Sherlock. The lad is destined for greatness. You, Sir, are not." With that, Elspeth abruptly stood with a rustle of her crinolines. Pinkerton jumped to his feet and I pulled my pistol.

"Surely, I'm not that dangerous to two grown men such as yourselves," she said.

"You murdered the Kiowa Kid just to take suspicion away from yourself. Yes, you are dangerous, to any man, woman, or child." I wasn't falling for her weak woman façade.

"Miss Kane, or whatever your name is," Pinkerton announced. "I have been given authority by the President of the United States to place you under arrest and escort you under close guard to the federal prison in Washington." He walked to the door and opened it, motioning for the two uniformed soldiers to enter. "This woman is under arrest. You will escort us to the local jail."

I found myself looking down the barrel of a Springfield rifle held by the soldier nearest me. The other uniformed man pointed his rifle at the Chief.

"I'd advise you to drop your weapon, Mr. Goodfoote." I looked at Elspeth and saw that she had produced a revolver from somewhere among the folds of her voluminous dress. Covered by two guns, I complied, putting my pistol on the floor at my feet.

"Ta-ta, Gentlemen," the nefarious Miss Kane said in a slight Southern drawl. "You have no idea how deep this campaign goes." She walked to the door separating the two rooms. "Get the little bastard from next door," she ordered.

One of the soldiers, the nearest to the room where Sherlock had been banished, thrust open the door and entered, rifle at the ready. He returned a few moments later.

"The room is empty," he said. "There's no one there. The window is wide open, and the fire rope has been lowered."

Elspeth spit out a word usually voiced by teamsters, buffalo skinners, and other men of rough ilk. From the gentle mouth of the lady, it was more than obscene. "Don't fire your rifles unless they move," she told the two rogues. "This hotel is crawling with Pinkerton's men and army troops. If they behave themselves, truss them up, then get rid of those uniforms. You know where to meet." Her voice had a clipped, hard edge I had not previously heard during the weeks I had been in her company. She slipped her gun back into her dress, opened the door and, with a brief wave and sardonic smile, swept out of the hotel room.

The rest of this tale is quickly told. The two men tied and gagged us, getting the knots cinched tight. Then they tossed their rifles on the settee with my pistol, slipped out of their uniforms to reveal laborer clothing underneath, and politely bowed themselves out of the room. It was only a moment after they had left that young Holmes appeared.

"They said the room was empty," Pinkerton wondered at Sherlock, after his gag had been removed and his hands and feet were being freed by the boy. "Where did you come from?"

"The simplest answer is, I was in the room but briefly," the remarkable young man said. "I slipped back into this room when you were both engaged with Miss Kane, but I opened the window and threw out the fire rope so the guards would think I had climbed down. The uniforms of the soldiers at the door were those of artillery officers, not infantry. The artillery would not have been assigned guard duty, and they should have been enlisted, not commissioned officers. I wasn't sure of the military protocol in America, so I ignored it until I saw that Miss Kane was to be detained. I've been concealed behind the settee in the corner, across the room from the lady, waiting for an opportunity to be of some service."

"You moved as quiet as an Indian, Sherlock," I said.

"Neva gave me lessons in stealthy movement when we spent our time together in the mountains."

Barely out of his bonds, Pinkerton, red-faced with rage, grabbed my revolver and rushed into the hallway. Holmes sat in a chair, his bowed head in his hands. I heard the Chief bellowing in the hall, but I closed the door and pulled a chair over to the young man.

When he looked at me, young Sherlock's eyes were red-rimmed. The lad who had handled months of hardships, both physical and personal, was crushed by the deception of Elspeth Kane. "I'll never trust a woman again," he said.

"Now, now, Lad," I said. "A disappointment, certainly. You're a young man who has suffered a blow. But, someplace out there is a girl who will send you into orbit around the moon. Don't harden your heart to her. Without love, life can be barren and cold."

Sherlock drew in air through clenched teeth. "No, Mr. Goodfoote. Miss Kane has taught me a lesson I shall never forget. Never."

CHAPTER 49

◫ ◫ ◫

"Some obscure mathematics professor at a small college"

A week later William Pinkerton, Sherlock Holmes, and I sat at dinner in the Green Room Eatery, a restaurant about a block away from the DeSoto Hotel. Also at the table were Stanislaw Stack and Seth Mahoney of the newly-formed Secret Service Division of the U.S. Treasury Department.

"You had a tiger by the tail, Mr. Pinkerton," Agent Mahoney said as he buttered a piece of bread. "With that filly as an opponent, we're lucky the damage wasn't greater."

"And you traced her back to England, Mr. Mahoney?" I asked.

"Yessir, we sure enough did. We traced her first to a boarding house in Ottawa in Canada. But she was gone before the Royal Police could nab her. Apparently, she took a first-class passage aboard *The Gloria Scott II* to England. Scotland Yard picked up her trail in Portsmouth. But again, they were an hour behind, arriving too late to catch her." Mahoney took a bite of his bread, chewed slowly, and swallowed before continuing. "According to the boys at The Yard, she was once an actress in England. Changing her appearance comes natural to her, and she seems to have a great amount of money stashed in various parts of the world. She posed as a man in Canada, full beard and all." Mahoney laughed. "And she sold some marital-aids to her landlady before leaving in the middle of the night."

"From whom did she get her funding, if not from the perpetrators of the railroad scandal?" Holmes asked. An insightful, pertinent question, I thought.

William Pinkerton set down his wineglass. "We don't have all the facts yet, Lad. There's a big investigation on-going in Washington regarding that whole railroad affair. Her stepfather seems to be an enormously wealthy aristocrat in England and she may have had access to some deep pockets."

Stack spoke up. "It's too bad she didn't follow in her step-brother's footsteps. He's as upright and boring as you can get."

"In what way?" I asked. I was sawing my slice of rare venison with a rather dull steak knife.

"Her step-brother?" Stack answered. "Some obscure mathematics professor at a small college. He spends his days, from what Scotland Yard tells us, plotting the orbits of heavenly bodies. Not at all like his half-sister."

I nodded and chewed silently on my venison. "Where did she learn her marksmanship?" I asked, after I had swallowed.

"Born to it, in a sense." Mahoney said. "Her father was the gamekeeper at a large estate. Apparently, he and his wife died suddenly when Elspeth was about eight. The family he worked for took the girl in, legally adopted her, and brought her up as their own. The Lord of the Manor, a proper English Lord at that, raised her to shoot pistol and rifle and ride like an Arab. Her benefactor's son, name of James, is said to be more bookish."

"Is that normal for the English gentry?" I asked. "Treat girls like boys?"

"The step-father seems to make his own rules, and the British authorities are being somewhat coy with his details. Apparently, Lord Moriarty is a man to be reckoned with in some parts of England." Mahoney put down his knife and fork, glanced first at Master Sherlock, then at me. He spoke more softly, as if betraying a secret. "In addition to teaching her to ride and shoot, this Moriarty hired a London trollop to teach her how to manipulate men." The Secret Service agent sipped his coffee, then dabbed his mouth with his napkin. "She left home shortly after reading for mathematics at Oxford and came to America when she was just a young woman."

"From her accent," Sherlock said as he looked over the rim of his teacup, "she must have resided in Virginia." We all stared at him.

"That's right, Boy." Pinkerton said. "That's right."

"You noticed an American accent?" Stack wondered. "I thought she spoke with a British accent."

Holmes ignored him.

Pinkerton signaled for the waiter to refill his wineglass. "She did land in Virginia and took the name Belle Brant."

"Belle Brant?" I said. "Not *the* Belle Brant? The Siren of the Shenandoah? La Belle Rebelle? The Rebel Joan of Arc?"

"None other. The most successful Confederate spy in the War Between the States. In fact," the Chief said, warming to his subject, "she was arrested twice and escaped a military prison both times by seducing the young officers in charge of her lock-up." He took a sip of wine. "We all know how charming she can be," he finished, glancing at Sherlock.

Stack spoke up. "The last time she escaped from prison, she ran off with the Union Lieutenant in command, escaping to England where they were married and reportedly had a child."

"So we have her married name, then," I said.

"Well, yes and no," Agent Mahoney said. "She changed it immediately after her husband, Lieutenant Adler, died of typhoid. She picked up the stage name of Belle Lamoure and toured as an actress, accompanied by her daughter. That's where her early trail ends." He spread his hands.

"How did she become Elspeth Kane? Is there a real Elspeth Kane?"

It was a question that had perplexed me for some time.

"Oh, there's a real Elspeth Kane with the Admiralty. Or, at least, there was." Seth Mahoney poured coffee from the silver carafe. "And she was assigned to accompany young Sherlock here, and Sergeant Davis, to America." He looked at Holmes. "Where did you first meet Miss Kane, Son? I bet it was aboard ship."

Sherlock nodded.

"Somewhere between the dock where she had left her colleagues, and meeting the boy and the Sergeant aboard ship, the real Elspeth Kane disappeared, and the woman we knew by that name appeared, complete with official papers and credentials, a British accent, and a plausible story. We haven't yet been able to locate the real Elspeth Kane, or more probably, her body."

"So her overall plan was to re-start the Civil War here in America? To what end?" Stack had stopped chewing to ask the question.

As everyone was quiet, Mahoney again answered. "We're not sure of her original intent. We believe she had no political motive, and no particular love for the Southern Cause. But her gang may have simply wanted the vast silver resources. Or to set up a little kingdom, without the interference of the Army. Kane, we suspect with Maldrome's backing, had ties to the Nightriders in Georgia and Indiana, the Tongs in Chinatown in San Francisco, and some Irish miners from an off-shoot of the Molly McGuires. On her signal, which was to be the assassination of President Grant, all hell would be let loose across the length and breadth of this country. Riots in our large cities, explosions on Wall Street, burning and looting in Washington, Atlanta, and other places were all parts of the plot. Various Cabinet members were also targeted, but we've thwarted all those plans."

"What about that fort?" Stack asked.

"No one would connect a little stronghold in the desert of Arizona Territory with the chaos and destruction in the cities. It was a safe place for a headquarters. And the rumors of a large vein of pure silver are more than just rumors. A British engineer discovered it two years back and told one of Maldrome's agents. The Brit's body was left to rot in the desert. Von Herder, working for Maldrome, was to buy up all the claims. It would have financed more schemes, more takeovers, more power for the arch villain."

We all sat in silence contemplating the enormity of the plot, and the ability of the woman at the center of it all, the trusted surrogate of a madman.

"You kept me in the dark about the other parts of the country that had come under Maldrome's influence," I said, looking over my coffee cup at the Chief. "You were already onto the plot before you dispatched me to Disenchantment."

"Well, I decided you would be distracted with too much information, Goodfoote. Each of the conclaves of rebellion was assigned to different agents. I made the mistake of taking Kane at her word. The real British agent was backed by the whole Royal government, and this impersonator had all the right documents and mannerisms. The villainess took me in completely." He sat forward and put both hands on the table. "I sent you to what I considered the hotspot of the scheme, and to guard the one person who could identify Maldrome. It was a major responsibility I laid on your shoulders. Unfortunately, the agent in San Francisco didn't fare as well as you did in Arizona." He gave a sigh and leaned back in his chair. "As a leader in this far-reaching criminal organization, Elspeth Kane is a formidable opponent, even if, as you suspect, she isn't the head of it."

"I was completely taken in by her treachery," Sherlock said. "Be assured, it won't happen again."

The table was silent, each of us with our own thoughts. Finally, I spoke. "She took in older and more experienced men than you with her acting ability and intelligence. You'd better just put it behind you and get on with your life. Most women are not a Belle Brant, if that is her name. Remember, she's the agent of the real villain, Maldrome, who is probably still in England. We may have stopped a coup, on one hand, but we only succeeded in chasing his factotum out of the country."

"Let's count our victories, Goodfoote," the Chief said. "This Agency cleaned up a whole snake pit in Disenchantment, probably stopped another Civil War, and rid the world of a tangle of wanted outlaws. It sounds to me like a job well done."

Stanislaw Stark cleared his throat. "What I don't quite grasp," he said, "is who murdered Sergeant Davis, and how did he get out of the room with the door locked?"

I looked again at Holmes. "The lad here can tell it better than I. He figured it out."

Holmes visibly brightened for the first time since Miss Kane had left us. "If we had been permitted to stay longer after Sergeant Davis' body had been found, there would have been no mystery. But Miss Kane directed that I move down the hall and retreat back to our rooms."

Stack tipped his head to one side. "And…?"

"Three deputies and the sheriff went into the room to retrieve the body. Four deputies and the sheriff left, carrying Mr. Davis."

I continued the explanation when Holmes fell silent. "One of the men, the murderer, was in the room when the sheriff blew the door open and filled the air with gun smoke. Bodkin made sure no one was allowed into the room to see the hidden deputy. Elspeth Kane quickly moved Sherlock down the hall, a move in which I unwittingly conspired. She had recognized his ability to spot details and knew he would have noted the fourth man when the body was removed from the room."

"She told me she was about to swoon," Sherlock added.

"Your report refers to footprints," Pinkerton said.

Holmes spoke up. "Yes. Mr. Goodfoote found footprints on the hardwood floor a short distance away from the body. Putting those together with the sheet from the bed which held smeared bloodstains, and various other clues, we logically made our deductions."

"So who did the deed?" Stark persisted.

"It had to be Blade," I said. "Sherlock noted that he was Bodkin's constant companion, but went missing when the body was found. From the size of the footprints in the room, we estimated the height of the murderer at six foot three inches, the same as Blade."

Sherlock Holmes looked at me, his tea cup poised in mid-air. "Several days later, Marshal Thompson found Blade hiding in my room. I would have been killed if the Marshal hadn't intervened."

"Well," Seth Mahoney said, "that does seem the most plausible answer to the locked room murder."

"Occam's Razor," Holmes said.

"Whose razor?" Stark asked. "You said he was killed with a hatchet."

"It's a philosophical rule," I answered. "It means that the simplest solution is probably the correct one."

Stark shot a hard glance at Holmes before posing another question to the table at large. "I wonder how many 'Maldromes' there are, and I wonder if any of them resemble the real Maldrome?"

"We may never know," Mahoney said. "We believe he has a host of actors, all looking roughly the same. All with the fake black mole and red-wine birthmark, which, of course, intentionally draw attention to their faces. Prendergast in Chicago, the man Sherlock saw in London, and two or three others have been reported. That's why he has the reputation of being fluent in several languages, and a master of disguise. As far as we can tell, he's never shown up in person. There must be a 'real' Maldrome somewhere, but he's more of a ghost than a man."

"The man who ordered Potty killed was real," Holmes said.

"According to Kane, he was an actor playing a role," Pinkerton said.

"What was the purpose of putting that actor, Prendergast, in our jail?" Stark asked.

"As I said before," I answered, "Maldrome and Kane don't do anything without a purpose. If Sherlock hadn't seen through the actor's disguise, we all would have thought Maldrome was out of the way. Then the President would have had Kane, Sherlock and me in for a private party to thank us. Kane had a pistol, and the guards were men in her employ. The life of The President would have been in serious jeopardy. It was young Mr. Holmes here who saved the day by discovering the subterfuge."

William A. Pinkerton put his white cloth napkin on the table and made to rise. It was a signal this meeting was over. Tomorrow, two detectives from Scotland Yard were due to arrive to escort Mr. Sherlock Holmes back to London. His mother had desired to come to America herself to retrieve her adventurous son, but young Holmes had assured her that that wasn't necessary. The boy's father and older brother, both members of the British government, had made all his necessary travel arrangements.

We rose and walked out onto an open, brick-floored area. The sun had long gone, and the gas lamps along Main Street were in full flame. The walk back to the DeSoto was short, and we said our goodbyes to Agents Mahoney and Stack in the lobby. Both men were due to leave on the early morning train so would be gone before the rest of us were out of bed. The hunt for Kane and Maldrome would continue in London, but none of us had any illusions about the success of that effort.

CHAPTER 50

◉ ◉ ◉

"This whole singular adventure has a Gothic ring to it."

The next morning, Sherlock, Pinkerton, and I ate in the hotel breakfast room. The Scotland Yard men had arrived on the early train and joined us in our repast. The train to take Pinkerton, Holmes, and the detectives back to Chicago was due to leave at noon. My plans would take me in the opposite direction, back to California to give Jubal T. Bedford a hand in finding the killers of the Pinkerton agent. Then maybe back to the Arizona Territories to look for Kaya.

"One more question, Goodfoote. When did you start suspecting this Kane woman was an agent of Maldrome's?" Pinkerton asked in the carriage en route to the train depot.

"It's hard to explain. I've spent a lot of time tracking animals and men. I was taught as a youngster that recognizing patterns is an important part of tracking. When the patterns don't make any sense, it may mean you're tracking the wrong critter, man or beast. That's when it's time to take a hard look at your assumptions.

"Early on, I wondered why there had been no attempt on the life of Sherlock. It made no sense not to go after the one person who had seen Maldrome. In other words, the pattern was inconsistent. When I mentioned my bafflement to Miss Kane, the Kiowa Kid, a man, remember, known for his skill with a rifle, appeared and fired a few rounds in Sherlock's direction. Elspeth had relayed my puzzlement to Bodkin and Von Herder, who soon after sent in the Kiowa Kid. And then it was the lady herself who killed the Kid. That set me to thinking. To believe Elspeth arrived just as the shooting started was a bit more of a coincidence than I was willing to accept at face value." I pulled my pipe from my jacket pocket and began to fill it.

"I suspected early on that Bodkin and Von Herder were in Maldrome's employ, which, I reasoned later, put them directly under Elspeth Kane's control, as she was Maldrome's agent in the field. But they had had ideas of their own, like the murder of the two ex-Army officers. I speculated that Miss Kane decided they would need a lesson. When she heard, by whatever means, that they had sent for the Kiowa Kid to shoot at Holmes, despite her admonitions not to put Sherlock in jeopardy, the lady took the occasion to drive home to her gang that any deviation from her direct orders would not be condoned. It's my contention that she left the hotel fully armed, and browsed in the millinery shop until the Kid fired his first shot. Then she left the shop, came up behind the shooter, and called his name. When he turned, she shot him in the heart. I don't think she necessarily feared for Sherlock's life, but she needed to be obeyed, and it also gave her an opportunity to throw off any suspicion I might have had of her. This is a woman who was thinking fast on her feet, modifying plans as the situation developed."

We arrived at the station and stood on the platform as the train was being loaded. I put a match to my pipe and puffed. The conductor waved to the engineer, who leaned out the window of the cab and returned his wave.

"In effect, however, some of her actions created the very suspicion she was attempting to dispel. What I initially had difficulty recalling was her skill in mathematics, a skill she demonstrated during a discussion with Sherlock about various mathematical philosophies. I reasoned she had the necessary skills to be Maldrome's agent in place and issue orders with the code book cipher. No one in Disenchantment knew it was she who pulled the strings. From the moment on the train when I remembered her defense of logic, a subject closely related to mathematics, I saw the pieces fall into place and my suspicions of her became my reality."

"All aboard," the conductor yelled. Pinkerton stepped aboard the train. The men from Scotland Yard positioned themselves beside Sherlock.

"The real Maldrome, and he is real," I said, "sits like a spider in the center of a web. Elspeth Kane is only one of his agents."

Sherlock Holmes, standing next to the train's steps, had been listening to our conversation with the shadow of a smile on his face. "Like a spider in the center of a web," he said. "It has a Gothic ring to it."

I chuckled. "This whole singular adventure has a Gothic ring to it," I agreed. "But we haven't seen the last of either Miss Kane, or the murderous Maldrome, whoever and wherever he may be."

As he climbed aboard the train, Holmes turned to me and held out his hand.

"Thank you for the lessons, Mr. Goodfoote. I promise to practice the skills you taught until they are part of me." Were his eyes moist from the dust of the train?

I gave his hand a quick grasp. "You'll do well," I said, as the train began to move. "Watch your back, Sherlock."

"I will, Mr. Goodfoote," he called, over the sound of the engine. "Watch your'n."

The End

Visit Tom Hanratty at www.thomashanratty.com

Follow the further adventures of Charles Goodfoote and Kaya in The *Wicked Affair of the Golden Emperor,* *The Crimson Cape,* and *Kaya and the Bone-Eater.*

Made in the
USA
Columbia, SC